Vanishing Breed

Vanishing Breed

Lon LaFlamme

Writer's Showcase presented by *Writer's Digest*
San Jose New York Lincoln Shanghai

Vanishing Breed

Published by Writer's Showcase presented by *Writer's Digest* an imprint of iUniverse.com, Inc.

For information address:
iUniverse.com, Inc.
620 North 48th Street
Suite 201
Lincoln, NE 68504-3467
www.iuniverse.com

ISBN: 0-595-09421-X

Printed in the United States of America

For Norma

Acknowledgments

My sincere thanks to American Trakehner Magazine senior editor Helen Gibble for her significant story and editorial contributions in helping bring this amazing moment in history to life. I'm also indebted to Daphne Machin Goodall (anthropologist Jane Goodall's sister) for her nonfiction book *Escape From East Prussia*, full of actual diaries recounting the torturous journey women and children faced in having only forty hours to escape Stalin's wrath. Thanks, too, to my wife Karen's encouragement and tolerance during my year-long journey into the Third Reich's darkest recesses. And lastly, to the relentless support of my agent, Nancy Ellis-Bell, and editor, Laurie Rosin.

Original cover art by Kat.

1

"Outrageous!" Colonel Matt Winn, the long-standing president of Churchill Downs, hammered a liver-spotted paw on the hand-tooled leather blotter. "Preposterous!" he added vehemently.

Hank Oscarson smiled lazily, turning from his idle inspection of his best friend and part-time employer's trophy-lined office to meet the colonel's eyes. "Exactly. And I'll do it." He settled into a high-backed leather chair opposite the desk.

The colonel harrumphed, a messy sound due to the man's asthma. "Not that you give a damn, Oscarson, but there's this little conflict going on in Germany right now."

Hank surveyed his new lizard cowboy boots with pleasure as he stretched his lanky legs across the colonel's polished cherry desk. A single piece of straw stuck out from one stacked heel embedded in a crusty substance Hank hoped was mud.

"Jeez, Hank," the colonel drawled, wrinkling his blotchy nose, "show some damned respect."

"I'm well aware of the war," Hand said, and swung his legs off the desk. "Fact is, I've been pouring money down a foxhole for three months trying to get a pair of breeding Warmbloods to safety. I'm going to have to do it myself, and from what I'm told, I'm almost out of time."

The colonel pulled a Cuban cigar from his custom-tailored jacket and rolled it between his fingers. "Hell, son, you were lucky enough to have a heart murmur that kept you out of the war. Now you're planning to go on purpose? What horse is worth that?"

"I don't expect you to understand what's at stake here," Hank said mildly, "besides the million I'm being paid to secure them. And I get the first foal. Warmbloods are my passion."

The colonel fumbled in his brocade vest, extracting a cloisonné matchbox. "I've spent my life with Thoroughbreds, but I'm sure you can straighten an old man out."

Hank grinned. "It took over two hundred years of ingenious breeding to create the East Prussian Warmblood," he began. "To my client and breeders around the world the double-moose antler brand is as precious as gold."

"Oscarson, you amaze me. You're one of the most successful breeders in the country. You're sitting on a gold mine right here in the heart of Kentucky Thoroughbred country. Your waiting list has clients from all over the world, and even with a war on, your standard five-percent breeder commission must've earned you your first million by the time you were thirty. What do you need with more money?" The colonel coughed, then reached for a silver cigar tip clipper. "Want one?" he asked, wheezing.

"When have I ever said yes?" Hank got up and crossed to the massive, parchment-colored globe next to the colonel's overstuffed sofa and spun the orb until one of his long fingers locked onto Germany. He stabbed at the upper right corner of the boldly outlined country. "Hitler bunkered and launched attacks on Russia out of East Prussia."

Colonel Winn heaved his bulk from behind the desk and waddled over to the globe, his head encased in a cloud of gray. "They're calling the area Hell's Gate."

"You know what your hero painter Frederic Remington called it? 'Horse Heaven.'" Hank closed his eyes and momentarily, visualizing cool, deep lakes and thick pine forests brushing the sky. "Stalin's one pissed-off communist," he continued. "His little buddy has betrayed him for the last time."

"Who, Hitler?"

"Yes, and there's a vendetta to pay. Millions of Russians have died, and millions more want that sniveling son-of-a-bitch hung up to dry like Mussolini."

The colonel swatted wafting cigar smoke from his face. "So you *do* follow the news. Then you also know that East Prussia's the gate to Berlin that both sides are using for a bloodbath. *That's* where you're going?"

"Damn right," Hank answered, scowling. "Another month, and the breed could be wiped out."

"Another month, and you could be married. Have you shared this plan with Victoria?"

Hank spun the globe impatiently. "I'll be back in plenty of time."

"If you say so, Oscarson." The colonel eyed Hank sharply. "Or you might be regrettably blown to smithereens. Want my advice? Stick with the filly. You and Victoria make a finer breeding pair than any East Prussian Warmbloods. Prime American hotbloods!" The colonel guffawed at his own joke.

Hank began pacing. "Wait'll you see them, Matt! There's no other breed like it! Its bloodlines are prettier than the 'Mona Lisa'—Arabian, Thoroughbred, and a touch of Coldblood. They're amazingly fast and tough."

The colonel rubbed out his cigar and rested it on a huge brass ashtray on his desk. "And you're just going to waltz into a war zone and snatch the best of the breed?"

"That's just it, Colonel. With a war going on, who's going to pay attention to one simple Swedish horse breeder?" Hank hooked a thumb through the denim belt loop closest to the shiny gold belt buckle he'd been awarded for service to the Derby. "I know this horse, Matt. I spent my summers growing up around them in Sweden. My father and uncle bred them for their Swedish Warmbloods. I saw them sweep the gold in the thirty-six Berlin Olympics for dressage and the three-day event."

"Good God, man," the colonel said. "Who in our world without their head up a horse's patoot doesn't know the Trakehner?" He rose and placed a fatherly hand on Hank's shoulder. "Your motives are certainly worthy, but—"

"So you do understand!" Hank knew he was ranting crazily, but couldn't stop himself. "Napoleon's army destroyed nearly seventy-five thousand of them. If they hadn't been moved to safety in the First World War, the Russians would have wiped them out. And they're about to do it again. But this time…"

The colonel raised his stubby hands. "Enough with this obsession, Hank. Just be careful. And save some of your passion for Victoria. She's going to need it."

~

Hank always loved the surge of power and freedom he felt when driving his Mercedes convertible, even with the top buttoned up. Today he barely heard the pounding hum of the stretch sports car's tires on the ragged pavement. He'd spent the hour's drive from Louisville to Lexington lost in visions of magically slipping between bullets and bombs to snatch at least one massive stallion and one fine broodmare before the Russians scorched the earth of Trakehnen.

His mind raced from one logistic to the next. The plan was foolproof. He looked Aryan, with his ash-blond hair, light-colored eyes, and tall, lanky frame. His uncle in Stockholm would get him a Swedish passport. Entering Germany would be almost too easy.

He made his usual gravel-kicking turn into Sunny Acres, jarring his thought back to his first hurdle. Victoria. Hank was almost twenty-four hours later than he'd said he would be. Victoria would be in the middle of her Olympic dressage practice at his show arena. She practiced daily, certain the war would be over soon and the Olympic games rescheduled.

He parked the Mercedes facing a snow-speckled green pasture, where a raven-black stallion tossed its head and pranced around his paddocks like a king inspecting his royal gardens.

He strode purposely toward the gleaming white mansion he called home. He would need a perfect setting to spring his plan. Someplace swanky, with soft lights and music. *DelMonico's.*

The front door swung open as he approached.

"Tell Miss Victoria I'm home, will you, Josh?" he called to his butler as he whistled his way through the house. Once showered, Hank selected a black tuxedo and dressed with care. He winked at himself in the full-length mirror, swung his double-breasted jacket over his shoulder, and briskly descended the marble staircase and out to the arena.

The shadows under the stadium bench allowed him an unobstructed view of Victoria's workout. *Elizabeth Taylor.* There could be no denying the resemblance between Victoria Logan and the star of *National Velvet.* Victoria's milky white complexion, English nose, and high cheekbones set off her rich lavender eyes and full black hair.

Hank watched with pride as his prized Lippizzaner stallion sidestepped to the sound of a piano concerto streaming from the loudspeakers overhead. At the last notes, the stallion bowed to the empty stadium seats above Hank's head. Victoria lifted her black satin top hat with a flourish.

"I see you, Hank Oscarson," she cooed in a lightly flavored Southern accent. "You'd better sneak around, making me wait for you all night— and after staying away for a whole week!" She posed with her hands on her hips. "Are you checking to see if the rider measures up to the horse?"

Hank stepped from the shadows and held out his hand in an open invitation. "He's a beauty, all right."

Victoria swung gracefully to the ground and led her horse over to Hank, walking slowly enough for him to appreciate her tight-fitting breeches and smart crimson riding jacket. "What am I to do with you? I arrived last night—and I don't mean to sleep. And here I've been, all alone..." Her voice trailed off provocatively.

He tipped her chin up and kissed her lips. "I'm sorry," Hank said sincerely. "I decided to spend an extra day in Louisville." He gathered her into his arms, pulling her firmly against his chest, then kissed her again, his tongue probing her lips. "You look great."

Victoria squirmed away. "You animal." She slapped his backside. "Too bad you're all dressed up with no place to go. After I tend to Shadow, I want a long, hot bath. Then—"

"Then I'm taking you out to dinner. At DelMonico's."

Victoria pursed her lips in a teasing pout. "You've talked me into it." She spun and walked Shadow toward the stable.

Hank stared silently after her. Victoria Logan was a woman any man would be proud to have as his wife, even if she was a little spoiled. And a divorcee. Her soon-to-be-ex had been a damn fool, carousing from one drunken escapade to another. No wonder she finally left him to seek sanctuary with her father, a nearby breeder and one of Hank's chief rivals. In a few more weeks, her divorce would be final, and Victoria Logan had chosen him, Hank Oscarson, to love forever. So why did his heart leap to his throat at the thought of that fateful word *forever*? He shook his head, trying to picture an eternity of bliss with Victoria. Persistent images of Trakehnen swarmed his mind. *You're a damn fool yourself, Oscarson*, he thought.

~

Victoria lounged against the red leather banquette at the intimate table for two Hank had reserved at the restaurant. She had chosen a slinky ice-blue satin gown, accented with a single strand of diamonds.

"You look gorgeous." Hank toasted her with his third cocktail, admiring the glacial color of her dress through the crystal martini glass. "You Vassar girls really know how to clean up."

"You Auburn boys aren't half bad either," she murmured, sipping her drink and scrutinizing him. He hated when she did that.

Hank drummed his fingers in time with the combo playing softly in the background. "That's you," he said, humming lightly. "'My Satin Doll.'" He breathed a sigh of relief when a cadre of waiters arrived with roasted quail, a specialty of the house. Hank ate with relish, making cheerful small talk as his lovely fiancée picked at her dinner. Her eyes seemed more clouded as the meal progressed, and finally she fell silent.

Victoria held her tongue all the way through the baked Alaska. Then she let her fork drop with a clatter. "All right, Hank, I give up. What is it?"

Here goes. "I've been waiting for the right moment to tell you," he said calmly. "I've got some really exciting news."

"Mmm hmm." Victoria raised a skeptical, perfectly plucked eyebrow.

"You know how many times we've talked about getting an East Prussian Warmblood for you to train and ride in the Olympic Trials?"

"Oh, darling! Have you found one?"

"Almost." Hank slid closer to Victoria and took one of her delicate hands, nervously stroking the enormous, unyielding diamond on the engagement ring he'd given her. He waited and soon felt inspiration strike. "You know, Victoria, there's no animal more sleek, proud, and regal than the Warmblood—just like you, my darling. That's why I've decided I must have this horse's foal as my wedding gift to you."

He paused. Victoria was gazing at him misty eyed. *So far, so good.* "So I'm going to Trakehnen—you know, East Germany—to bring out a stallion and a mare."

The mist turned to steel. "You're going to Trakehnen?"

"I've tried everything else. I've got to go myself." Hank spoke in a rush. "After Normandy, Germany is about to fall. I can get in and out in twenty-four hours."

"How, Hank?" Victoria demanded angrily. "You can't charm your way in and out of Germany. Europe will be leveled before this war is over. If you were captured by the Nazis…" Her eyes grew wide at the thought, and she withdrew her hand from Hank's.

Hank grasped her hand again, pressing it between both of his. "Victoria, listen. The timing is perfect. But I have to go *now*. If the Russians do charge into Germany through East Prussia, they'll destroy everything in their path." Victoria looked as if she were about to flee for the safety of her father's home once again. "Imagine yourself accepting the gold medal in the Olympics!" he urged.

Victoria's eyes narrowed, and she spoke in a low voice. "Somebody's paying you to do this?" She didn't wait for the answer. "You're not just gambling with your own life anymore!"

Hank dropped her hand and pulled away, frowning. "Come on, Vic, you of all people. I thought you'd understand."

"This is certainly one imaginative way to break an engagement."

"Darling, that's not what I'm doing! I'll be back in two weeks at the most. I could save the breed from extinction. Isn't that important enough for you?" Hank's voice softened as he continued. "Now listen. I've planned the whole thing. According to my uncle in Stockholm, Sweden provides all the iron ore for Hitler's war machine."

"Bombs don't care if you're Swedish or—"

"Hear me out, Vic. Even this late in the war, Swedes can get in and out of Germany with no problems. I can get a Swedish passport. I speak fluent German and Swedish, so Trakehnen will be a breeze. They're expecting me. I'll buy the finest stallion and mare I can find. I'll fly in and out, and I've already arranged rail transport to ship the horses to Stockholm, where I will be waiting at the docks."

"You made all the arrangements without telling me." Victoria lifted her tear-brimming eyes. "You're going to go whether I agree or not."

Hank embraced her and held her quietly, waiting for the quivering to stop. He brushed his lips against her tear-streaked cheeks and whispered, "I love you, Vic. The wedding is a month away—I'll be back before you even order the flowers."

She wriggled closer in his arms. "Then stay until my divorce is final. I don't need a big spring wedding. Let's get married before you go."

Hank gulped. "I can't wait, darling, even a day. It's now or never." He stroked her silky shoulders until he felt her distress ease. "Don't worry, I'll be fine."

"Then I'll go with you," she whispered. Victoria gently extracted herself from his arms. She smiled wanly. Her cheeks were streaked with mascara.

Hank smiled back and dismissed her plea. "In case anything happens—like I slip on sauerkraut or something—I've drawn up a will leaving Sunny Acres and everything to you."

Victoria whirled on him, her eyes filled with sudden rage.

"I don't give a damn about your money or Sunny Acres!" She sprang to her feet and hurled her evening purse at him. "You're not leaving me standing at the altar, Hank Oscarson. War or no war, you'd better come home, or I'll fly to Germany myself and kick you all the way back!"

2

Leap-frogging giants from ancient legends couldn't have made the paddock ground shake more violently beneath Katja Haffmann's riding boots. The bleak winter skies above Trakehnen whistled and sparked with the fire of Russian bombs hurtling to the frozen earth. Farmwomen and their children dropped tools and buckets and ran screaming toward the main house.

Katja wrapped both arms around her head as she raced toward the stable. She called to the horses, and miraculously they turned toward her voice and followed her inside. Speaking in a soothing, quiet voice Katja tried to calm the animals as she led each one to its stall. Quickly, she filled the feed bins with hay and oats. The small amount of water in their troughs would have to suffice. Then, holding her breath, she closed the stable doors and bolted.

As Katja reached for the door of the huge red brick Haffmann farmhouse, she heard the sound of kicked-up hooves and a horse neighing behind her. A familiar voice called out as another explosion burst a few miles away.

"Kat! Kat!" Dr. Ernst Brunner, the most influential man in Trakehnen, slid his powerful frame from his horse, dropping the reins as he ran toward her.

Katja waved a welcome and ushered him inside. The spacious living room was packed with sobbing women and children who clung to their mothers. A few old men huddled near the fireplace. Katja wound her way through the mass of people to the hearth, where she turned to face the gathering.

"Is everyone all right?" She raised her clear voice to be heard. "*Achtung*, everyone! The radio says we're only days from winning the war. Soon my father will return from the front, and the Russians will be beaten back for good!"

"Hah!" shouted Wolfgang Haffmann from the back of the room. "The Russians will be feasting on us before the week's out." He licked his cracked lips and snarled like a starving wolf. Katja turned a scorching look on her burly, grizzle-haired cousin. He stared back in blatant defiance.

~

"Oh, God in heaven, help us!" Eva Scheider, a buxom young housemaid, clutched her three-year-old daughter and began to cry.

"Not another word out of you, Wolf," she said acidly. "My father's not here to protect your lazy ass. He's already more than repaid his debt to your father by keeping you off the front lines and making you stable master."

Wolf turned his venomous eyes to Dr. Brunner, then spat tobacco juice onto the floor. "I spit on your dearly beloved Fuehrer! He is a madman! Tell them, Brunner. Tell them the truth." He stomped out into the howling winter wind, slamming the door behind him.

Dr. Brunner turned as scarlet as the trim on his gray uniform. The middle-aged Trakehnen farm director cleared his long, lean throat, then slowly wove his way to Katja's side, never taking his eyes off hers. "Kat, we must talk without an audience," he whispered.

Katja nodded, unable to conceal her brief look of alarm from the gawking onlookers. But she quickly mastered her expression. Although she was only twenty-four, her father had entrusted her to run the stud farm while he served as commander of the Reich's horse-drawn artillery unit, and she wouldn't disappoint him by behaving like a frightened little girl in front of the staff.

"It seems the bombing has stopped," she announced happily. "We all know how close the fighting is. We'll be leaving before there's any real danger. Stay in the house for a few more minutes, until we're sure it's over." She turned to the woman closest to the kitchen. "Gerda, get everybody something to drink and eat. This house has seven bedrooms. Anybody who wants to spend the night is welcome." She tousled the hair of a boy who had lit up at the suggestion.

Dr. Brunner tapped Katja on the shoulder, then led the way out of the house. He grabbed his horse by the reins and trudged some fifty yards toward the stables. Despite her dread, Katja decided to wait out his silence. Like Dr. Brunner, she preferred to speak only when she had something to say.

He put a warning finger to his lips and before speaking searched the stable for curious ears. Dusk had fallen, rendered even darker by an encroaching storm. Katja lit a kerosene lamp, and the two settled on stacked hay bales, aglow in a pool of soft yellow light.

"I've got some bad news," the doctor began. Puffs of December mist enveloped his words.

Katja shivered, a spasm that went far deeper than the cold. "It's Father, isn't it?" She searched Brunner's kindly eyes. She'd known the ruddy-faced horseman with the huge Prussian mustache since her girlhood.

Dr. Brunner rested a hand on Katja's slender thigh, then quickly removed it. "No, Kat, it's nothing like that."

Katja barely breathed. "Then what?"

"The Fuehrer hasn't given word that any of us can evacuate." Brunner whacked his open palm with his fist, flushing with suppressed fury. "Damnit, Kat, he still thinks we're going to win the war."

Katja gazed frantically around the stable, picking objects out of the shadows beyond the lamp. "Of course we're going to win the war! My father…" Her throat tightened. Until this moment she had felt certain her father would burst through the door, whisk her and her bedridden mother into his arms, and set the world back to normal. Could the whole world be caving in around her?

Brunner looked to the eaves as though seeking inspiration. "It's different here in East Prussia, for the two-and-a-half million of us whose entire life's purpose is to farm and breed. We're simple people." He took a deep breath and expelled a visible cloud. "I've been traveling from one stud-farm master to the next. You're the last of the nine."

"What are you saying, Doctor? I've read the newspapers, and listened to the radio, too. Once the Bolsheviks are destroyed, everyone is ordered to return to sowing their winter grains. The Fuehrer—"

"Forget the Fuehrer! Kat, believe me, he has no idea what's going on at the Russian frontier. Stop any German soldier passing your farm in retreat, and you'll learn more about how near the end is than the Fuehrer could tell you."

Katja dug her work-worn fingernails into her palms. *How dare he?* she wondered. She felt her nostrils flare and her jaw lock as she wrestled to keep from spitting the word *traitor* at her trusted overlord. Ernst Brunner had been a second father to her. How could he insult the Fuehrer, impugn her faith in the cause that might take her father's life?

"Katja, you would give your life for Germany, wouldn't you?" he asked gently.

Katja answered at once, fiercely. "As fast as my father would."

"My dear, this isn't about love for your country or whether Claas is committed to an honorable pursuit." Brunner lowered his voice. "Kat, it's about a reality so horrible, I wish I didn't have to share it with you. But it's time you hear it—all of it."

Katja's anger reached depths she had never plumbed. "Get on with it, Doctor. I've got a farm to run."

Dr. Brunner smiled sadly, not even raising an eyebrow at Katja's outburst. "You know, my dear, I never joined the Nazi party. Still, I agree with almost everyone in Germany that the Treaty of Versailles gouged out a piece of our homeland we should have kept. The chancellor caved in to every international commerce restriction imposed on us. By the early twenties poverty and hopelessness had grown so rampant, we were ripe for a Hitler."

"Indeed we were," Katja said defiantly.

"Without that treaty the German people wouldn't have been desperate enough to allow Adolf Hitler to spread like a disease."

"Dr. Brunner, I don't want to hear another word against our Fuehrer. You are speaking treason—" She gasped as the doctor abruptly yanked her arm, forcing her to silence.

"You'll listen, young lady, before it's too late." Brunner fixed his eyes unflinchingly on her. "It's over. Our soldiers on the Russian front are freezing to death. The Allied invasion of Normandy was a disaster for Germany."

Katja jumped reflexively. Her father had been stationed in Normandy. She pictured him buried in an icy unmarked grave. Anguish escaped in a soft groan.

"Let's talk about what's happening right now," the doctor said firmly. "On my way to Berlin two months ago, I passed through Thorn, about a hundred miles from our borders. Sources had told me there was a prisoner camp at Chelmo where horrific crimes were taking place. I couldn't get anywhere near the camp without being stopped, but I didn't need to." He held her gaze and lowered his voice.

"The sky was a rich blue, with not a cloud in sight, but a fine ash was falling from the sky, dense enough that I had to use my windshield wipers. I stopped and got out of the car." Brunner shuddered and looked down at his boots. "Kat, I knew I was smelling burning flesh."

He stared at her direly again, his eyes grown large with horror. "Imagine how many bodies were being burned for that wretched odor to reach out. The camp must have been five miles from where I stopped. I knew at that moment..." His voice broke. "Kat, I've had reliable information about unspeakable horrors of the Reich since Hitler started gathering his group of cutthroats in the twenties." He glanced furtively around the barn, as though informers might be lurking nearby. "They have SS posted at my front door."

Katja swallowed. *As well they should.*

"Until that trip," Brunner stammered, "I found the stories hard to believe. But at that moment, with human ash coating my skin, my clothes, my car, I knew in my soul that everything my sources had been telling me about Himmler's ethnic cleansing plan was true."

Katja recoiled, twisting away from the man she once loved. Now a steel door had slammed down in her heart.

"The Nazis are exterminating Jews, gypsies, even handicapped Germans. Millions of them. Day after day."

Weeping, Dr. Brunner reached out and clasped her freezing hand in his stiff riding gloves. Katja ripped her hand away and ran through the darkness for the closed stable door. The doctor followed close behind and grabbed both of her arms. She struggled against him, writhing in fury, but he held her tightly against his chest.

"There's more," he whispered. "The Russians won't be satisfied with killing us."

Katja threw her head back with full force into Dr. Brunner's jaw, jolting him hard enough to break his lock on her. He staggered back, then put a hand to his forehead and dropped to his knees.

"Run, Kat!" he sputtered hoarsely. "Take everybody and leave now. Make sure everyone has papers. Take every man, woman, and child, or they'll shoot you as spies or deserters."

Katja met his pleading eyes, grieved at the trickle of crimson running onto his coat from his lip. She felt paralyzed with compassion, scorn, horror, uncertain whether to help or to flee.

"I have already evacuated the heavy-in-foal mares and most of the best stallions." Brunner wiped the blood from his chin and dragged himself to his feet. "I'm not the enemy, Kat. It's true, I could be hanged for treason—but I'm urging all the farm masters to flee now. You may only have hours to get out before the Russians reach us."

"The Fuehrer…" Katja whispered.

"The Fuehrer has given me personal instructions through Province Governor Kock to keep all three thousand Reich farm employees to the end. He wants us to go down with the army."

"My father wouldn't have left," Katja stated flatly.

"Don't be so stubborn!" he shouted, then pressed his hands to his temples. "I'm sorry. I shouldn't have yelled. I've done all I can. The rest is up to you. You've managed the farm directorship beautifully and now you have to accept another heavy responsibility. You've got to get those women and children to safety."

"And what about all your people at the main stud farm?" she asked, suddenly exhausted.

"That's *my* nightmare."

Katja nodded. "I'm staying, but I'll send everyone away at daybreak."

The doctor dusted off his clothing and regained his rigid posture. "Of course. To honor your father. How's your mother?"

"She's in no condition to travel."

"If I get official word that we can leave, would you go then?"

"Yes, when it's official."

Dr. Brunner licked his split lip and approached Katja as if she were a horse about to be put in harness for the first time. When she stood passively, he put an arm around her shoulder, opened the stable door, and walked her back to her front steps. At the front door, he leaned over and kissed her forehead. "Your father would be proud of you, Katja. You're a brave woman. And as foolish and headstrong as he was."

3

Hank stepped from the cab, dropped his light valise, and surveyed his Uncle Gustav Oscarson's Swedish Warmblood breeding farm. He had spent every summer of his youth there. Although he had never seen the estate in winter, the farm still looked exactly as he remembered, untouched by time or a warring world. The main house was still pale yellow, stately and impassive; the nearby stone guest house with neat, symmetrical shrubbery; the stables, the snow-covered grazing land, all snobbishly fenced.

"Welcome, stranger!" Hank followed the sound to an outdoor arena fence on his right. A huge man wearing a broad smile strode toward Hank, hand outstretched.

Hank needed a moment to recognize Erik, his cousin and boyhood best friend. In the fifteen years since Hank last saw him, Erik had thickened into a younger version of Gustav, a comic book hero with bright honey-colored hair; a square oversized jaw, and the height and breadth of an oak. Though Hank and Erik shared the same piercing blue eyes and blond hair, Hank had inherited his father's wiry build. He wouldn't be pinning Eric to the mat in wrestling matches anymore.

Hank hesitatingly reached out and got back what he feared, a hand-crushing welcome, followed by a bear hug.

"Trip was good?" Erik asked in typical singsong Swedish.

"Ja, no problems." Hank gestured to the farm. "Looks like things are going well." He knew he was stating the obvious. Gustav Oscarson had been long established as Sweden's premier trainer and breeder, and his clientele included royalty and Sweden's wealthiest equine sport enthusiasts.

Erik slapped Hank on the back. "Oh, nothing changes. And we've heard all about you, our American millionaire. Come to the house. Father can't wait to see you."

Although both cousins were thirty, Hank felt like a scrawny little brother as he hurried along, trying to keep up with Erik. As they entered the house Hank stopped to inhale the familiar aromas of furniture polish and pastries baking.

Aunt Bibi emerged with open arms from the kitchen, chattering nonstop. Hank had never noticed how tiny she was. The farmwoman had never made concessions to fashion or to the Oscarson's high-society guests. Her straight skirt and sensible hand-knit sweater allowed only a glimpse of her ankles and neck. She wore no jewelry and had pinned her hair into an unruly bun.

"Welcome, welcome, Henning," she said, her eyes tearing with joy. "My, and so much like your father. I've got everything all set for you in your old room in the guest house." Aunt Bibi pushed against her towering son's barrel chest. "Move aside, Erik. Please sit down, Henning. You'll eat, ja?"

Before Hank could respond, his uncle's booming voice rolled through the dining room to the kitchen.

"My brother's son is here?"

Hank thrust his hands into the back pocket of his pants to avoid another painful family handshake.

"Sit, sit!" Erik urged. "Let Mother fix you something. Get some flesh on those bones. Rich men do not eat in America?" Before Hank could sit, Gustav crushed him in an embrace, then burst into a jolly laugh. "Our boy! Our boy is back!"

~

Whatever Aunt Bibi lacked in elegance she more than made up for in culinary mastery. The huge, juicy roasted beef tasted sublime. Hank found he needn't have worried about his rusty Swedish: father and son never stopped talking at the top of their voices.

"You see, Erik?" Gustav demanded jovially. "Henning followed in his father's footsteps and became a famous equine veterinarian. But little by little, all those lessons we taught him here at the farm began to bubble in his blood. Isn't that right, Hank?" Gustav didn't wait for an answer.

The Swedish Oscarson clan had clearly heard this story before. "He caught a taste for horse-trading!" Erik chimed in, winking at Hank.

"He caught a taste for horse-trading!" Gustav boomed over his son's statement. "He sold his first yearling colt…When was that, Henning?"

"In 1937," Hank answered. "In Saratoga, New York."

"For six thousand American dollars," Gustav continued. "And from that moment on, he left his father's side because his Uncle Gustav's training was the wiser course. And today our Henning is an—"

"—an internationally known horse breeder," Erik and Bibi finished. "Just like his Uncle Gustav."

The family joined in hearty laughter, followed by a round of toasts to Oscarson geniuses.

~

After dinner Uncle Gustav invited Hank to join him to inspect the breeding farm's finest stallions and mares. He didn't have to be asked twice. Erik stood, too, but Gustav waved him back to his seat. Disappointment soured his expression, then disappeared in a bland countenance. Hank thanked Aunt Bibi for dinner, then followed Gustav out the door. Once beyond earshot of his son and wife, Gustav looped his arm in Hank's and turned sharply away from the stables and guided him toward an open field. "Let's stroll for a while," the older man suggested. "I'd rather not be interrupted by the staff. It's best not to get Mother or Erik involved. I only told them you were traveling on business and would stop overnight for a visit."

Hank nodded slowly. His uncle's lighthearted banter had shifted to a stern, businesslike tone.

Hank cast a quick look toward the stables. The war had made Gustav cautious. This was not a bad thing, Hank thought, all too aware that his own life might be in Gustav's hands.

"I read and reread your idea to go into Germany," the man said. "I want to make sure I understand you, Henning. Your message was brief, so I decided to wait until you arrived to address your purpose and motivation fully."

"It's simple. You know, it was you and my father who taught me to appreciate East Prussian Warmbloods. Without them where would you be?" Where indeed, Hank thought, admiring the idyllic setting before him. Uncle Gustav's farm and outbuildings had seemed a magical village to his child's eyes, and the adult Hank still fell under its spell. No air seemed as clear and crisp, no green so true, no water so delicious. The Oscarsons had prospered here for generations.

"So you want to go buy a pair before the Russians destroy them? This is right?"

Hank smiled eagerly. "That's about the size of it. All I need are Swedish papers and—"

Gustav barked a laugh. "Ridiculous! The Nazis would discover your ruse, and you'd be killed before the horses are."

"With all due respect, Uncle, I'd be in and out in less than twenty-four hours. I can hire a pilot to fly me to Trakehnen and pick me up at the same spot, allowing me, say, six hours to negotiate a final price."

"I can't allow you to do this."

Hank stopped walking and put his hand on Gustav's shoulder, speaking earnestly. "I have it all worked out. I met with a ship captain in Stockholm this morning. Transporting the horses will cost a bit more than I had planned, but I'm sure I can trust him."

Gustav shrugged off Hank's hand. "You'll have to get that money back or lose it. I won't let you do this."

Hank felt puzzled by his uncle's resistance and certainly did not appreciate being treated like a child. "Okay, Uncle. I don't want to put you to trouble. I'll find a passport in town. I'm sure they're easy to come by."

"You don't understand, Henning," Gustav said angrily. "Now listen. You've heard of the Wallenburgs. For over half a century the family has represented the Swedish establishment, like the Rothschilds or the Rockefellers."

Hank shook his head, slightly embarrassed at his ignorance.

Gustav grunted. "It's not so surprising. Unlike other industrialists, the Wallenburgs have always shied away from public attention. But the Wallenburg dynasty stretches all over the world. Banking, shipping, railroads, electronics, tobacco. The list is too long to keep track of."

Hank nodded blankly. "What about them?"

"Two weeks ago word reached the press that the Russians had arrested the Wallenburgs' twenty-six-year-old son Raoul in Budapest for forging thousands of Swedish citizenship papers to help Jews escape."

"This only proves my point!" said Hank. "These people come and go with no questions asked because they're Swedish."

"No, Henning, you don't see. Sweden and Switzerland walk a delicate line. We represent the kind of Aryan world Hitler is trying to create, but our governments are still terrified he'll turn on us next. The Swedes have bought protection by providing Hitler's war machine with iron ore and other favors."

"And the Swiss?"

"The Swiss are trafficking and hiding the spoils from conquered countries." Gustav leaned forward and whispered, "They're helping the Reich in other ways, too."

Hank studied his uncle's troubled face, so like his father's and, at the same time, so different. "How do you know all this? And what does Raoul Wallenburg have to do with my plan?"

"Wallenburg has disappeared, and his family and the king are so embarrassed about a Swede saving Jews, they aren't doing a thing to find the young man." Gustav stabbed a finger at Hank. "These are tense times, Henning. Wallenburg has made all Swedes suspect right now, even with Hitler."

Hank shrugged. "I still believe I'll get in and out so fast, they'll never know I was there."

"Nobody is allowed in and out of Germany without official approval," Gustav said flatly. "Forget this idea. I can't have you stain the Oscarson name. This family will not join the disgrace of the Wallenburgs. Do you understand? We've worked too hard to be caught forging papers for some insane adventure."

Hank felt both saddened and relieved that he had not unpacked his belongings. He turned and started toward the guesthouse. He would not spend the night; he had too much to do. "I won't use the Oscarson name, then. Will you call for transportation into Stockholm? I'll do this on my own."

Gustav beat Hank to the cottage door and blocked it, folding his rock-hard arms over his chest. "We're going to settle this here, Hank. You are an Oscarson. If you were caught, it would be the same as Erik getting arrested. You would cause untold grief to your family, and it could ruin us."

Hank felt his resolve harden, but he knew the best tactic would be to let Gustav think he'd won. "You know how I respect you, Uncle," he said. "I would never endanger our family."

"Good, good," Gustav said, softening. "Why don't you stay the night and think it over, Henning? You didn't know until now the danger you would be in."

Out of deference to the relationship they used to have, Hank pretended to give serious thought to his uncle's demands. "Good idea. You're probably right."

The next morning, however, Hank knew he would say farewells to the Oscarsons and be on his way.

~

Back in downtown Stockholm just after breakfast, Hank headed directly to the American embassy where he learned that Gustav hadn't exaggerated.

Finding Stockholm's seamy underbelly proved to be a challenge. Civic and personal pride left few dark corners where he could network to find a master forger. He was beginning to wonder if he had undertaken a fool's errand. On the third night of moving from one cargo waterfront bar to the next, however, his luck changed. He was sipping his third vodka on the rocks in a dark, nameless tavern when a tap on his shoulder jolted him from thoughts of Victoria and Sunny Acres. He looked straight ahead into the bar mirror.

A starched wisp of a man, surprisingly elegant in a gray pinstriped suit, was staring back at him in the glass. "May I join you, sir?" he asked in a dry British accent.

Hank nodded cordially.

The man took the next barstool. In perfect Swedish he ordered the same "his friend" was drinking. "It has come to my attention you are in need of certain papers," he whispered.

Hank turned to the man. The muted bar light caught a twitch of cheek muscles as the Englishman attempted a polite smile.

"What papers would those be?" Hank asked.

"You are the American trying to pose as a Swedish citizen in Germany, are you not?"

"I might know the man. Who are you?"

"Somebody you need, for the right price, of course." The Englishman reached his spidery fingers into his coat pocket, extracted a folded piece of paper, and slipped it to Hank.

"Meet me at that address with five hundred American dollars," he murmured.

Hank maintained an impassive facial expression and spoke in a low, casual tone. "A thousand more if you can line me up with a pilot who will fly me directly in and out of East Prussia."

"When would you require this service?"

"Tomorrow. The next day at the latest."

"Such dangerous sport ups the ante. Three thousand dollars total."

"Two thousand. My last offer."

"Done. I will have your pilot the day after tomorrow. He could lose his license. Your deal with him is separate."

Hank nodded.

"Five hundred right now, or this conversation's over."

Moving slowly so as not to attract attention, Hank tucked five folded one-hundred-dollar bills under his bar glass.

The Englishman never broke eye contact while his hand spirited the cash from counter to pocket. "Meet me at the address in an hour for the photo and papers," he said, then faded back into the darkness of the smoke-filled room.

~

Hank held the meticulously lettered paper up to the street lamp a second time. The address matched a prestigious men's hat shop in the business district not more than two blocks from the king's palace. The name of the shop, painted on the window in shimmering gold leaf, glowed in the lamplight: Cromby and Svensen.

He saw movement within. The Englishman waved; signaling the front door was unlocked. Hank scoured the street in every direction. No suspecting eyes. He entered, momentarily spooked at the pleasant chime of the shop's bells in the silence.

"You have the money?" asked the Englishman.

Hank displayed his billfold, opened wide enough for peeking eyes. The Englishman's hand darted out of the shadows. "Not yet," Hank snapped.

The Englishman dropped his hand, then beckoned Hank to follow him behind the sales counter to a wall of shelves. He removed a hatbox from a nose-level shelf and pushed a button, activating a revolving wall. As the shelf of hats moved, dim light spilled into the darkness.

Hank's eyes were still adjusting as the wall thumped closed behind him. The room was at least fifty feet deep. A dark-haired man and a chic, red-haired woman, both in their early twenties, waited to receive him, partially hidden by a dated printing press and photographic equipment.

"Ada and Mark Moscowitz, let me introduce you to…" The Englishman paused. "I don't even know your name."

"Henson. Oscar Henson. Call me Hank."

The couple moved forward and heartily shook Hank's hand.

"I don't know what I'd do without them," the little man said, placing a hand on each of their shoulders. "Every good forger needs capable apprentices."

"You're the American?" the fawn-eyed young man asked. "Is there any word about the Allied Forces? Are we—they—winning?"

"Who are you?" Hank asked slowly.

"I haven't properly introduced myself, Mr. Henson," the Englishman said quietly. "I am Aaron Levy. Also known as Steven Cromby in this part of the world."

Hank felt puzzled. "This is your hat shop?"

"Ostensibly." Levy raised a pencil-thin finger. "We make papers," he said simply. "All the money you give me tonight will go toward saving one more Jew."

"I heard about Wallenburg," Hank ventured. "Tragic."

"Let's be clear, Mr. Henson, or whatever your name is. I don't care whether or not you're concerned about the plight of my people. Your money is what I need." Levy turned to the young couple. "Let's get this man his traveling papers."

"What about the pilot?" asked Hank.

"It's all taken care of." Levy turned his back to Hank and busied himself with the camera equipment. "It'll cost you another ten thousand."

"Forty-five-hundred."

The Englishman turned, half smiling. "Did I say ten? I meant eight. But you'll have to put up some kind of collateral for the pilot's family. There's always a remote chance you won't make it back. You understand."

Hank glanced at Ada and Mark Moscowitz, who seemed relieved they weren't handling negotiations.

"Make it ten thousand, then." This time, Hank turned his back, loosened his shirt, and pulled a wad of bills from the belt he wore across his chest. He rearranged himself and counted out the money into the Englishman's open palm. "The pilot's name?"

"You don't need names. Be at the Stockholm airport passenger luggage area at exactly five A.M. You'll be meeting a man about your height, balding, with brown hair and a mustache."

"How will he know me?" Hank asked cautiously.

Ada Moscowitz laughed long and hard. "Swedes don't wear yellow cowboy boots," she said, wiping tears from her eyes. "You stick out like a lighthouse in the desert."

4

Katja had been up before the cloud-smothered sun. She pushed all thoughts of Dr. Brunner's twisted story from her mind, and looked in on her sleeping mother in the adjacent bedroom, then stole her way to the kitchen. There, speechless, she could only gasp in outrage at the sight of Wolf's shirtless gorilla chest, shoulders, and thick arms moving at lightning speed to shove as much cheese and bread into his mouth as his bulging jowls could hold.

"What are you doing?" she demanded.

Wolf raised a finger to hold her off while he gulped down his last mouthful. "I heard you and the doctor." He smiled devilishly.

"I knew I'd need a good breakfast before setting out."

"You bastard," Katja whispered. That food was to be shared. "I curse the day you ever came here."

Wolf's dark, pocked face beamed in indignation and delight at her remark. "But you would never have been able to handle this place without me."

"That's a lie," Katja retorted. "And much as I'd like to be rid of you, you're staying here with me and Mother, until the Russians are ramming down our door, if that's what it comes to."

Her blazing look quieted Wolf. He turned his attention back to a still-sizable portion of cheese and bread.

"Stop eating, you disgusting pig. The women and children are going to need all the supplies we can pack into wagons." She felt sure the evacuees could make it safely to Danzig, about fifty miles out of East Prussia. The journey would take them about two weeks. Unfortunately they'd have to stay on main roads because the snow was so deep.

Wolf kept chewing until Katja bolted to her feet, grabbed a carving knife from its slot on the counter near the sink, and drove it a foot from Wolf's chest into the wooden table.

His hands shot up. "All right, all right," he said through a mouthful of food.

"Now get to work. I want to get everything done before we tell Mother and the rest of them about the evacuation."

Wolf nodded reluctantly and rose to his feet, brushing breadcrumbs from his chest.

"We'll have to load the covered wagons properly with enough food, cooking utensils, and warm winter clothes."

"Jawohl, commandante," he said, saluting. "Great idea. We give them all the food, so we starve before the Russians get to us."

Katja huffed at her cousin's boundless selfishness. "The Russians aren't going to get to us. We're going to win the war before that happens." As angry as she was with Wolf, her forced certainty sounded as unconvincing to her as it must have to him.

~

Every morning, Katja prepared a hearty breakfast, brought it to her mother, then outlined the day's activities. Early on, she had read her father's correspondence aloud to her. Although the letters had stopped, mother and daughter often remarked that the escalating war had interrupted mail delivery. Each visit still ended with ritual reassurances that husband and father would be returning any day.

Sonja Haffmann was holding on to reality by her fingertips. She had taken to her bed with a mysterious illness only days after her husband had proudly donned a Nazi uniform and kissed her good-bye. Each night before she closed her eyes, Sonja kissed the photograph of her husband that stood on her bedside table, flanked by tiny, bright-red swastika flags.

That morning Katja had seen the gray-haired, moonfaced woman glaring out her bedroom window at her and Wolf as they worked to harness, pull up, and load four wagons with what seemed like the entire contents of the Haffmann household. The morning's conversation was going to be tougher than usual.

Now, Katja knocked, then opened the door slowly enough for her mother to dive into bed and pull up the covers.

"You awake, Mother?"

"Yes, dear. Come in, but be very quiet. My head is splitting."

Katja set a breakfast of three fried eggs, two pieces of thickly buttered bread, and coffee before her mother. The comically long moan as the rotund woman struggled to straighten her nightgown and sit up was also part of the morning ritual.

"What was all the fuss?" Mrs. Haffmann sat up high enough to demonstrate her ability to see out the frosted-over bedroom window. "I saw some running around. Don't tell me I didn't. I did." Her voice rose a quavering octave. She gave a small cough and patted her chest. "Somebody going somewhere, dear?"

"Yes, Mother. The Russians are getting a little close. You heard the bombs last night."

Mrs. Haffmann dropped her fork and grabbed her daughter's hand. "You never even came upstairs to see if I was all right." The false sniffle was the usual signal for Katja to coo over how much her mother meant to her and tell her that Father would be home soon. *Not this time.*

"I'm just about to tell the women and children that those wagons are for them."

"If your father gets home and finds you've sent the last of the help away, well, I don't have to tell you how upset he'll be. Now you go down and unload those wagons right now. At once." She waved her daughter away.

Katja left her mother without further explanation. At the top of the staircase, she heard worried voices. Wolf had already provoked protests and terror. She hurried down the stairs and found a small gathering in her kitchen.

"Mistress Haffmann, we can't take little children out in that freezing cold," a fresh-faced mother of a two-year-old boy said timidly, then turned her eyes away in embarrassment.

Katja assumed her leadership position by the stone fireplace. "I don't know what you've been told," she said, and shot a scorching glance at Wolf. "Your leave taking isn't by choice. You must think of your children's safety. Yesterday's bombs were just the beginning."

Wolf rose lazily from the table. "Why should we believe you, when Berlin radio assures us we're winning the war?"

"Get out of here, Wolf. See to the wagons and horses. Now."

With an unresponsive shrug, the stable master pushed his way through the tight circle of stunned faces, then slammed the door behind him, as usual.

"There isn't a moment to lose," Katja said urgently. "You'll find room in the wagons for your warmest clothes."

"Mistress?"

She caught sight of a narrow arm raised. "Yes, Elsa?"

The speaker was a petite blond housemaid with high Slavic cheekbones. "Two of us with no children have decided to stay until you leave."

Katja had seen a whiskey-laden Wolf breathing lustful enticements into Elsa's swanlike neck on more than one occasion and hoped the girl knew the risk she was taking.

House cook Hildegarde, as round as she was tall, nodded in agreement. "I've already unloaded one of the wagons, Miss Kat," she added in her baritone voice.

She accepted the welcome improvement on her plan.

"All right. The rest of you, hurry up now, and eat all you can of the cheese, bread, and milk I've set out in the kitchen. Marion, you and Frieda will make the best wagon masters. I've got a map for you."

To the drone of approaching aircraft, the women and children clambered into the wagons but had no time for farewells. Before they could pull away, the whistling of bombs started again, this time sounding close enough to level the house. The lead stallion reared as far up as his harness would allow, whinnying in alarm.

Katja ran from the front porch to the horse, calming him with pats and words of comfort. She jerked her head skyward, squinting above the copse of pines at the edge of their cleared pasture. Just clearing the trees, low-flying Russian aircraft roared into view, then streamed directly overhead without firing a shot.

"Get to the woods!" Katja screamed to the wagon masters. The horses' nostrils flared, and like living locomotives, the heavily loaded wagons lurched away, toward the protection of the tree-lined cart path a mile from the main road.

Katja stood rigidly waiting for the enemy's return. Minutes passed with only the sound of her heart pounding in her ears. Then she noticed a muffled clanging sound from the back of the house. Katja slogged stealthily through the deep, wind-blown snow along the side of the house, then peeked around the corner. Unaware of spying eyes, Wolf dumped his last load of food into the wagon Elsa and Hildegarde had abandoned. He arched his sore back, then trudged back into the house.

He's probably after Mother's silver. Katja had held her own on elk, deer, and wolf hunts with her father since she was old enough to steady a firearm. Now the familiar killing instinct filled her mind and chest causing her fingers to tingle. She wheeled around and ran at a snow-exploding pace for the front door. The rifles were in her closet, moved there after her father had left home. Her mother would not sleep in the same room as the weapons now that she was alone.

Katja took the stairs three at a time without alerting Wolf, whom she had spotted in the kitchen. As she suspected, he was flinging the family silver into a pillowcase.

Katja charged through the bedroom door, then sent garments flying from the closet in search of her father's single-bolt action 8mm Mauser hunting rifle. Weapon in hand, Katja pulled down the box of shells, shoved the lid open with one hand, then loaded three internal magazine rounds as fast as a seasoned marksman.

"Katja?" her mother called in a thin, reedy voice.

Without answering, Katja crept down the creaking stairs. The kitchen was empty. From the open back door, she saw Wolf secure the canvas drawstring on the wagon. All was ready for his escape.

"The only place you're going is right to hell," she told him in a voice so full of fury, that she hardly recognized it as her own.

His carnivorous smile dropped like a trap door when his eyes focused on the barrel of the rifle pointed at his head. "Now, Cousin Kat, what are you doing?"

"Catching a thief."

Wolf gulped. "What are you talking about? The Russian bombers will be here any minute. I've got us ready to go."

"How thoughtful of you to pack my mother's silver," Katja said.

"Your mother would never have left without it." He paused, and a look of exaggerated surprise crossed his face. You thought…I can't believe you actually thought I was leaving."

"Get moving to the stable. Don't turn around. Make any fast moves, you're dead."

"You're acting crazy, Katja," Wolf said in a patronizing tone that fueled her anger. "You've got your enemies mixed up. I was only trying to help get ready."

Katja jabbed the barrel of the rifle into the small of Wolf's back.

"Hey!" he barked, and stomped through the snow and through the door, to the first empty stall.

"On your knees, you thief." Katja thrust a booted foot into the back of Wolf's knees, forcing him to buckle to the ground. "I begged Father to get rid of you."

"But because my father saved his life, he couldn't. Uncle Claas would have bled to death from—"

"I know the story, and I'm damn sick of it. If your father's the good man everybody says he is, then how was a monster like you spawned from his home?"

Wolf twisted around, as if gauging how far he would have to reach to yank the rifle from her hand.

Katja took two steps backward and retrieved the harness rope from the wall.

"Now how do you plan to keep that gun on me while tying my—"

The butt of Claas Haffmann's prized elk-hunting rifle provided the answer.

~

Katja slowly approached Senta, her three-year-old dark bay brood-mare, and spoke evenly, affectionately. "It's okay, baby, we're going on a little ride to the castle. After we see Dr. Brunner, we'll stop by and see your father."

She considered Senta her closest friend. The slightest turn of an ear, widening of an eye, or toss of the horse's mane communicated more clearly to her than any words she had ever exchanged with her peers in the village.

Senta had come from Sadorus' lineage; one of Trakehnen's finest large-framed, well-muscled horses with plenty of bone and powerful elastic paces. Since her birth Senta had been more horse than most could handle, but she and Katja had bonded from the moment their eyes met.

Katja had trained Senta under her father's tutelage. He had taught her never to raise a hand, ram a stirrup, or use a whip with the uniquely sensitive East Prussian Warmbloods. A mere shift in tone of voice would make the point.

Now, Katja's mind filled with worries over the harsh treatment her horses might receive from the ignorant and inexperienced women wagon-masters. She'd only had time to give them feed-rationing instructions, six pounds of oats per day and some hay wherever they could find it.

Senta's ears gradually moved high and forward from an anxious, pressed-back position at the gentle sounds of Katja's voice. The woman harnessed the saddle on Senta's back, and soon the two were trudging through the woods, surrounded by a curtain of falling snow.

"I guess we should have taken the main road," Katja said to Senta, as she labored through the virgin snow of a no-longer-short shortcut. Katja envisioned the countless summer days they'd made the same journey, with centuries-old oaks throwing long afternoon shadows across the dusty path to the main stud farm. She recalled the song of the cuckoo birds above, an elk standing over its fawn, and other common summer sights as she and Senta wandered past the lakes, pastures, and forests of her beloved Trakehnen.

Katja finally emerged from the woods near the village. During a brief respite from the relentless snowfall, she tugged down the hood of her fur coat. Senta lowered her head and broke through a natural space in the village's eight-foot hedge wall. The normally sleepy winter main street was full of people dashing in and out of the marketplace. But no one appeared to be fleeing, and Katja relaxed her tense shoulders.

Senta whinnied lightly as they passed the open barn door of the blacksmith. The ox of a man was bent to his task, silhouetted by the golden glow of his fire pit. Two men stood watching as he worked, while others impatiently waited for their horses to be shod.

Katja bit her lip and began to grow nervous as she passed the Swiss chalet-styled Hotel Elch. Not only were there no signs of life, the aroma of dark coffee that wafted day and night for nearly a half a block was absent. She nudged Senta into a gallop to the director's estate. The stone castle was set back in a formal park. A life-size statue of the world-famous stallion Tempelhüter, sired by the Thoroughbred, Perfectionist, guarded the towering front doors.

The province governor's Nazi-flagged black Mercedes was parked in front of the mansion. Katja reined Senta to a stop at the guest stable parallel to the house.

"I won't be long," Katja said to the startled stable boy. "Rub her down, blanket her, and feed her, will you?" She dismounted, handed him what coins she had in the pocket of her riding breeches, and sprinted to the house.

One of the front doors had been left ajar. She slowly pushed it open. Nazi Gauleiter Koch's voice echoed in the expansive marble entry from the chandelier-lit living room. "The planes never fired a shot. There's no need to overreact!" The tall, sour-faced province governor paused in surprise at Katja's entrance.

Two other soldiers were among the small group of village elders and farmers. Outlying breeding farm managers shifted uncomfortably in the unfamiliar luxury of the gilt and damask furnishings. Ernst Brunner smiled and waved her into a tapestry-covered armchair.

"May I present Katja Haffmann, Herr Koch," said Dr. Brunner. "You remember Claas Haffmann left his daughter to run the farm."

"Haffmann, yes." The governor beamed at the mention of one of the most vocal Nazi loyalists in Trakehnen. "Please, join us."

Katja inclined her head, removed her heavy fur coat, and sat down. She turned her eyes down angrily, embarrassed at the governor's open appraisal of her appearance.

"Meaning no disrespect, but we must be allowed to evacuate while there is still time." Farm master Bruns Vogel's Adam's apple bobbed as he swallowed hard. "Almost everyone has gone or is packing."

The governor narrowed his eyes. "Are you questioning my authority?" he snapped. "I just spoke to a group at the County Farmers' Association, and not one man questioned the outcome of the war. I told them what I'm telling you, that the Russians will be beaten back from the borders of East Prussia in less than two days. There is no reason to panic." His tone discouraged further discussion. The governor turned to Dr. Brunner and indicated the meeting was over.

The village leaders and handful of outlying breeding farm masters extracted themselves from their seats and filed out of the house. Katja lingered in the entryway, within earshot of the governor's low, stern words to Dr. Brunner.

"We know you have transported horses without official approval, Doctor. If you disobey orders again, I will have you shot for treason."

Dr. Brunner's eyes darted briefly over the governor's shoulder to Katja. "We both know the Fuehrer will leave us all to die rather than surrender, don't we, Gauleiter Koch? He has proved that already with his army."

The governor moved a hand to his holstered revolver. "If you speak in that tone of the Fuehrer again, I'll shoot you myself. Suddenly Koch seemed to sense somebody listening. He whirled on Katja. "Surely the daughter of Claas Haffmann understands that following orders without question is critical in a time of war."

Katja held her stony expression. "I let most of my women and children ride to safety after the Russian planes flew directly over our farm.

I came here to tell this to Dr. Brunner and to plead that we all be allowed to evacuate, sir."

The governor's mouth tightened into a vicious line. "You should have learned more from your father while you could."

"Have you heard from him?"

Dr. Brunner coughed loudly.

"Regrettably, I have no news for you," the governor replied. "But you should know that your father has dedicated his life to the greatest cause in human history."

A week before, Katja would have agreed with the governor. Today his words of allegiance to the Reich sounded twisted. Today the war had extended its razor-sharp claws into her world.

"Go back to the farm, Katja," Dr. Brunner said softly. "The second we are cleared to evacuate, I'll get word to you and your mother."

Katja stuck out her chin defiantly. "Nobody's mentioned the horses. Why not herd them away before they come to harm?"

"The horses, the people, everything in Trakehnen is the property of the Reich." The governor shook his head in disgust. "You're nothing like Claas Haffmann. Your father would be ashamed."

The thought of her father's anger or disapproval sent a wave of nausea through Katja.

"I see you still hold your father in great esteem," the governor said. "As well you should. These are confusing times, my dear. Never let fear overpower your loyalty to the Fatherland and the Fuehrer. We are lucky to be witnessing this history-defining moment."

Katja tried to clear her head of the poison Dr. Brunner had been feeding her about the Fuehrer and the Nazi party. She nodded numbly, as much in exhaustion as agreement. Her father's voice echoed in her mind. *We are building a greater Germany, Kat.*

~

Katja stomped snow from her riding boots and entered the farmhouse.

"Mistress Haffmann?" A voice wailed from somewhere near the fireplace.

Housemaid Eva Scheider moved from the shadowy corner of the room, her little daughter attached to her like a leg brace.

"Eva, you were supposed…What happened? Where are the other women and children?"

"They took it all." Eva flopped onto the couch, forcing her teary-eyed daughter to break loose of her grip. The child knelt on the sofa cushions, allowing herself enough height to clutch her mother's disheveled blond hair.

"Take your time. Tell me everything," Katja said in a level tone, even though her insides were churning.

"We weren't ten miles from here when we ran into them."

"Them? Who, Eva?" Katja sat next to the housemaid on the couch, and the girl buried her face in her mistress's shoulder.

"German soldiers. All the roads are full of them, running from the Russians," she sobbed. "There were so many of them."

"Did they help you?"

Eva sat up; her stringy hair stuck to one side of her face. "No!" she wailed. "They're the ones who stole everything." She took a deep breath and stared into the flickering fireplace flames. "They were skinny, like skeletons. They stopped us. While two of them were talking to Gretchen in the front wagon, the rest circled us. One of them jumped in the back of my wagon. My baby started screaming, and one of the soldiers hit her face."

Katja put her hand on Eva's back. "You're still soaked. Where's the wagon? Wolf get loose and take it?" She got up to build the fire.

"They took that, too. They took everything," said Eva.

"Did they…"

Eva put a hand to her chest. "Thank God no, miss. They were starving. They took everything, though."

"Where's everybody else?" She struck a match and put it to the tinder.

Eva wiped her eyes with the back of her hand. "Wolf's still here. I untied him."

"The women and children, where are they?

"They kept going. They begged me to go with them, but we weren't prepared—none of us were—to walk to who knows where in the freezing ice and snow with no food or night's lodging."

Katja straightened and put a hand to her forehead, trying to think of a plan. "I'll reload the wagon. We can tie Senta to the back and go find them."

"No!" she pleaded, her shrill voice cracking. "They'll do the same or worse to you. They're beasts."

A greater Germany. The thought was like swallowing sour milk.

5

"The name's Hank." He offered a country smile and an outstretched palm to the apple-cheeked man who would have to be his pilot; no one else in Stockholm was out of bed yet.

"Aren't you a sight?" the man said in Swedish, rubbing his button nose with an infectious chuckle. He scanned Hank from head to toe, grinning most broadly at the unmistakably American belt buckle, cowboy boots, and fur-lined cowhide coat. "You'll need to do a little shopping to convince anyone you're a Swede."

"I've got a change in my bag," Hank said, feeling slightly defensive.

"Okay, then, cowboy." The elfin man grabbed Hank's valise. "This will be a ride you won't forget." He took off with surprising speed, considering his lack of height, toward the outlying field for small aircraft. "They call me Jergie," he called over his shoulder.

Hank nearly had to break into a sprint to keep pace. "They told you where I'm going, I hope."

"Someplace in East Prussia," Jergie said. "My little prop will just about make it." The pilot halted abruptly and dropped the toothy grin. "This trip never happened."

Hank raised his eyebrows. "What trip?"

Jergie turned and picked the pace up again. "She's probably a little cold. I took her out of the hangar about an hour ago." He pointed to a bedraggled-looking six-seater.

Hank's stomach acid didn't like its looks. "That thing still flies?" he mumbled, then glanced up at the dark anvil-shaped clouds. He wondered if the craft had the wherewithal to break through the cloud cover.

"I wouldn't trade it for a model ten years newer." Jergie elbowed Hank. "You see? I painted the Swedish flag on the tail so there would be no mistaking us. A free bonus service." He pried open the rusting passenger door and hefted Hank's valise onto a seat.

Hank flinched at his further examination of the aging craft. "I'm sure Mr. Cromby took good care of you."

Jergie's grin reappeared. "Mr. Cromby and I have been doing business together for some time. Now what's the name of this place again?"

"Trakehnen. I've got a map." Hank settled nervously into the copilot's seat.

Jergie buckled up and turned the ignition key. The engine coughed feebly. "She's still a bit cold. Runs like a river when she...there." The engine thundered, reverberating at a jaw-bouncing pace. They taxied briefly, then abruptly lifted through the lowering sky.

"We'll need to fly to Copenhagen first to refuel," Jergie yelled over the engine's steady hum.

"That's out of the way. Why not fly directly across the Baltic?" Hank yelled back.

"Too far. I can refuel in Rostock on the German coast."

"I know where that is. That's where I'm railing my horses. Should be a good spot for a Swedish flag." If he didn't have confidence in the airplane, he did, at least, like Jergie's strategy.

The pilot turned. "I've got a good idea for every dollar you're spending." He extracted a document from his coat pocket and handed it to Hank. "Cromby printed it. Official Swedish government approval for our short trip into Trakehnen."

Hank examined the paper, satisfied his plan would go smoothly.

The flight proceeded flawlessly once the teetering plane was aloft. Jergie hugged the German Baltic coastline in hopes of avoiding Allied bombers. Hank soon fell into the first deep sleep he'd had in more than four days.

"Hey, Hank!"

Hank opened one eye, then the other. "We there?" He sat up, stretched, and studied the snow-covered forests and frozen lakes below.

"Soon. We just entered East Prussia's airspace. What's this Trakehnen place?"

"Trakehnen is where the central stud farm is. I wish it were spring or summer so we could really see it." Hank leaned closer to Jergie's ear. "It's written about all over the world. There are nearly a hundred thousand stallions and mares in East Prussia." Hank pointed out the window. "Fly lower, Jergie. You can see some of them now on our right."

Jergie banked the plane and dropped down just above tree height.

"See there? They separate the herds by age and color. There are bays, chestnuts, and blacks, all in their separate areas, and all magnificent."

Jergie lifted to a smooth traveling elevation. "They know you're coming?"

"Yes, the central stud director loved the idea of saving his horses. Even two of them. He's got twenty chief stallions and nearly four hundred broodmares I can choose from. Every horse undergoes a year of training over the most beautifully designed obstacle course in the world."

Jergie's bouncing eyes encouraged Hank's love of storytelling.

"The stallions at central stud are so valuable, they're treated like kings. Their summer paddocks are so big, they're like villas, each for just a single horse. Four times a year the residents have an all-out foxhunt.

The horses not suitable for breeding are used for sport. Until the war I had every intention of going on one of those hunts."

Jergie nodded sympathetically. "This war has destroyed a lot of people's dreams, hasn't it? Maybe some day you'll still get to do it." He banked the plane to break through a thick layer of fluffy cumulus clouds. "I'm going down for a closer look."

"Soldiers! Back up! Back up!" Hank screamed.

The biting blast of German rifles ripped through the air.

"Are we hit?" Hank yelled, gritting his teeth as the plane rose straight up.

"No, it was just rifle fire," Jergie choked out through a dry throat. "We're real close, Hank. Soldiers could be jamming the roads everywhere."

"Where are we going to land?"

"I don't know." Jergie tapped his fuel gauge. His brows furrowed deeply. "On the road, I guess, if we can find an empty spot. I've got to get you down and get out of here. The flight took more fuel than I calculated."

"You going to be all right?"

Jergie forced a smile. "We'll break down at cloud line. Bullets can't reach us there."

Hank gasped as they swooped down, following the line of a snow-heaped road. "A little farther, Jergie, until we can see the central stud farm buildings. With over seven hundred of them, they should be easy to spot. There, up ahead. That's got to be the village."

Jergie didn't hesitate. He dropped the wheels, lowered the tail flaps, and headed toward a narrow, muddy road.

"You're going to land *here*?"

"No choice. Hold on, it's going to be rough."

The wheels grazed, then bounced and settled onto the wagon-rutted, half-frozen ground.

"Get out!" Jergie hollered.

"Here—right here—is where you'll pick me up." Hank consulted his wristwatch. "It's noon. Come back from Rostock before dark at four o'clock, okay?" Hank glanced down at Jergie's bare wrists.

"Here." He unfastened and thrust his Cartier watch at Jergie. "Exactly four o'clock."

The pilot nodded.

"Be careful," Hank said.

"*You're* the one who needs to be careful! I hope these horses are worth it."

Hank grabbed his valise and stepped out of the plane into a half a foot of mud and slush. The freezing air hit him like a shower of glass needles.

"Have my wheels got clearance?" Jergie shouted over a revving engine.

Hank guessed. "Enough."

"Turn the tail around so I can take off."

Hank dropped his valise on the crusted snow. He needed all his strength to turn the plane about. He watched the tail slither like a snake, then lift off the road and disappear, swallowed by the security blanket of clouds.

For a moment Hank had never felt so abandoned. Then he took a quick look around and started out. He didn't have much time.

6

"*Halt, dummkopf!*"

Hank spun on his heel in response to the sharp voice, then slowly raised his hands in the air. Five pale, bearded ghouls in Nazi helmets confronted him. One held a rifle aimed at his throat.

He glanced at his valise, then back to the brazen stares. "I'm a Swedish citizen," he said in careful German. "I'm here to see the Trakehnen stud master. My papers are in order."

"I'm a Swedish cowboy," one of the human skeletons mocked.

"I breed horses in Stockholm. I'm trying to..." Hank stopped talking. The men, drawing closer, rearranged themselves to form a tight circle around their fresh game.

The soldier with the most haunted stare tilted his head in the direction of Hank's valise. Another, the shortest of the five, backed out of the circle, ripped open the suitcase, and dumped out its contents from chest height. Shoes, socks, shirts, trousers, underwear, and a zipped leather case of toiletries tumbled onto the hard snow. The birdlike heads turned in wonder and unconcealed delight at such a find.

"You can have it, all of it. Just let me pass." Hank's appeal in perfect German had no more effect than trying to cut through steel with a feather. He followed the leader's eyes, which dropped from Hank's coat to his feet.

Two of the tattered soldiers grabbed his arms while the burly leader tugged on one of Hank's boots so hard, he fell back into the mud.

"Hey!" Hank shouted, then instantly regretted the impulse.

A soldier leaped to his feet and hurled his gloved fist into Hank's open mouth. This time the leader appropriated both boots with vicious yanks. Icy mud oozed through Hank's socks.

The instant the wolves stripped off his coat, Hank gasped at the cold. Freezing wind penetrated to his very core, starting his teeth chattering uncontrollably. Hank wrapped his arms around his chest and huddled on the ground, hoping to conceal the money belt beneath his shirt. The strapped-on wallet bulged with five thousand German marks. Trakehner stallions and fillies were going for up to six hundred marks, the rest would pay for rail and ship transportation, if the Nazis didn't shoot him.

Apparently satisfied with his misery, the soldiers, arguing heatedly, parceled out the suitcase contents. They trudged away, still squabbling.

While Hank wasn't one to pray, he silently muttered heartfelt thanks for being allowed to live. He stumbled in the opposite direction, following deep cart tracks filled with soupy slush. Within a minute his feet had graduated from freezing shock and pain to a numbness that crept up his legs with every step. The thought that frostbite could result in amputation shook him. He forced the thought—and its terrifying images—from his mind.

A wave of realization that he had placed himself at hell's door surged through him like stomach flu. A second wave followed shortly thereafter when, as he neared the town square, he found himself weaving unnoticed through throngs of frantically evacuating villagers. Oxen and horses pulling crudely covered wagons bore down on him as quickly as a twelve-foot wall of water. The passing carts brimmed with odd assortments of belongings, pathetically representing generations of hard labor. Squeezed between the family treasures, crying children and mumbling elders rode in fear or stunned disbelief.

Hank surveyed the darkening clouds. No sign yet of enemy aircraft. A single, dreadful thought played at the edges of his mind. *Give it up, Oscarson. You're too damned late.* Yet he commanded his ice-block feet to fast-step against the tide, willing himself toward his destination, an imposing three-story chalet with an inviting sign: Hotel Elch.

Hank stumbled up the entry steps, pushed open the door, and staggered into the relative warmth of the lobby. The hotel had been decorated in alpine manner, with inviting rustic wood furniture. A hand painted mountain landscape adorned the wall behind the long reception desk. A wood-banistered staircase led to guestrooms upstairs. He saw no signs of life.

"Hello? Some assistance please!" Hank called at the closed door behind the reception area. He heard nothing but a series of clicks as two little carved yodelers, a boy and girl, circled in and out of a massive cuckoo clock high on the wall leading up the staircase.

One explosive gunshot, then another, shattered the silence from behind the closed door. Ignoring the sudden stabs of pain in his feet, Hank vaulted over the reception desk and threw the door open.

A German Luger dangled from an old man's claw-like fist where he had fallen. An elderly woman, her white hair in a neat, tight braid coiled on the back of her head, slumped peacefully in a well-worn armchair. Blood marked a hole in her forehead.

A murder-suicide. The woman's face held a slight smile, but when Hank pulled back the shoulder of the killer, who had crumpled on the carpet, the old man's eyes bulged, frozen in a look of horror and grief. He was undeniably dead, the shot directly through his own heart. Hank looked away quickly, scanned the tastefully accented room, and then forced himself to examine the man with the gun. He was easily eighty years old, with wisps of white hair barely covering a pink scalp.

Hank did not allow himself to dwell on the bittersweet tragedy of two old lovers who had chosen to take their own lives rather than join the procession outside. They had met their maker; he had to go on. He needed a coat, dry socks, and boots.

He found a wool coat hanging on a peg behind the door. The socks, no problem. The old man's drawer was full of them. He searched the closet, the bureau, under the bed. No shoes, no boots. He saw only the shoes on the dead man's feet. Hank eyed the possible fit, then knelt so close to the oozing, pooling blood he had to hold his breath to keep from vomiting. The black leather shoes were laced tightly. Squeezing his eyes shut, he pulled them off the still-warm corpse.

The fit was tight and worse than uncomfortable, exacerbated by the searing pain caused by the blood returning to his frozen feet. One shoe had an odd built-in lift. But they would have to do until he could find or buy another pair.

He gritted his teeth and headed back out into the cold and through the crowds to an eerily silent, poplar-lined road. He tried in vain to wiggle his cramped toes in the ill-fitting shoes, and soon the cold and lack of circulation numbed the pain for the entire two-mile walk from the village to the central stud farm.

At last he spotted the turrets and spires peeking over the treetops, the legendary estate well known among horse breeders. The road soon opened to acres of snow-covered rolling pastureland lined with white fencing. Red brick stables, stable hands' quarters, and training and performing arenas flanked the towering storybook mansion. Hank closed his eyes, then slowly opened them as if raising the curtains on a breathtaking stage set.

A broad smile split his face. "Colonel, have I got a story for you," he breathed aloud in puffs of frozen air. *How Victoria would love this!* He imagined his exquisite fiancée at his side.

A round, hunched-over woman, wrapped in a blanket from head to toe, waddled out of the first stable building and brushed past Hank as if he weren't there.

"Excuse me! Can you help me? Where is everybody?" Hank asked, following her for a few steps.

The woman turned her leathery face up to study him. Her lips sank into her large, toothless mouth. "They're all gone," she finally pronounced.

"The stud director, too?" he asked as she moved to leave.

"Maybe. I know I'm going." She stared for a moment at Hank's shoes, and then her blue-veined hand flew to her mouth. "I know those shoes. They were made for Franz Schmidt! How…" She backed slowly away from the newest face in town, then wheeled around and started running for the mansion, dropping the blanket as she waved her hands above her head.

"Help! A thief!" she screamed. "A murderer!"

Hank made no attempt to catch her. He hobbled at a safe distance and managed to grasp the front door before she could slam it in his face.

"Doctor, Doctor, a killer's after me! Help!" The old woman lugged herself up the right side of a double marble staircase that swept from the spacious entry hall to the second floor of the mansion.

From the corner of his eye, Hank saw a man in a form-fitting gray and red-trimmed riding uniform emerge from what appeared to be a drawing room off the entry hall. His cap—resembling those worn by high-ranking German officers—accentuated a long, stony face. His lip was split and swollen. "Who are you looking for?" he demanded.

"Stud master Dr. Brunner," Hank replied, drawing himself up to his full height and dignity, in spite of his shabby appearance.

"What might you want with him?"

"That's him, Doctor!" the crone shrieked from the top of the staircase. "He killed Franz Schmidt!" The old woman stabbed an accusatory finger his way. "Look, his shoes! Those are Franz's."

The fellow narrowed his eyes at Hank's mud-caked shoes.

"Please, allow me to explain," Hank said sharply. "My name is Henson. Oscar Henson. I wrote to Dr. Brunner using the name Henning Oscarson. I've come from Sweden. My boots were stolen almost as soon as my plane dropped me off. I sought refuge in the hotel and found that the proprietor had killed himself and his wife."

The man studied Hank's face, then nodded curtly. "It's not what you think, Mrs. Muller," he called, his eyes never leaving Hank's. "I invited this man here to buy some horses." He extended a hand to Hank. "I am Brunner."

"The shoes!" the woman shrieked.

"This is not your worry, Mrs. Muller. Get your things now. The last wagon may have even left." He returned his attention to Hank. "I'm afraid you couldn't have picked a worse time to drop from the sky, Herr Henson." He bowed slightly with an outstretched arm, welcoming Hank into the drawing room.

Hank smiled. The world was in chaos on the other side of the front door, and the doctor's demeanor was a leisurely as a Southern gentleman offering a mint julep on a muggy summer's eve.

Hank felt too tense to sit. "Doctor, I've got less than four hours before my plane comes back for me."

The doctor consulted his pocket watch. "No one has much time. Exactly seven hours ago the province governor officially allowed my eleven hundred staff members to evacuate. The Russians have been conducting frequent bombing raids and are about to overrun us." The doctor seated himself. "Please sit down."

Hank relented, but his fists were balled from tension.

"If you can imagine, and who could, the Fuehrer..." Brunner paused long enough for the venomous way he spit out the name to settle into his guest's mind. "Hitler has given us less than seventeen hours to evacuate. The women are desperately trying to gather up all they and their children will need to survive the rest of their lives. If January's snow or the Allied Forces don't kill them, that is."

The doctor's voice sounded heavy with responsibility for the masses under his charge. He sat up, his eyes blazing. "This edict affects more than my people. In October a half million were moved from the eastern frontier to the western edge of the province, but now everyone—over two million of us—is supposed to escape from the Bolsheviks at the same time, in less than a day."

The doctor rose, planted both hands on his hips, and studied the oil portrait of Adolf Hitler posed astride one of Trakehnen's world-class stallions. "The plan is as insane as Hitler himself." He turned back to Hank's pensive gaze. "He never rode, you know. He loves animals— dogs and birds and the like—but he is terrified of horses. That painting is a complete fabrication, just like his peace promises to the world since 1937."

Such blatant treason from one of the Reich's most powerful men in East Prussia meant the war was over for Germany, Hank realized. With the impending collapse of the region's political and military structure, he could feel the second hand ticking on his mission and his life.

"Doctor, forgive me, but I must leave at once to save Hyperion. Where are the stallion and mare? I've got the money, right here." He patted his shirtfront.

"I don't want your money. I never did. I just want as many of my horses to survive as possible." Brunner returned to his seat, crossed his legs, and reached into a silver-plated box for a cigarette. He lit it, dragged deeply, and slowly released the smoke at the ceiling. "After the first evacuation, I knew I would have to take matters into my own hands. Ever hear of Brigadier General Bolten?"

"Of course, one of England's best-known horsemen. He participated in the Berlin Olympics."

"He arranged the rescue of twenty-eight mares and two central stud stallions."

"Hyperion?" The name caught in Hank's throat, and he felt his stomach lurch.

"No, not Hyperion's line. Bolten sent the horses across the Elbe, the narrows of the Baltic Sea, after it iced over in early December. They were quietly distributed to farms and estates until they can be sent from Wiemerskampsecond to Trakehnen for Warmbloods, near Hamburg."

"And Hyperion? Where's his line?" Hank glanced at his wrist and mouthed a curse for giving his watch to Jergie.

"At the Haffmann Farm, less than an hour's ride from here." The doctor rose and ushered Hank to the entry hall. "Wait here a moment, Herr Oscar—er, Henson." He returned minutes later with a map and a pair of high-topped leather riding boots.

"This will get you to the Haffmann Farm. With so little time you'll have to use the main road or risk getting lost. And please take these." He handed Hank the boots. "The only mare you can take is early in foal. Tell Kat my thoughts are with her and her mother, if they haven't already left."

"Kat?"

"Katja Haffmann. Her father died during the Normandy invasion." Dr. Brunner shook his head. "She doesn't know that yet. I never found the right time to tell her. Her father was her whole world, you see, and Kat's been running the farm since he left to serve the Reich."

Horse breeding was a male-dominated business. Hank tried to picture haggling with a woman but couldn't. She could be unreasonable, stubborn, unbusinesslike, and ruin the whole mission. Damn! Nothing was going as planned.

Brunner smiled sympathetically. "I can guess what you're thinking, but Kat knows horses like no woman I've ever met." He chuckled. "I'd put her a bit taller than you," he said, fingering his bruised lip, trying unsuccessfully to hide a grin, "and probably a lot tougher."

~

Map in hand, Hank dismissed the doctor's suggestion to use the refugee-jammed main road. With less than four-and-a-half hours to Jergie's touchdown, he decided to save time and go through the woods.

He pulled lightly on his pregnant mare's reins, guiding her onto the trail of broken snow leading in the direction of the Haffmann farm. As he ducked under a snow-laden pine bough, he patted and rubbed the horse's long neck. "You're a beauty," he whispered.

The mare tossed her mane. For a moment Hank released his fearful anticipation and bathed in a respite of twinkling sunlight and crisp-scented woods. Never had he felt so alive, so connected to the natural surroundings. The mare felt as comfortable under his seat as a longtime riding companion.

A faint buzzing sound disturbed his reverie.

"What's that?" Hank whispered to the broodmare. Her ears perked up.

The buzz rapidly grew to a deafening roar directly overhead. Hank was caught in the open. His upward glance caught a broadside flash of silver, and for a morbid moment he wondered if a bomb would drop out of the belly of the plane to end his life.

He lingered in the silence left behind the whining plane. He kicked the mare to a walk and passed through a copse of thick pines. Not fifty yards ahead, the woods broke into an open snow-blanketed meadow. Hank nudged the horse into a trot, and then a gallop across the open field, heading for the barns and large house that came into view along the main road.

Reaching the road, Hank spurred on the mare. Even the clacking sound of her hooves kicking up gravel and snow couldn't muffle the distant engine hum, now rising to a scream overhead. "To the house, girl. Run like hell!"

The horse broke out into a full stride. Hank crouched low in the saddle like a four-foot-eight jockey dashing to the finish line. A crackling staccato sound directly above him didn't register at first. Then plugs of snow exploded straight up like geysers in rows to his right side.

"Jesus!" Hank screamed. He weaved erratically to avoid being such an easy target for the machine gunner having sport with him. He twisted his neck to identify the swooping plane. *Russian insignia.*

The pilot and gunner were making sport of him. Lines of bullets pockmarked the ground to his left. The main farmhouse loomed to his right. Hank tugged on the reins, and the frantic mare headed dead on for the rapidly approaching pasture fence that separated him from the house.

Hank squeezed his eyes shut as the mare bunched for the jump, then flew over the fence rail, soaring as high as any jumper Hank had seen in Olympic competition did. "Holy shit!" Hank yelled as the mare made a perfect landing, barely breaking stride.

The shooting stopped as the plane banked to the right and disappeared. Hank reached with a shaking palm to rub the mare's sweating neck. "Hell of a ride, baby," he cooed to the horse. "I guess you put on a good enough show to save our skin."

He dismounted, petted the mare's regal forehead, and hurried to the house, holding her reins in a still-shaking hand. His heart had been hammering with adrenaline at his close call, and now it nearly burst with anticipation. In the yard in front of the house, he saw three filled wagons, each fitted to be pulled by two East Prussian Warmbloods. He wasn't too late.

7

Hank didn't bother to knock. "Hello?" he called as he opened the door to the farmhouse. "Miss Haffmann?"

Thick hairy arms lurched from the shadowy interior and grabbed him by the front of his coat. A sharp pain erupted in his groin. A fist slammed into his face. His head banged against a hard wood floor as he curled into a fetal position. He cupped his hands over his throbbing groin and tried to roll out of range of the heavy work boot, about to swing like a pendulum blade straight into his face.

"Stop!" a woman's voice commanded.

The boot halted a foot from the intended victim's right temple.

"That's enough, Wolf. We don't even know who he is," the woman snapped.

Hank took one hand from his groin and feebly lifted it in the air. "Henning Henson," he choked out in German. "Are you Katja Haffmann?"

He took a deep breath. The shooting pain was beginning to subside. He peered up at the woman in riding breeches and boots. From his angle, her legs looked impossibly long, and she was beautiful. Thick, flowing, coffee-colored hair framed her wide-set eyes, full lips, and chiseled high cheekbones. Brunner's label of tough had caused Hank to visualize a very different image than what stood before him.

"I am Katja. You're a German?" she asked.

"A Swede. Dr. Brunner sent me here to buy a stallion and mare. Hyperion."

"A customer!" Katja let loose a short manic laugh. "I regret the rude greeting you have received from my *temporary* stable master." She glared at Hank's panting attacker. "Wolf, feed the horses and recheck to make sure we have enough oats packed in each wagon."

The stable master wasn't taking his eyes off Hank, who slowly knelt, then stood. Katja shoved Wolf on the shoulder, drawing a scorching look. "Now, or you can escape on your own, all right. On foot. You're just lucky we need you to drive a wagon," she barked. The stable master nodded and grudgingly left the house.

Katja turned to go upstairs, as though Hank was of no consequence.

"Miss Haffmann, I've got only a couple of hours before I'm flying out of here in the village. I need those…"

Katja stopped and turned. Her cocked eyebrow signaled the need for a new tack.

"If I could just see the horses, fraulein, I'll get you the money and be gone in less than ten minutes."

"They're not for sale."

"Didn't Dr. Brunner—"

"I know nothing of this. But it wouldn't have mattered anyway. I need those horses for our trip to Hamburg."

"Damnit, your stable master nearly made me sterile, I just missed being made a human pincushion by Russian bullets, and—"

Katja started up the stairs again. "And they'll be back here any minute," she tossed over her shoulder "Forget the horses and run for your life."

"No! I need those horses. I'll pay you twice, three times what you could ever sell them for."

Katja furrowed her brows. "Money is of little consequence to me right now, Mr. Henson. I'm responsible for a household of women and children who may be lost in the woods."

Hank tried his most charming smile. "You don't have to select the horses. I'll pick 'em out myself. Surely you have enough horses to pull your wagons?"

"I don't have time for this." Katja started up the stairs again, then paused at the top. "If I find you still here when I come back down, the Russians won't need to kill you. I will."

The two froze in a locked stare. Hank finally broke into a grin. "The doctor said you were tough. I'll bet you've done a hell of a job with this place since your father, ah, since your father left."

Katja gripped the stair railing, her knuckles white. "I'm sure you seem suave to all the girls at home, but here you're just an idiot with an hour to live before the Bolsheviks shoot you. Enjoy the rest of your life, Mr. Henson."

Homicidal thoughts filled Hank's mind, replaced by the scheme of abducting Katja, gagged and bound, taking the horses, then leaving the woman somewhere she would be safe. He dismissed the fantasies for what they were and said, "Somebody needs to throw a saddle on you, woman!" He cleared his throat. "I'm taking those horses." He yanked his money belt open beneath his shirt and without counting, peeled off a third of the German marks. He balanced them on the staircase post. "That should be more than enough to compensate you. It'll come in handy on the road." Then he smiled appeasingly. "Show me Hyperion's line, or I'll pay your hairy friend to get me what I want."

Katja shook her head in disgust. "Meet me in the stable in fifteen minutes."

Elation burned bright in his soul. With each passing moment his fervor to complete his mission grew. He hurried to the stallion stables first, where Wolf had already gathered between the wagons nine of the twenty horses Katja had chosen to herd. Hank raised both arms. "I'm not your enemy." He lowered them as he drew closer and held out twenty marks. "They're yours if you can point me to the stallion from Hyperion's lineage."

Wolf snatched the money and pointed to a black stallion. "I can sell you more than Crusader."

Hank's eyes narrowed. "Get me his sister, and there's twenty more. You've got to drop what you're doing, though, and get the broodmare now."

Wolf leered greedily. "Make it fifty. My crazy cousin will shoot me if I don't do as she says."

Hank grinned. "Yes, I'll bet she would. Hurry."

Katja stormed into the stable as Wolf disappeared. "You're not done yet?" she snapped.

"Believe me, lady, nobody wants to be done and gone more than I do. This isn't my war."

"And it's mine?" she demanded. "You Swedes are despicable. You don't stand for a damn thing but what keeps your little world comfortable." Katja looked around in fury. "Where'd that bastard go? Help me steer these horses into the corral just outside."

Hank did as ordered. Once the horses were gated, Katja pointed out a chestnut stallion. "You can't have Crusader, but you can take that one."

Katja kept her eyes on the horse, but Hank couldn't take his eyes off the horse's master. *She's a feisty one, all right. Victoria could teach her some lessons in manners.*

"Progeny of Charm, one of Trakehnen's best bloodlines," Katja continued. "Look at the strong, thick bone, correct joints, the depth of his girth. Hell of an animal. He's got an Arabian's heart, too."

"I trust your—"

A shrill whistle slashed the air. Katja grabbed Hank by the arm and pulled him down to a crouch.

"Russian bombs," she said, then broke into a low-to-the-ground run back toward the stable. A bomb exploded less than a hundred yards from them. They dived over to a wall of hay stacked against the stable in bales.

"They're here," Katja hissed between clenched teeth. "Where the hell is Wolf?" Her expression turned from frustration to terror. "Mother!" She bolted toward the house.

A second whistling zinged overhead. In an instant, the back third of the stable exploded, hurling splintered wood in every direction. "Shit!" Hank exclaimed in disbelief, hiding his head in his arms.

When the flying debris had settled, he squinted through particle-filled air at the gaping hole that seconds before had been the building's rear wall. The shrill wail of a horse's pain pulled him to the devastated area. A downed tar-black stallion was kicking and snorting wildly as blood gushed around the six-foot fragment of barn wood that had pierced his underbelly.

"Jesus!" Hank shouted in rage. He searched the room for something to end the animal's pain and spotted a sickle hanging by a leather strap on a wall just beyond the exploded area. He lifted it and clutched the cold, smooth wood handle. The second his hand made contact, bile rose in his throat. He imagined hacking through a tree trunk rather than the dying horse's neck. The sordid task was taking too long. Hank dropped the sickle and broke into a run for the house.

~

Katja was on the porch yelling orders at Wolf. "The herd will be controlled between the second and third wagon. The only way we'll be able to keep them together is to travel at a trot. I want you to…" She stopped at the look of numbed horror on Hank's face as he approached from the stable. "What happened?"

"Downed stallion. I need a gun, or a rifle."

"Which?" Katja caught herself. What did it matter? All the animals were her children. She hurried upstairs and marched directly to her father's closet, again causing her mother to gasp.

"Who died? The bomb…"

Katja glanced at the terrified woman, propped in bed fully dressed with a bag packed by her bedside. The photograph of Claas was gone from the table. Probably the first thing her mother had packed. Katja avoided her mother's eyes. "You need to get yourself down to the second wagon, Mother. I've got all our papers in case we're stopped." She pulled out her father's hunting rifle and filled her coat pocket with bullet boxes.

"My God, child, what now?" Mrs. Haffmann pressed her hand to her heart, then uttered a low wail. "The Russians…they're here! They're going to—"

"No, not here yet, but they will be any minute." Katja pointed to the door with a parental gesture. "Get down those stairs and into the wagon right now."

Mrs. Haffmann shifted her legs over to the edge of her bed, then stood like the physically capable woman Katja knew lived behind closed doors. "Why the rifle?" she asked in a quavering voice. "Who's that blond man downstairs?"

"A horse buyer from Sweden caught in the same mess we are. Get going."

The old woman took a long, panning look at the room she had shared with her husband for twenty-eight years. Katja put her arm around her mother's stooped shoulder. "Don't worry, Mother, you'll be back. And so will Father as soon as we win the war."

Mrs. Haffmann nodded unquestioningly, then tried to lift her overstuffed bag.

"Let me help you with that." Katja jerked the bag from the floor. "What did you pack in here?"

"Our picture books, my silver brush and mirror…"

"I told you we'd be back." Katja hoisted the suitcase onto the bed and opened it. A full set of silverware glistened in the window light. The heavy-framed picture of her father in uniform was tucked between a folded sweater.

"You think I was going to let Wolf get away with my best silver again?" her mother demanded.

Katja laughed. "You don't miss a thing from this room, do you?" After making sure her mother had packed adequate warm clothes, Katja buckled the fabric suitcase and started helping her mother down the stairs with one arm while the other braced the rifle.

"My God, the horse! Mother, you'll have to get yourself into the wagon." Katja raced out of the house. Wolf was lining up the third wagon at an adequate distance to accommodate the twenty-horse herd. The Swede was nowhere in sight. Katja ran to the bomb-ravaged stable. She nearly ran into the stranger's arms as the two collided at the entry.

The man righted himself and ran a hand through his hair. "I'll take my horses, now, Miss Haffmann."

"The injured horse?"

"Already dead."

"You…"

"No, I didn't need to. He was dead when I got back to him. I'll take Charm's yearling, but I still need…"

Katja gawked at the brazen horse-trader. "You-son-of-a-bitch! All you can think about is buying a couple of horses." She took one hand off her rifle and braced a fist on her hip. "How are you going to get these animals to safety?"

"I've arranged rail transportation in Trakehnen."

Katja laughed derisively. "You think the trains will be running on schedule? They're probably not running at all." She shook her head at the man's naive stupidity. "Everybody's getting out. There won't be enough room for people on those trains, let alone horses."

Hank took a deep breath and clenched his teeth. "You may be right. It's not your problem."

"That's the truth. Now take your horses and get the hell off my farm. We're leaving right—" The telltale whistling of bombs sounded nearby. "Run!" she ordered. She and the Swede raced shoulder to shoulder to the wagons.

"They're coming!" Wolf yelled, his hands cupped around his mouth. "We have to leave now!" Katja's cousin climbed into the front seat of the third wagon. "Come on, woman!"

On the front porch Hildegarde, the droopy-faced cook, stopped wringing her pudgy hands and scurried to the wagon bench next to the stable master.

The Swede stood frozen. Detached, he watched Katja help her mother into the second wagon and direct a hesitant young housemaid and daughter to the lead wagon.

"No, Miss Katja, I can't drive a wagon," the girl protested. "I've never…"

Katja grabbed her by the arm. "You'll learn by doing, Eva. I've got to take lead on the herd. You and Andrea must get up in the wagon. You can do it."

"She doesn't need to drive that wagon. I will."

Katja whirled around to the voice behind her. That infernal Swede. "You? You're more trouble than you are worth. Just take your horses and get out."

"Where the hell am I to go? I'll never catch my plane ride out of this insanity. Besides, I'm a veterinarian. Have you packed a medical kit?"

Katja shoved the hair out of one of her eyes and tilted her chin defiantly. "I don't need you telling me how to take care of my herd."

The Swede sidestepped, blocking her attempted move around him. Katja turned back to her mother. "Mother, hand me that rifle. It's right behind you."

The man raised his hand to the old woman before she could respond. "Mrs. Haffmann, I'm a horse vet. Besides driving the lead wagon, I could care for the horses and help push the wagons when we get stuck." He shot an icy glance toward Wolf's mocking stare. "Besides, you need a man you can trust on a journey like this. Not being a German, I may be able to help get you to safety. I speak English perfectly."

Katja sighed in dismay. This handsome blond stranger was charming her mother.

"Listen to the man, darling," Mrs. Haffmann said. "We'll need all the help we can get."

"I packed only enough food for five of us and the little one," Katja responded without turning back to her mother.

The pushy horse trader stared at Katja resolutely. "Look, you think *I* want to go with *you*? I haven't got a choice."

Wolf's face had turned a bright fuchsia. "We don't need him," he growled. "He'll just eat our food. What could he do that I can't?"

"I'll eat half rations," the Swede said in a brisk, businesslike tone. "I'll more than earn my keep, especially if you fall into Allied hands."

Or Wolf's hands, Katja thought. She looked from the Swede to her cousin and back again. "Get up to the lead wagon," she told the stranger. "Eva will ride with Wolf." She turned to Wolf's brightening face. "Just during the day. You two men will sleep together in the wagon at night so Eva and Andrea can have a wagon to themselves."

"He's not getting into my wagon!"

"You'll do what I tell you, Wolf," she replied evenly, "or he'll be taking your place."

The stranger nodded with the first frank look of appreciation he'd given Katja since his unwanted but perhaps not unlucky arrival. "Oh, and Swede—"

"The name's Hank."

"Well, Hank, you'll need more than that scruffy old coat. Get my father's fur one out of the closet in the first bedroom at the top of the stairs."

"Katja, you're giving away your father's coat? What will he say when he gets home and finds out some stranger's wearing it?"

"There's no time to argue, Mother. He'll be of no use to us if he freezes to death." Katja gestured to the house. "Get the coat and let's go."

"I don't know whether to say thanks or go to hell," Hank retorted and half-smiled.

Katja stopped her always-in-motion body as though to consider which she preferred. "Go to hell."

8

Hank looked up at an overhead patch of Trakehnen countryside blue sky. "Visibility is good. We'd better get out of target range."

"Our planes will blast them from the sky any time," Katja said quietly.

"When we've got a minute, I'll explain the facts of life to you, young lady," Hank said.

"What's a stupid Swede know about the war?" Katja spit out when she stepped up to her wagon. "Got to keep the horses at a canter at least or some of them will break out of the herd."

Hank looked out at the snow, ice and mud-rutted road.

"Won't be easy. Roads look like hell. I'll look back for directions on when you want to turn."

"Use the main roads as long as you can. We've got to make up to sixty miles a day," Katja said.

"Excuse me, miss," Eva said in a high crystal voice.

"What Eva?" Katja said. "We've got to move."

"It was on the road the soldiers got us. We didn't have papers proving who we were. You said we were supposed to use the cart."

"Soldiers? Russians already this far?" asked Hank.

"Germans!" Wolf said. "Desperate for anything they can get their hands on."

"Enough talk," Katja snapped. "After we get about eight miles from the farm, the roads will be jammed with other wagons. We'll at least start on the main road to make time."

Eva looked down at her clinging child and nodded.

"It'll be all right, Eva," Katja said. "We'll get you and Andrea to a safe place until the war's over and we can come back home."

"At a trot?" Hank said. "Horses wouldn't last two…" Katja's hardening expression required no words.

"We'll do what we can," Hank said.

Hank muttered the word "bullheaded" before his horse trudged away from Katja's wagon. The stark contrast between Victoria's genteel nature and his rip-roaring female task master shot adrenaline, and regret, through him until he felt nauseated with guilt.

They hadn't traveled seven miles through thick snow-stacked woods when an intolerably bumpy ride caused Hank to pull the reins, step down and inspect his two harnessed, steam-puffing stallions. "Damn woman," he yelled after lifting his sweat dripping hand from Crusader's raven black neck. He turned and stormed back to his taskmaster.

"What did you stop for?" Katja demanded. "There isn't much daylight left."

"Got to stop trying to kill the horses," Hank said evenly. "We'll rest them for ten minutes. Oats in your wagon?"

"What in the hell do you think you're doing?" thundered Katja. "You're going to get us killed. We've got to make at least another ten miles before it gets dark. Get back to your wagon."

Hank slacked his jaw and repeatedly ran his index finger and thumb to a point on his chin while contemplating what insult fit best.

"You a Nazi?"

"What does that have to…"

"'Cause from what I've heard, you sound just like one. Giving commands all the time as if you ruled the world." Hank yanked off the knit hat Katja's mother had given him to save his ears from frostbite.

"Look lady. You need those horses. When they need rest we'll give it to them. They need food; we'll give them some of ours if we have to. Without them, we're dead."

He watched Katja glare into his laser blue eyes. She stepped down from her wagon, threw her arms up and back to stretch. The unintentional focus she caused on her small, pert breasts, poking out from under her unzipped coat, made her blush. She stepped back from Hank and the wagon and looked in both directions.

Katja finally spoke. "Going to let the horses rest for ten minutes. Give them a few oats and some water."

"Thank you," Hank silently mouthed to Katja so her craned-neck mother couldn't hear.

Wolf leaped from the wagon to catch up with his sauntering road companion before she reached Katja.

"Miss Haffmann. Miss Haffmann," the portly housemaid, Hildegarde yelled with her arm waving.

Wolf passed her by and ran up to Hank and his farm master. "That old woman is driving me crazy. Have her drive the lead wagon and let—"

"Not a chance, Wolf," Katja snapped. "Get some oats out of your wagon and feed your horses. We'll only be stopping a few minutes."

"Miss Haffmann," the old woman patted her balloon-sized bosomed chest to catch her breath. "Miss, I can't ride another minute with that man." She nervously kept Wolf in her peripheral vision while pleading.

"See, it would be better for everybody if Eva and…"

Katja raised an open palm to Wolf. "Shut up. You have no say in this." She turned her attention back to the maid.

"What's he done?"

"It's what he says, Miss. He keeps trying to scare me, telling me horrible things about what the Russians, or our own soldiers will do to us if they catch us." She put a quivering hand to her cheek. "I can't listen to it anymore."

"We had better get off the main road, Missy or..." Katja turned to her strained appeal.

"Don't let that monster scare you any more than we need to be."

Wolf's face was a dark mask.

Hank stepped to the edge of the road and returned to the huddled group. "We can't run these horses. There's a saddle in my wagon—"

"In all three wagons," Katja interrupted. "What's your point?"

Hank took a deep breath. "If you'd let me say a word without interrupting, I will ride with the herd so they can walk instead of trot. They'll never make it. Hell, they're not even shod. Their hooves are going to be bloody stubs as it is if we have to make it all the way to Hamburg."

Katja turned to Hildegarde. "If I let you ride with Eva and Andrea, will you drive the wagon? You know these roads much better than she does. And you're stronger."

The old woman's chin dipped into her thick, flabby neck when she enthusiastically nodded.

"Okay then, best we make the switch now."

Wolf softened his voice. "But Eva and I get along well. We could..."

Hank took a step forward. "You heard the woman, now get back to your wagon."

Wolf eyed the average-sized Swede. He moved in close enough for Hank to smell a mix of foul odors. "I'll get my chance with you."

"Leaving in five minutes," Katja yelled to the assembly. "Feed your animals and we're gone." She turned her eyes upward. "Planes could be by any minute."

"Hey, Swede. We'll take turns riding with the herd. Sound fair enough?"

"Suits me," he said smiling.

Once settled back into the journey, Hank trailed close enough to Katja's wagon to keep his full attention on her. He smiled as he watched her eyes getting droopy, trying to stay awake while shutting out her mother's wandering chatter from a reclined position behind her.

Hildegarde and Eva were in a hardy laughter with a giggling child.

The thick woods thinned out then edged open to another frozen pond. Everybody's eyes were trained on the distant moving centipede of refugees, wagons, horses and oxen on the intersecting main road to and from Trakehnen when the ground exploded.

9

Hank was ripped from his stupor by the roar of the sound. The force of the annihilating blast stopped all movement from Katja's pull horse and threw her upper body back so radically that she somersaulted back on top of her screaming mother.

Hank's chestnut broodmare reared up at the moment of detonation. He instinctively nudged his boot heals into his horse and broke out into a full run for the lead wagon. Splinters of wood, human and animal bone and flesh, glass, metal and everything else in Hildegarde and Eva's wagon were still settling to the frozen earth when he pulled on the reins. At the sound of the explosion the herd scattered like the flying debris.

"Holy, Jesus!" Hank screamed. He leaped off his horse and ran to the edge of the four-foot deep and twenty-foot wide hole the cluster of land mines had sharply bit out of the road. A raven black horse's hindquarters and a part of what had to be the upper torso of the old housemaid shot nauseating spurts of adrenaline through his veins.

"Crusader," he choked out.

Hank whipped his head back to Katja, righting her position on the wagon seat and trying to calm her mother's nonstop screeching and muttering.

Wolf was already thirty feet from the bombsite when Hank climbed back on his horse.

"What the hell?" Wolf's shrill voice was the next boom to crack the silence of the woods.

Katja clutched her stomach and vomited. She crawled from the wagon to the ground, her wrenching stomach unrelenting.

"Nothing, nothing left of 'em," Wolf moaned. "That beautiful child and mother. She was my friend. Oh, Eva." Wolf dropped to his knees, put his hands to his face and let out a strangled cry.

"Wolf, we can't let Katja see this." Hank's tone was calm, controlled. "Get up and go back to your wagon." He glanced to the edge of the road. "Shouldn't be a problem making it around the hole if the snow's not too deep. Hey, don't let Katja see this. Do you hear me?"

Wolf's quaking shoulders stopped long enough to nod his head.

Hank pulled the reins to the side and walked his horse back to Katja, who was still doubled over in agony. He moved slowly, intentionally, approaching her in a warm, soothing voice. He tentatively stroked her hair on her downturned head. "They're gone. There's nothing we can do now but try to save ourselves."

Tear-pooled, molasses-colored eyes turned up to him. Hank's pounding heart fluttered at her vulnerable beauty.

"I killed them! I killed them!" she shrieked.

"What are you talking about? It was a land mine, not a hole."

"Eva, Eva pleaded not to take the main road." Bile was erupting in Katja's throat again as if it were an active volcano. She turned away and began spastic vomiting between wrenching moans. Hank kneeled at her side, holding one shoulder while rubbing her back.

"It's been tough since your father left, hasn't it, kid? Let it out." She was too sick and disoriented to resist his comfort; his gentle touch and warm words started settling her down.

"Of course, it's not your fault," Hank whispered. "She was talking about the—" Hank's head shot up at the sense of being stared at. Wolf's face was now filled with raw terror. Hank's eyes traveled from the man's wild eyes to where his outstretched arm was pointing. He fought his own sudden panic.

"Katja, get up. Soldiers, German soldiers." He eased his trek master to her feet, feeling more than paternal when she laid her head on his fur-coated chest. His thoughts turned to snatching Katja's moose rifle, but while still at a distance he could count at least twenty-foot soldiers.

Katja tensed in his embrace. She moved away, wiped her mouth with the back of her glove and reached out to Hank's hand.

"They're ours," she said. She quickly dropped Hank's hand and cleared her throat. A steadiness returned to her voice. "My father's a top officer in the army. They won't harm us." Her sense of confidence and control was growing with each word. She took off one glove and wiped the tears from the corners of her crescent-shaped eyes. Katja glanced into Hank's eyes, seeing a worried affection that made her jerk her head away to the direction of the advancing platoon.

When the soldiers got within fifty yards of Wolf's wagon, she waved her arms and began running in their direction.

"We need your help. We need your help," she yelled. The soldier in the lead of the V-shaped formation was waving a metal detector inches above the uneven road when she approached him. "Thank goodness you're here."

The watery, blue-eyed soldier, Katja guessed not older then eighteen, held up his hand, fingers protruding through the worn-through wool glove.

"Halt. Do you want to get blown to pieces, too? This road has been mined."

"We've had a herd of horses fill every inch of where you're walking. I don't know what's up ahead, but it's safe where you're walking."

The pale, hollow-cheeked boy dropped the long handled device to the ground and took a deep breath. He turned back to those behind them. "It's all clear until we get past the wagons," he yelled. He rigidly turned back and looked up into the woman's inviting smile.

"Clear the road so we can get through," he commanded in a voice cold as the air they were breathing.

"We need your help gathering our horses from the woods. I'll give you a little food. We don't have much." Katja was already regretting the offer. The young man's eyes transformed from icy to ravenous.

"We will take whatever we have to. Show me your papers," he hissed.

Katja planted her fists on her hips. "Well, you little bastard. My father is commander of the horse drawn artillery unit of the entire army. You had better behave."

"I'll decide what we take." He pulled a P-38 light round pistol out from under his filthy, near buttonless overcoat and rammed the barrel into her ribs. "Don't move," he said with no more emotion than saying hello to a passing stranger. The leader turned and waved the rest of the soldiers to his side. Katja realized they were deserters. One by one Hitler youth his age and younger stood beside their self-appointed leader. Soulless unblinking eyes set in frozen, starved bodies started to form in a huddle around her.

"Clear away, my wife is always talking too much," Hank said in a no-nonsense voice outside the circle and Katja's sight. An area opened long enough for him to enter the circle then closed again. Hank thrust papers into the leader's hand.

The man narrowed his eyes while scrutinizing suspicious papers, suspicious differing last names, and suspicious Swedish origins. "All lies. You're too young. He shoved his pistol barrel into Hank's chest. "Probably a deserter."

"Of course you are welcome to whatever you need." Hank stepped back, then patted the leader on his frail shoulder. "What would the Fatherland be without boys like you? We offer you everything we have. I hope you will leave your countrymen enough for us to survive, too. We're trying to make it to Berlin, to the protection of our great Fuehrer." Hank put his arm around Katja and kissed her on the forehead. "My wife can be a little strong-headed, but she loves our country and will do anything to help hungry soldiers." Hank turned her scorching eyes to his. Her lips were curled in disgust.

"Now come on, honey. That's no way to act." Before she could get a burning word out, Hank pulled her lips to his and kissed her deeply. His arms locked around her back, ebbing any chance of resistance. She stood motionless. He relaxed his forced lips, unintentionally allowing her an opportunity to strike back. She bit lightly through his lower lip with a deep growl.

"Ouch!" Hank released his grip and she pulled away. Blood started running down his chin.

The soldiers one by one started to chuckle, then break into the first belly laugh they'd had since leaving home for the Russian front months ago.

"She needs a beating," the leader said through a laughter-drowned voice. The laughter stopped as fast as it erupted. "Enough play. We are hungry. You'll get us all the food out of your wagons. We'll find the horses ourselves."

Katja started to object, but Hank clamped a hand over her mouth. "If you would leave us the wagons and our horse teams, maybe a touch of food, we would greatly appreciate it officer," he said. "If you'll allow us we'll fix each of you a big meal and give each of you enough food to pack your pockets."

"We don't have anything for a hot meal." Hank put his hand over Katja's mouth again.

"You said you've got horses scattered everywhere," the leader said.

Hank tightened his grip around Katja and clamped his hand even harder over her muffled screaming.

"With all this snow, it'd be hard to start a fire. Besides, when the blast hit, those horses took off like race horses." Hank got on his toes and tried and look over the surrounding soldiers. "I don't even see one of them out there. They're lost."

The leader studied Hank's relaxed smile. "I like you," he declared, as if passing a live or die judgment. "We will do as you wish. Now let's be quick about it."

Katja finally dropped her pinched shoulders. Hank slowly took his hand off her mouth. He still held her tightly, lingering long enough for the soldiers to pass them momentarily.

"Katja, don't be a fool. These kids are half-dead. They don't care about right or wrong, even your precious crazy leader any more."

Katja reeled back a leg and kicked her captor in the shins as hard as she could. Hank grabbed for the injured leg, teetered, then fell backwards.

"Serves you right, Swede. And one more ignorant remark about the Fuehrer or my country and I'll leave you behind."

Hank studied her expression, then broke out into a broad smile. "You make a Thoroughbred seem calm as a plow horse."

"I mean it, Swede!"

"Hank, Kat. The name's Hank. Now settle down before you get us killed." He stood up and felt his cold mud-covered rear. "That's cold as hell."

At first tempted to apologize, Katja huffed, then directed his staring eyes to the audience of soldiers enjoying the scuffle.

Hank got as close to Katja as she'd allow. "Look, it's safer for you and me if they think you're my wife. And if they want horse meat, it's better to sacrifice one of the herd than have them take all our food."

"I'd rather die," said Katja. She marched away from him into the middle of the soldiers and finally shoulder-to-shoulder with the leader.

"How close are we to winning the war?" she asked.

"Our Fuehrer will save us. He has a plan."

"The Bolsheviks, I mean the Russians," Katja insisted.

The leader stopped abruptly. "We cannot beat the Reds. There are too many of them. It took too long to get us food, gas for our trucks and tanks." The leader's cracking voice sounded more to Katja like a boy forgotten by his father than a German soldier. "We couldn't even get warm clothes."

"We've got a long journey ourselves. Please…"

The leader turned and slapped Katja's face. "You think I care about what happens to you? Hurry up and get us food right now or we'll take it and the wagons, too."

Katja looked into the young man's crazed eyes long enough to realize Hank's tack wasn't so misguided. She looked over her shoulder, this time disappointed that Hank wasn't right behind her to step in and calm the maniac she would now attempt to humor.

Once full of bread, chicken, and cheese, the leader undid the two buttons holding his closed knee length coat, rubbed his concave stomach and swaggered away from his troop to Hank, Katja and Wolf standing motionless by a wagon wheel.

He gave a dismissive gesture to Hank and Wolf, then bathed his eyes in the lean sassy woman's raw beauty.

"You two aren't married," he said coyly. He raised a finger and wagged it close to Katja's nose. "You can't stand this man."

Hank stepped between the soldier's hungry eyes and Katja. "Of course we're married."

The leader pulled his pistol from his holster. "Shut up. It's obvious; she can't stand the sight of you. As soon as you forced her to kiss you, I knew you had never touched those beautiful lips before." With each word, the leader studied Katja's reaction. "See, I can see it."

"Don't worry, Hank," Katja said, eyes glued to the predator. "He knows we're married. Now that he has a full stomach, he's hungry for something else. Listen you little bastard, we're not the enemy." Katja pointed back to the East Prussian border. "They are. Remember?"

The leader dropped his dripping smile. He leveled the barrel of his gun at Katja's stomach. "Clear out everything from both wagons."

"Hold on. There's nothing but a few old household possessions my mother-in-law threw in to the wagon before we left."

The leader turned on one foot to Hank. "Everything, right now." Hank nodded. "Dear, go tell your mother what he has ordered us to do. It'll be all right. I'm sure he's just trying to get what he needs to see his men make it back to Berlin safely. We're all on the same side here."

The soldier lowered the pistol. "Do what your husband tells you."

"My husband, my husband is right. We'll do whatever we can to help."

"You, you look like a servant," the leader said to Wolf. "Unload the wagons. Hurry, more soldiers will be by any minute."

Wolf stormed to the closest wagon and began unloading. After he pulled the last silver platter out of Mrs. Haffmann's steadfast grip, the leader motioned for four of his men to join him.

"Remove all the food. No, not all the food." He turned his eyes to Katja. "There is a way you could keep enough food for the four of you until you make it to the next village."

Katja understood. "Half the food." While her tone wasn't inviting, she'd dropped the indignant edge that made the soldier want to kill as much as rape her.

"Can I talk to you a minute? Alone?" Hank said to the young man. Without awaiting a response, Hank draped an arm over the soldier's shoulder and walked away from Katja and ambled away from every-body. A few stomach churning and lip biting moments later the two returned in whispers and laughter.

"Leave them enough for a couple of days travel," the leader said.

The boy soldiers stuffed their clothes so full of food there was scarcely a day's meal left. They reformed a V-formation and moved on without saying another word.

"Wolf, help me unharness Kat's team. We haven't got more than two hours before dark," said Hank.

"I don't take orders."

"Wolf," Katja said testily.

The stable master glared savagely, shrugged his shoulders and did as ordered.

"All right, Mr. Henson, what did you tell the soldier?" Katja asked once Wolf and her mumbling mother were out of earshot.

"What I had to tell him to get his eyes and hands off you…" Hank said with a smirk. "Not that I blame him…"

"Probably that—"

"That you're colder than the ground he was walking on. I told him that under that big fur coat, you're built like a man and with a flat chest."

"You arrogant bastard." Before Katja could lower a closed fist, Hank grabbed her arm.

"You even fight like a man, too."

"Let go of me. You're the most conceited man I've ever met." She looked up and down her captor. "Legs skinnier than a new colt. Bowed, too."

"See? We're both funny looking enough to make a great team." Hank let her now-relaxed arm go. "I'm one other thing too, Kat." Hank dropped his voice an octave. "I'm an American, not a Swede."

10

Hank had no premeditated plan to unveil who he really was, but he was too cold and tired to care about hiding it from the Haffmann party any longer. What would they do?

Hank moved closer. "Listen to me, Kat, this could save our lives. My relatives are horse breeders in Stockholm, but I'm an American passing as a Swede to get a couple of your magnificent Warmbloods out of here."

"I don't believe you. Who'd be crazy enough to jump into the middle of a war to buy a couple of horses? Now hurry up. Those Russian planes are coming."

"I thought I could slip in and out like a ghost."

"You're a liar and a fool."

Hank looked over at Wolf and back to Katja's puzzled expression. "A fool, yes, but not a liar."

Katja moved in close to Hank's unblinking eyes. "You're really good. They just might believe your stories if you speak English as well as you lie."

"Katja," her mother called, what's that man doing with our horses? We have to go home right now. I'm cold and hungry. I want a hot bath."

Katja turned to her mother's first coherent words since the explosion.

"That's Wolf, Mother, our stable master. We have a long journey ahead."

"Those boys took our food. We'll starve and freeze to death." The old woman rubbed her exposed hands on the folded arms of her jacket. "It's time to go home, dear."

"We'll get to Gumbinnen in no more than two hours, Mother. I'm sure we'll be able to find some more food and a warm place to stay. Lay back down."

"Turn this wagon around right now and take me home, Katja Haffmann. That's an order." The old woman closed her mouth and puffed out her cheeks like a two-year-old holding her breath until somebody listened.

"We'll get you back home soon, Mrs. Haffmann," Hank interjected. "After this war is over and everything can settle back down." She shook her head, dropped the wagon canvas flap and returned to her bed.

"First you lie to me, now my mother," she said after a moment. "I think I can trust Wolf more."

Hank shook his head. "I don't give a damn who you trust."

The midday sun broke through the clouds. Both of them shot their eyes up to the sky. A flock of birds trying to find winter refuge made them sigh in relief. In silence they stood and watched them soar slowly over to the woods until they disappeared into an encroaching gray wall of clouds.

"Let's round up what we can and get the hell outta here," Hank said.

They were only able to find six mares just inside the tree line and straight across from the wagons.

"We've got to keep looking for the last two stallions," said Katja.

"Out of time, Kat."

"I'll tell you when we're out of time."

"Hey, I'm not one of your farm hands. We might decide things together, but I'll be damned if you're going to be deciding for me."

Katja bit her bottom lip. "I don't care what you do. I'm going to find those stallions."

Hank shook his head and without another word turned for the wagons.

"Where are you going?" she called, but couldn't raise a response. She rode with blinding rage back to the wagons a few paces behind Hank. As they neared Katja's mother's wagon, she rode up alongside Hank.

"You know you never even thanked me for saving you from those boys," he teasingly prompted.

Katja shoved the hair away from her eye. "I could have handled him. I've sent boys twice his size home limping."

The sound of Hank's laughter carried across the open field.

"Fair warning," Hank said with a smirk. "You'll just have to fall in love with me from a distance then. I'm not about to be your next victim."

Katja stopped her horse, not sure if she heard him correctly. "Telling me stories as if you're the enemy. We've got more than enough problems."

Hank got off his stallion, approached Katja and grabbed her horse by its reins. "What do you mean the enemy?"

"An American. Who's going to believe that?" Her eyes narrowed and voice dropped. "You'll get us all killed if you keep talking like that. It's obvious you say anything that pops into your head."

"Look lady, I am an American. You'll be damn glad of it when the Allies come in and kick Nazi asses all the way to Berlin."

Katja dismounted and snatched the reins from Hank's hand. "If you're an American, I'm Winston Churchill's sister. You had better figure out who your friends and enemies are."

"That's easy. Fascists."

Not quite understanding exactly what a fascist is, Hank caught Katja at a loss for words.

"Nazis," Hank spit out.

"My father's an honorable man, and a Nazi. You know nothing about my people, you conceited traitor."

Hank waved Wolf over to Katja's wagon. "Somebody should have put a bit in your mouth years ago."

Wolf and Katja finally gathered close. Hank looked in all directions, then proceeded. "Here's how I see it. We're down to hardly any food. It was almost a blessing the horses scattered. We've got to travel light and fast. Let's only use cart paths and do a lot of our traveling at night." Hank glanced over at Katja's not yet disagreeing expression.

"Good, we agree." Hank patted the map in his coat pocket. "We'll search out food at every village we stop at."

"That's all obvious. Let's get moving. We can make…"

Hank held up his hand to stop interruptions. "What's not obvious is that I am an American." Hank turned his eyes on Wolf. "Won't do you any good to know that. I'll just deny it if you tell a German officer. I've got all the Swedish papers I need to prove you a liar."

"A filthy American," Wolf hissed.

Hank smiled and turned to Katja. "See, it's not impossible to believe. We all know you'll be better off captured by the Allied troops than the Russians. Now you can find comfort in knowing that as long as you're with me, they won't even hold you as prisoners."

"Don't listen to him," Katja blurted out. "He changes his stories once an hour. I'll get us through this, and all the way to Hamburg." Katja turned everybody's attention to the never-ending line of refugees up ahead. "We'll lose days if we don't use the main roads like everybody else."

"There will be bombs overhead and along the roads," said Hank simply. "Not to mention retreating German soldiers."

"We're not going to follow you into enemy hands, you lying traitor," Wolf said.

Hank raised open palms chest high. "I'm just after the same thing each of you are, waking up another day."

"He says he's an American?" Mrs. Haffmann yelled down from the wagon to her daughter.

"Just a ploy to try and save his backside, Mother," Katja said. She turned back to Hank and stared into his unblinking eyes.

"Don't listen to anything he says. He's just so scared he makes up a new story every mile." Katja reharnessed the two stallions and climbed up into her wagon.

"You ride with Wolf, Swede," Katja said icily to Hank.

Without responding, Hank climbed into Katja's wagon and yanked the reins from her hands. "We'll take turns. Lie down in the back and get some rest. You said this village is about two hours away?"

There was no getting back the reins short of a wrestling match. Katja motioned to Wolf. "Main road at least until the village. We'll decide roads or cart paths in the morning."

Katja's concession was enough for Hank at the moment. As they fell into line on the main road, a lean, freckled refugee wagon train man galloped up the road alongside Hank.

"Hear the news?" he yelled in a squeaky adolescent voice.

"News?" Hank responded.

"The Bolsheviks have surrounded East Prussia. There's no border crossing anywhere, except for the Frische Haff."

Hank turned to Katja for an explanation.

"Can't do that. It'd be impossible to cross."

The young rider kept pace with the Haffmann wagon's increasing speed. "I know, but there's no choice. Where you going when you get away from the Reds?"

"Hamburg," Katja yelled over the clanking hooves.

"Can't do that either," the young rider said matter-of-factly.

Katja's face was darkening. "You're just full of good news. Why the hell not?"

"Bombed to bits. About everybody's dead from bombs dropping like raindrops."

"How do you know all this?" Katja yelled.

"Folks about three wagons back with family there. They got word somehow about the bombing." The young man's voice cracked. "Had to change their plans."

Katja turned to Hank. "Just stories. Nobody knows for sure."

"And you believe Germany's still going to win the war?" Hank asked.

"Of course." Katja leaned across Hank to the rider. "Thanks for the information. Any main roads blowup?"

"Blockades and German troops. No bombs yet. Everybody's going to be forced off the main roads after Gumbinnen."

"Everybody's going to the same city?" Katja asked.

"If there's anything left of it. Do you have any food you can spare? There's just me and my mother about five wagons back. We're fine, but the family in front of us didn't get out in time to pack any food. I'm going from wagon to wagon to get even just a little of anything you've got so they don't starve."

"We got robbed by our own soldiers," Katja boomed out.

"A lot of that," the young man said, then rode up ahead to the next oxen hauled cart.

Hank turned to Katja, but as usual she was posed to get in the last word. "I know, we can't ignore what the young man said. If we get confirmation from others when we get to the village, I'm willing to consider crossing the Haff. But only if we have to. My mother would never make it across the ice."

"And Hamburg?"

Katja's full lips curled up in disgust. "If I reacted to everything somebody says," she stared Hank down with a long pause, "we'd never make it out of East Prussia. Everybody's scared. People will say anything. Stick with the plan."

Hank nodded. "We'll do some asking tonight. I don't think we should make any decision yet, but I suspect you're right. We'll hear something new every day."

~

It was dusk. Charcoal and powder gray steams of smoke off scattered demolished homes and businesses were still rising reminiscent of departing spirits when the Haffmann party stopped at a knoll above the town below.

It would soon be dark and ice was thickly caking on Hank's stubbled beard. "Think there's anything left?" Hank asked.

"I see a few lights and homes that didn't get hit." Katja glanced over the continuing line of wagons passing by. "Question is, how long has this parade been going on? There's probably nothing left down there."

Katja was wrong. As the Haffmann wagons entered the village well after dark, a more than half moon in the black winter sky illuminated a ghostly Holstein cow mooing in prolonged pain from swollen udders. Starving pigs, a bloated cow, dogs and cats were running wild across the town's main road and in and out of doors left wide open to the freezing night air.

"Looks like everybody's gone," said Katja while rubbing her mitten-covered hands over her arms.

"Let's stop and stay in one of the houses still standing. Cold?"

"Damn right it's cold," Mrs. Haffmann spouted off from behind the canvas drop. She bolted to an upright position and stuck her head out between Hank and Katja.

"Find us someplace warm and some hot food right now, before we freeze to death."

Hank pulled off the village's main road. He guided both wagons to a two-story, snow-caked house that appeared deserted. Hank sprang down from the wagon seat.

"Scavengers have probably already gone through everything, but I'll go check it out. If there's no sign of anybody returning we'll stay here tonight." Katja was too tired to dispute his decision. She nodded.

Hank used his glove to rub a circle out of the lacy frost covering the living room window. The furnishings were all in place. No sign of disturbance. No sign of life. He shuffled to the front door, took a deep breath and turned the knob. It opened. He reached and found the light switch, but got no light. He entered quietly as a burglar. The fabric and leather furniture, wood tables, bookshelves and accent pieces were as nice as in Hank's Uncle Oscar's home. His acute hunger was mixed with embarrassment and shame for violating someone's home.

"Hello, anybody here?" he called. All was silent. The night sky casting a soft light through the dining area window revealed a hardy roast beef and potatoes dinner half eaten on six plates. Hank picked up a slice of meat and ate it. While cold from last-second abandonment probably as long as a day before, he couldn't stop grunting sounds of ecstasy with each bite and swallow. He regained his senses and vision to see a generous half of a roast still uncut on the center of the table. His eyes then turned to the small stack of wood on the stone fireplace hearth. A child's excitement filled him. He ran out of the house waving his arms to his freezing companions.

"You won't believe it. Meat, potatoes, bread. Milk probably still good 'cause it's freezing in there."

Mrs. Haffmann was out of the back of the wagon and into the house before Hank could take a breath. He burst out laughing when she dashed by him.

Katja held herself back from giving her adversary the satisfaction of gushing about the welcome news. She slowly got out of her wagon and looked up and down the road for possible competition for their find. While the main street was still filled with passing wagons, the back street with four large homes amply spaced apart was temporarily all theirs.

Hank couldn't be so coy. He ran to Katja and gently grabbed her arm. "You won't believe it, Kat. There's enough meat to last us for days if we're careful. And wood to start a big fire."

"No fire, or lights. Every wagon in town will be here before we even warm our bones. Let's eat, pack up everything we can use, and you and I go on more house searches along this street to see what else we can find."

Hank was too relieved and happy to argue. "Sometimes, not often mind you, you have wisdom beyond your years."

Katja let a half-smile slip out before reassuming her stony mask with him.

Assuming the town was full of riches, they all ate until their stomachs ached. The cupboards were too full, Wolf had guessed over their moonlit dinner. The owners of the house had to have been killed in the streets. There was no sign of attempted evacuation. After dinner every one of them, including the now highly animated Mrs. Haffmann, searched a different area of the house in quest of warm blankets, clothing, and every bit of preserved food stored for winter.

Mrs. Haffmann eventually tired from her daughter's reprimands for sneaking expensive porcelain figurines, jewelry, and select silverware she needed to complete her own wagon-packed set, and even an evening dress that wouldn't have fit her in the bloom of her youth.

"Ready for our search?" Katja asked Hank after they had darted from the house to the wagon for the last of the treasures.

"There's no more room."

Katja ignored Hank's practical assessment. He followed close behind at a jog, driven by curiosity more than need. The neighboring house showed no signs of evacuation, but the front door was locked.

"Wonder if they all went to some kind of bomb shelter," Katja said with furrowed dark brows. "Imagine if the house we just raided isn't abandoned. If those people are alive."

"They would have been back by now. We've got enough to worry about without inventing things." Hank trudged through knee-high snow and peered into the window. "You wouldn't know anything about that," she said. While not nearly as opulent as the home of their still-settling feast, he again felt the eeriness of personal violation at the undisturbed living room. A tall, broad shadow moved inside.

"Let's get the hell out of here," Hank said dropping his voice an octave. "They're still home. He's probably getting ready to blow our heads off." The two crept from the porch to the center of the street.

"We've got all we need," said Katja, more of a command than request.

"Should we go to the last house and see if anybody's there? This might be the best chance we get for supplies for the rest of our journey."

"Until your comrades, the Americans, swoop down and save us, right?"

"Now you're starting to get the picture."

The modest one-story wood frame house edged an expansive open snow-covered field Hank assumed the owners used for farming. Hank crept to the porchless front steps, reached out for the front door knob and found it slightly ajar. He stuck his head in far enough to detect movement or noise. "Hello. Anybody home?"

Silence.

"Let's go," Katja said, shifting her weight from one foot to the other more out of anxiousness than cold.

"Hello," Hank boomed out. He turned to Katja and waved her in after him. The interior of the house was as characterless and spartan as the outside. Unlike the first house, Hank immediately sensed someone was living there after the bombing, maybe even hiding now.

"There's somebody here," Hank whispered and pointed to the red glowing embers in the fireplace. He stood erect and cleared his throat. "Hello. We aren't the enemy," Hank hollered.

"We're Germans like you. Come out and don't be frightened."

Katja heard something move in the corner space near the threshold from the living room to the kitchen.

"Hank, see that?" Katja whispered. "Light that lantern on the end table."

"Don't anybody panic. I'm lighting the lamp so we can see what we're doing. Nobody shoot or anything." This time Hank heard a child's high-pitched cough shut off by a hand to mouth.

Katja started walking to the source of the noise. "I think I hear a frightened little girl, too."

The silhouette of a young woman wearing an ankle-length tattered dress; low matronly-heeled shoes and oversized coat draped over a thin frame, sprang into the doorway and snatched the child to her side.

"Get out of our house!" the shrill voice was rising hysterically.

Hank struck the match and touched it to the kerosene-soaked wick. The woman and child clung tighter and gasped in surprise.

"My name is Katja Haffmann, from Trakeh—"

"I don't care where you're from. You say friends, then break into our house as if you're thieves." The young woman's eyes looked wildly around the room for others who might leap out from the shadows.

The woman and child cowered at Hank's slightest movement toward them. "I said hello, when I opened the door. Would a thief do that? We're only—"

"My own neighbors, those bastard boys, came into our house looking—oh, get out of here!" she screamed.

Hank turned to Katja. "Come, let's go. We're scaring the poor woman to death."

"You're too late. We have nothing. They took it, food, warm clothes, everything," she choked out through tears.

"Where's your husband?" asked Katja.

The woman broke out into such deep sobs that she couldn't speak.

"Daddy's hurt." The child said and pushed away from her mother far enough to point into the dimly visible kitchen.

"Get out of my house," a distant wooden voice called out from the kitchen.

"We can help if you need food," Katja said.

Hank elbowed Katja's side, and then put his arm around her and force-marched her out of earshot. He leaned down to her ear, first pushing away her long hair with a feather touch.

"Kat, we've got to protect ourselves and the horses. Everybody's hurting."

Katja catapulted away from his grip and rushed to the woman, now on her knees comforting her whimpering child. "I meant it, we have food."

The mother gazed up into Katja caring eyes. "I think my husband's back is broken."

"Don't trust them," the voice said from a prone position on the kitchen table. "They'll try to...Oh!" An attempt to sit up shot paralyzing pain through the man.

Katja turned to Hank, halfway out the front door. "Hey, you're a doctor. Come and look at this man." Katja kneeled down and put her arm on the woman's shoulder.

"Everything's going to be all right. I'll do all I can," Hank said.

Hank shook his head, picked up a lantern and started toward the kitchen. "Damnit, I don't even have a medical bag," he muttered.

He held the yellow glow up to the man sprawled out on the kitchen table. The cocoa-colored sweating face set in tar-black hair and a raggedy half beard winced through clenched teeth.

"Pretty bad, huh?" Hank said.

The man nodded. "You a real doctor?"

"If your favorite food is oats. I'm a horse doctor." Hank's attempted try at charming bedside manner passed by the man wrenching in pain.

"The back. I think it's the back. I broke it when they shoved me down the stairs."

"Your neighbors did this? I'm surprised you didn't shoot."

"No gun. I don't keep a gun." A snarl of agony sweep over the man's face. He clamped his eyes shut as the slightest movement ripped excruciating pain through him, no different than it would feel to have a broken bottle being dragged down his bare-skinned back.

"We're going to need to see that vertebrae. Kat, come in here, please." When he looked up she was already at his side with her coat off and shirt-sleeves shoved up to the elbow. "Hold this lantern. What's your name?"

The man mouthed the words, then repeated in a raspy voice. "Dreyfuss, Hendrick." He winced again and closed his eyes.

"Mrs. Dreyfuss, I'm going to need your help turning your husband enough so we can see if we have a break or strain here." The young woman scurried to her husband's side.

"We ready? This is going to hurt, but I have to see." Hank gently started to turn the shoulders. The man's veins jetted out into livid ridges along his temple and throat. He didn't make a sound.

"Hold the light closer," Hank ordered Katja. He gently felt along the man's spine, feather touching and probing.

"Okay." He and the man's wife eased him back to the table.

"How near is your doctor?" Hank asked Mrs. Dreyfuss.

"He's gone. He left with most the others. Hendrick thought it was less dangerous to stay with our ten-year-old and wait things out." She turned her moist downcast eyes from Hank to Katja. A slight head movement motioned Katja to join her in the living room.

Hank glanced at Katja then back to the mother. "I'm afraid you're right. It appears he has seriously dislocated the disks in the lumbar, lower back area. The backbone is swaying similar to a backyard garden snake."

Hendrick clutched Hank's wrist. "I'm paralyzed. I'll never walk again."

"Heavens no," Hank responded, patting the man's white knuckles with his free hand. "You do need to have the vertebrae aligned and be set in traction for a time. No, you'll walk again." Hank turned to Mrs. Dreyfuss and motioned her and Katja to join him in the other room.

"No," Hendrick snapped. "I need to know what to do. It's my wife and daughter, Alena, that really need the help."

Katja's eyes turned on Hank's. She couldn't read his cloaked expression.

"First, as much as it's going to hurt, we have to move you to the floor, so you don't roll off the table," he said to the injured man. "Mrs. Dreyfuss, get a mattress from the bedroom and we'll lay it right here."

"No gentle way to do this I'm afraid," Hank said while pushing matted hair off the man's forehead.

"Kat, I'll take the center, you and Mrs. Dreyfuss each grab an arm and leg. Mr. Dreyfuss, try to stiffen your body the best you can."

Hendrick bit his lip to contain a need to scream as the three lifted him to the floor.

Once shifted, Dreyfuss tugged on Katja's arm until the two were alone in the shadowed living room.

"We were wrong not to go with the others," she said in a hushed voice. "I pleaded for our little girl's sake, but my husband wouldn't, still can't believe what's happening to us all."

Katja said nothing, anticipating the desperate woman's next words.

"Please, please, take our daughter. We can't go now. She'll be killed by the Russians." Mrs. Dreyfuss rushed her hand to her gaping mouth with visions of worse than death for her blonde silky-haired daughter. Katja read her thoughts and pulled the woman to her chest.

"Of course we'll take her."

"Kat, come here a minute and pull that chair over for the man to raise his legs," Hank yelled from around the corner.

"You would do such a thing for us?" Mrs. Dreyfuss could hardly choke out words from her throbbing throat.

"Write down your full name and give me a picture of you and your husband. When we make it to safety at Berg Haffmann's house in Hamburg I'll attempt to get word to you in this village. If you leave…"

"I know. I'll remember Berg Haffmann, Hamburg." Mrs. Dreyfuss wiped her running nose with the back of her hand and released her grip on Katja. She stuck her head around the corner and stared at the wheat-haired doctor gesturing to her husband on the best way to protect his back until help arrived. She returned to the young woman's caring eyes.

"Will your husband take our Alena?"

"He's not my husband, and I don't know what he'll say." Katja guided the two back to the kitchen.

Katja paused, then as usual let it all out assuming she could control the outcome of whatever she said. "The little girl goes with us."

Hendrick beat Hank's explosive reaction to the order.

"Nobody takes my daughter. How dare you enter our house."

Mrs. Dreyfuss rushed to her husband and dropped to her knees. "It was me. I asked that they take her."

Hendrick shot up until excruciating pain forced him back to the floor. "You what? Without even talking about it?"

"Mr. Dreyfuss is right," Hank interjected. "Crazy idea."

"It's not crazy to leave a helpless child here for the Russians to steal, rape or murder."

Each word pounded Mrs. Dreyfuss as if they were bare fists. She wailed and pleaded with her husband to allow the child to go. She collapsed in tears on his chest. Patting his wife's stringy mouse-colored matted hair, Hendrick raised his eyes to Katja and nodded.

"Not this time, general. I've got a better plan for them, and us," Hank said.

Katja yanked away from his light grip.

"You don't have a say in it." She threw up an open palm and gestured his dismissal.

"I don't have a say in the matter?" Hank took a deep breath. He'd never felt such fury for a man or woman before. The words caught in his throat like a fishhook.

Katja pulled her hair back from the nearly-always covered eye, self-righteously lifted her chin and turned her back on him.

"It isn't as if I don't care about the child. She should stay with her family."

"The doctor's right," Hendrick yelled to his wife.

Hank nodded. "Thank you. I'm going back to get plenty of food for your family, then we'll find a place for you to hide until the Allied Forces arrive."

"Allied Forces?" Mr. Dreyfuss asked.

Katja shot a thumb over her shoulder in Hank's direction. "Says he's an American caught behind enemy lines. We're the enemy." She turned her head to Hank. "Right? Whoever the hell you are."

"More than ever," Hank said, then headed for the door. "The child stays". He slammed the door behind him.

The sheet of ice air caught Hank by surprise. He loudly gulped and pulled his fur jacket closer to his body and exposed neck. He broke into a run through the deep snow, sensing something was wrong back at the wagons. The thick cloud-covered sky offered little light, contributing to a slip, then both feet flew up in the air and Hank landed on the hardened ice-rutted dirt road between houses.

"Shit!" he shouted, then stood back up and looked around to see if his outburst was heard. As he approached the house with their wagons, he broke into a full run.

"Where in the hell…Wolf, you son of a bitch." He burst into the house and found Mrs. Haffmann gagged and tied to a chair in the dining room. A steady hum of attempted speech came from her muffled mouth. Hank pulled down the gag.

"That beast. That monster. Untie me!" Mrs. Haffmann commanded.

Hank took the meat-carving knife from the table and sliced open her bonds.

"Stupid. We should have tied him up before we left."

"He took everything. All the food." Mrs. Haffmann kept patting her well-endowed chest. "My silver. Everything."

"Bastard took the main wagon, didn't he? I'll unharness the stallion and track the son-of-a-bitch down. Couldn't have gone three miles pulling the wagon," Hank shouted over the woman's near-comically exaggerated breathing while releasing her bonds. She raised her fat dangling arm as if her last words were about to be imparted.

"The gun. He got the gun and all the bullets. Let him go." She took another deep-jagged breath. "He'll kill you. He told me he'd be ready for you. He held the rifle up to my face." She burst into a hooting cry that sounded more like a mouse call than a woman's wail.

Hank turned at the sound of the door opening and the sound of a child's voice.

The situation required no explanation. Katja led the child to the living room couch and started the already-stacked wood ablaze in the fireplace.

"You all right, mother?"

"Of course I'm not all right. That cousin of yours is the devil himself."

"Warm yourself here, dear." Katja said to the child. Hank stared at Katja's attractive sharply defined facial features in the light of the flaming logs.

"Everything, right?" She shoved her hair back over one ear. "Wolf took it all…Gun, too, right?" Katja's voice was ascending to a murderous falsetto.

Hank sighed and sat next to her, too exhausted to engage in another confrontation. "Right. Everything."

They sat as still as mannequins staring at the fire, Katja's arm draped over the cuddling child.

"Well, well what are we going to do? Don't just sit there," Mrs. Haffmann haughtily said.

Hank slowly rose. "I'm going to tell the child's parents after a couple of hours sleep that I'm going to search more houses for food." Katja stoically remained fixed on the fire. When Hank got to the front door he turned back to the woman and child. "I'll also tell them the child will be safest with us."

Katja didn't turn back to Hank until after the door had close behind him. She was too exhausted and emotionally empty to say thank you.

11

Hank returned less than a half-hour later. When he entered the fire embers were still radiating heat. The child was draped on Katja's chest in a deep sleep. Mrs. Haffmann was snoring in the living room chair; a blanket pulled tightly up to her neck.

He tiptoed over to the woman and child. Hovering over them, Hank took his time to study Katja's face lying peacefully with a slight smile he assumed arose from the closeness and warmth of the child. She hadn't hesitated to cling to Katja like a mother since they first met.

Hank stretched in front of the fire with a sofa pillow and blanket. While his first thoughts were to douse the fire to minimize the danger of more desperate neighbors or retreating soldiers, the warmth overtook caution and he fell asleep in moments.

Katja stirred him from his recurring dream of Victoria's beautiful face writhing in pleasure while he tenderly made love to her in his Sunny Acres master bedroom canopy bed.

"Mr. Henson," she whispered. "Wake up. Time to find food before it gets light." Hank rubbed his eyes. The fire was now no more than dark embers. The room once again held a dark, cold, hostile feeling.

They slipped back into the night air. Hank stepped to the blanket-covered unharnessed horses tied to a hitching post in front of the house. He crouched down and lifted each hoof and gasped.

They couldn't survive like this. He rubbed the freezing back of one of the two stallions. They critically needed to be shod. They needed shelter. He patted the nose of one of the two. "Kings to paupers, hey, guys," he whispered in one of Katja's favorite stallion's ears.

~

At that moment Katja forgot how, just hours ago, she was angry enough to shoot the gentle horseman now whispering soothing words into the ears of her beloved horses. She tucked one of her arms around Hank's to softly pull him away from the horses.

"Come on, we haven't much time," she said.

They walked without a word past the village's once main street and to the houses in a thicket of pine trees. They perched on a slight rise with an overlooking view of the formerly picturesque town.

The first two of the eight houses on the rise were stripped of everything, from furniture to wall hangings. All seemed lost when, in approaching the third house, they saw a single candle light in a distant room.

"Maybe somebody's there that can help," Katja said.

Hank stopped and put a finger to his lips to be silent.

He leaned to her ear, pulling back her thick, long hair. "Stay here. I'll sneak up to the window and see what's going on." She nodded and retreated to the side of the house as Hank crouched down and eased his way to the drapeless living room window.

A half-finished bottle of wine and fresh bread and cheese could be seen by the candle's glow on the living room coffee table. Hank saw no one. He decided their odds of trouble were less in scavenging through deserted houses. He lowered his head and began to creep away when the front door flew open.

"Dinner? Dinner?" the young German soldier said. Hank stood up and approached the inviting cherub face.

"Dinner? Yes," Hank responded. "We'd enjoy some dinner."

"Where are the others?" the soldier said in a high singsong tone.

"No, just me. I meant the people back at the wagon outside town."

The soldier pointed to the side of the house where Katja was hiding. Katja soon appeared with two more young soldiers acting as a moving wall behind her.

"Her. Yes, my wife. We would appreciate some dinner."

The greeter crossed and rubbed his arms. "Cold, cold," he said with a smile and a mock shiver. Katja and Hank were to be guests for dinner or whatever else the young desperates had planned.

On entering the modest house, Hank counted four other young soldiers with liquor bottles in hand or gulping.

"Now we party," a man with a Hitler-style haircut and short mustache moaned while gyrating from a stretched out position for Katja as she passed him by on their way into the kitchen.

The door greeter bowed and motioned for the two to have a seat at the dinner table.

"Homemade vegetable soup, bread and wine. Please be our guests."

Hank and Katja hadn't slurped more than a couple of spoonfuls when the seated, drunken soldiers began querying them about where their wagon was located.

"It wouldn't do you any good to take our wagon," Hank said over the strained polite small talk. The room went silent.

"Friends, friends," the lead soldier said, rising with a half-full glass of blood-red wine. He signaled to Katja to bring two glasses from the living room to the kitchen for the guests to share in a toast. Katja looped her arm around Hank's, sensing impending danger.

"No, no, I insist on getting it," Hank said, pulling away from Katja and hurrying out of the room before their host could respond. The host followed close behind, flanked by two of the five soldiers. The two blocked the doorway while the host rushed to Hank and put his arm around him.

"Thieves?" he asked innocently as a child.

"No, no, we're not thieves. Just hungry like everybody else. Trying to get away from those monstrous Bolsheviks."

Hank stepped up his rambling to get past the curious staring. "We're from Trakehnen. Raise Warmbloods for the Reich. You, where are you from?"

"Thieves," he repeated, shaking his head.

Hank cleared his throat while he craned his neck to see past the soldier in the doorway to Katja. His heart pumped at the speed of a locomotive at the thought of her in danger.

"Where are the people who live here?" Hank said brisk, businesslike.

"They were generous. Understanding of what a sacrifice we've made for the Fatherland." He coldly smiled and waved an arm around the room. "They left us everything. Their clothes, cupboards full of food. Plenty of wine."

One of the two soldiers blocking the doorway scratched his bristly black beard and chuckled. Hank's eyes shot over to the two still unable to get a glimpse of Katja in the other room. He hadn't heard a sound from the kitchen since darting into the living room. No question now, she was in trouble.

"They were generous. Now it's your turn. We want, no, need to—in the name of the Reich, of course—take your wagon and horses."

Hank nervously smiled. "Of course. A reasonable request. Would it be too much to ask to enjoy a little cheese, bread and wine together before meeting your request?"

The host glared into Hank's eyes, detecting no fear or spitefulness. "Of course, there's no hurry. We just need them by daylight so we can get to the safety of Berlin and our Fuehrer."

Hank patted the white-haired, blue-eyed Aryan on the shoulder. "That's exactly our plan. The Fuehrer will squash those Reds before they ever step foot into Berlin." The soldiers at the doorway relaxed, opening up a space large enough for Hank to glance into the kitchen. Katja and the other two soldiers weren't in sight.

Hank started singing a little German song his father had taught him as a child. He raised his hands urging the young men to join in. The four of them plopped down on the living room sofa and chairs while Hank nursed them from one stanza to the next.

He rose to lead them in a second verse. His mind and mouth couldn't have been more disconnected. A slight movement around the room got him within reach of the gun. He'd have to take the life-and-death chance it was loaded and the safety was off. Using his hand as a batten, on a down note he pumped his arm over to the MP40 sub-machine gun leaning against the wall, locked it to his waist belt high and widened his stance. The exploding noise was followed by the spray of blood from scalps, faces, necks and chests. Hank stopped short of emptying the gun's thirty rounds on his victims.

He bolted into the kitchen, through to the back to a closed door. When he kicked the door open two soldiers were still trying to pull up their pants up when he rammed the butt of the weapon into the closest head and emptied the gun in the chest of the last one.

Hank looked into Katja's glazed eyes. Her painfully vulnerable nakedness stretched before him. A sheet that tied her wrists and ankles at each twin bedpost was crimson, screaming evidence of a brutal struggle. He moved closer in the cramped space, with barely enough room for a dresser and bed, and hovered over Katja. A razor thin cut between her breasts had eased out a single drop of blood where the cutting stopped.

He turned to the man with the exploded bare chest propped as though he were a rag doll against the wall, then to the soldier he bludgeoned when he kicked in the door. A knife was dangling from the still body's fingertips. With a crazed look nearly as distant as Katja's, he roared and drove the butt of the machine gun through the downed rapist's skull. His eyes jetted from the horror he'd just created to Katja.

"Jesus, I'm sorry, Kat. I couldn't get to you any sooner."

Hank sat on the corner of the bed, gently untied each appendage and rubbed them to help circulation return.

Once untied, Katja couldn't stop the spastic shaking. "I…I stopped them. Moved…so much they couldn't get—"

Hank pulled her to his chest and held her cheek to his tightly.

"'Course you did, Kat, 'course you did." He rocked her naked body in his arms until there was some sense of life returning.

"Okay kid, we're going to get dressed now." His movements were deliberately slow. Her bra and panties had been ripped off her body, leaving too much damage to even begin to make them usable. He helped her on with her now buttonless shirt, then pants, socks and boots. She moved as if she were a mechanical doll. Once he seated her at the edge of the bed, he got down on his knees in front of her and lightly rested his hands on her knees.

"You're the one with the Arabian heart, Kat. You're going to be all right." Hank glanced at the corpse against the wall. "If I wouldn't have got them, you would have scared them to death." Katja didn't, couldn't, smile.

Both men had spewed their venomous sperm into her: a fact Hank was all too aware of when he wiped away the evidence before pulling up her pants.

"I'm going to get the wagon."

Katja clung to his arm.

"We'll go together." He helped her to her feet and braced her against him past the body blocking the doorway and out into the darkness.

"My mother, don't tell her."

"Of course not. We'll get you back to the house, then I'll bring the wagon over here and load up food and whatever else we need to keep going."

Katja was staggering on her own as they neared the house. "We'll stop at Alena's house to leave them some food."

"Alena?"

"The child. We'll have to make due with half of what's in the house."

While he disagreed, Hank nodded. He welcomed any signs of Katja spitting out orders again. "That kid was talking about some kind of escape."

"The Frische Haff," Katja said, then took a deep breath and shoved strands of hair out of her lifeless eyes. "I need a brush."

"How about a bath…a hot bath before we leave," Hank said.

The suggestion sparked Katja's last few steps to the front door. The child and Mrs. Haffmann were still asleep. Hank paused with the strange thought that he had killed five men and the woman with him had been raped in their brief time away from those still sleeping.

Hank steered Katja into the kitchen. He pulled her close so they could speak without waking the others.

"You go upstairs and take the first bath. I'll take care of everything." Katja's face was still ashen.

"Go on now," Hank said, patting her shoulder.

"It'll be freezing crossing the Haff," she said through grinding teeth.

"One of our stallions already has colic from exposure. Damn, I wish there were a way to remove their harnesses to give them half a chance of making it. Three pounds of oats a day with no hay or straw. How in hell have they made it this far? We've still got another five weeks to Hamburg if the Allies don't save us first." Hank looked into Katja's face, expecting at least a raised eyebrow at the word "Allies." Not tonight.

12

The moody skies drooped as low as their spirits. The long procession of wagons only feet apart bumped over fields, woods and rocky ice and snow-packed crags never intended for road travel.

The Haffmann wagon had journeyed from Kreis Bartenstein to Ratzen-Rendenau-Landsberg in over five days of seldom-interrupted near-blinding snow. It gnawed at any exposed skin it could numb, then destroy.

Hank tugged the ice-crusted scarf down from his mouth and slightly turned his head to Katja while opening and closing his near rigid fingers holding the reins.

"Every village is the same: businesses ripped to shreds, bloated, starving or dead animals that stink like hell and people running from one hideout to the next."

Katja nodded and pointed back to the rutty, muddy path he was about to veer off from into a ditch. Hank yanked up the reins and righted their course.

"Check on your mother and Alena, will you? It's getting cold enough to kill us."

Katja lifted the drape to find the old woman and child huddled together with their heads down and out of sight.

"Mother?"

Squinting possessed eyes rose to meet Katja's.

"You and Alena are all right?" Katja asked.

"Wait until your father hears about this. He's going to give the Fuehrer an earful, I'll tell you."

As crazy as it sounded Katja sighed in relief and enthusiastically nodded. They were Mrs. Haffmann's first words since losing the last of her possessions. An occasional childlike voice humming nursery tunes to the child beside her wafted up to Hank and Katja from inside the wood-sided cart.

Hank had heard the exchange. When Katja turned about he patted her leg and scooted close to her.

"I know nothing about our two stallions here, Kat," Hank said. "Tell me about them."

Katja's eyes lifted to her companion. He looked nothing like the cocky Swede that sauntered into her life nearly three weeks and a lifetime earlier. His blue eyes were still shining out through a haggard, filthy and half-frozen bearded face with a self-pleasure she envied.

"You haven't been eating," she said.

"What are you talking about? I'm eating."

"I've been watching when you ration out the food. You're eating half of what we are. It's got to stop."

Hank remained silent.

"It's Alena, isn't it? You're making sure she gets enough to eat."

"I don't know what in the hell you're talking about." Hank absently flipped the reins up and down to return her attention to her horses.

"The black on the left, with colic, is named Noble. His lines go back to the King's court as a favorite fox hunter for the royal family." Katja sighed. "Is he going to be all right, Hank?"

Hank rose in his seat to see the ever-growing breadth of ox-and horse-drawn wagons and carts along with hundreds of men, women and children dragging themselves through the freezing snow.

"Must be three, four-hundred of us all crossing that ice at the same time. Damnit, I wish there was another way besides trying to cross some frozen waterway." Hank looked up at the near black sky, finally resting from relentless snow. "Going to be dark soon. We're too damn freezing and tired to attempt a crossing tonight."

He glanced down at his gloved hands. He wasn't anxious to examine the tips of his fingers. People might be uncomfortable buying thoroughbreds from a man with stubs for fingers.

"Your fingers as cold as mine?" he asked.

"Not as bad as my feet. I don't think I could walk right now."

"We'll be stopping soon, kid. You're tougher than any man I've ever tangled with is. We've got a little firewood left. Let's use it tonight. Won't do any good on the Haff's icy floor."

Katja nodded. "A kid is a goat or a child." Katja dramatically slid over to the edge of her carriage seat.

Hank broke from chuckled breathing into a full out laugh.

"Just a friendly expression where I come from."

"Rude, just the same," Katja snapped.

"Okay kid, I get your point."

Hank's smiling eyes wouldn't let hers free until she relaxed her pursed lips.

"We'll wait at the Haff's edge for daybreak to start across," she said through chattering teeth. "Maybe we can make it in a day."

Hank shook his head. "No way. One of the men in the other wagons showed me a map. It's thirty-nine kilometers lengthwise. No way to make it in a day. We'll have to survive a night on the ice."

She elbowed Hank's arm. "Hey, you're not getting soft on me now, are you?"

Hank reared back to watch Katja's expression. The same woman only days before raped and nearly murdered had eyes full of fire and sass. Katja could read his examining glare.

"We Germans are toughest in the world. Haven't you learned that by now?"

Hank shook his head in amazement.

"A lot of the wagons are too overloaded," Hank said, leaning over the edge of his seat peering at the two wagons less than twenty yards ahead of them. "They're killing their horses. If we had a hot meal for every horse that's died for silver and furniture, we'd wouldn't go hungry all the way to Hamburg."

"This is my wagon," Katja huffed. She grabbed the reins away from Hank. "You'll eat exactly the same amount as we do. You're getting weak and negative. I don't want to hear it!"

Hank chuckled, pushed back the fur hood on his coat and ran a hand through his hair.

"You can be what Americans call a little brat. Is it better I call you that?"

Katja's daggered eyes gave him his answer.

"Now tell me about the damn horses."

"Henning Henson, you are the most conceited Swede, American or whatever the hell you are, I've ever, ever met."

Hank broadly smiled and took back the reins. "Now that's the Kat I've grown to know and love."

While the "know and love" line was a casual phrase often thrown around by Americans, he could see it was new to Katja, as was his bold proclamation that he loved her. He watched her blush and look away with a nervous smile.

"What? What did I say?"

"The other stallion is—"

Russian planes broke through the low-hanging dirty gray clouds with machine guns blazing.

"Holy hell!" Hank yelled and tried, but couldn't move any faster than the long procession of evacuees headed for the Haff's embankment, within sight less than a half mile away.

"Run for the Haff!" Katja screamed.

Hank made a sharp right yank on the reins. The stallions were quick to respond.

"Where are you going?"

"The woods, it's our only chance." The thunderous rattle of aerial machine-gun fire grew closer, popping out a path of death less than ten feet in front of their teamed horses.

"Run boys, run!" Hank yelled. He looked behind him and saw Russian tanks and ground troops.

"Jesus, Kat!" He let go of the reins long enough to point.

Though slowed by the deep snow, the Haffmann stallions ripped through the meadow as if they weren't lugging over a thousand pounds behind them. Four other wagons followed their lead. They crossed into the thick woods bordering the vastly open area before any Russian planes diverted their fire to them. Less than one hundred yards into the cover of trees and well apart from the other wagons that made it to the woods safely, Hank pulled on the reins.

"Hold up, you gorgeous creatures!" Hank yelled. Alena popped her head out of the canvas curtain separating the driver's seat and its passengers and cargo. "What happened?"

"Mother, are you all right?" said Katja, lifting back the curtain. Her mother was still trying to right herself from the hellacious ride.

"I think I'm all right," she muttered. "I might have broken my arm." She moved it up and down, back and forth with no impediment in movement. "Yes, I think I did."

"You'll be all right. We should be safe here until the Russian troops—"

"Troops?" Mrs. Haffmann shrieked.

"We should be safe here."

"Kat?" Hank said, yanking her head back from behind the canvas. "Don't go counting on that too soon. Let's pull the wagon into a covered spot and sneak to the edge of the woods to see if they're going to follow us."

Katja nodded and stuck her head back into the passenger area.

"Now look, you two. We won't be gone long," said Katja, eyes locked on Alena.

"Get your father, dear. I think I broke my arm. Where is he? Never around anymore when we have trouble. I'm going to give him a piece of my mind, I'll tell you. Dear, go get him right now."

Katja brushed the hair away from her right eye. "You all right, Mother?"

"Just go get him. Go child, do as you're told."

"We'll be back as soon as we can." Katja looked back at the wild-eyed child. "Watch over her, Alena. Mother's a little shaken up. Can you do that? I really need your help right now."

"I want my mother. I want to go home," Alena said, her voice a quavering squeak.

Katja reached her hand far enough back in the wagon to comfort Alena. With it nearing dark she fumbled, then found, the quivering limp wrist.

"We'll find your parents when all is safe. I promise. Now watch after Mother."

"Come on Kat, let's go," Hank said, just above a whisper.

He lifted the cart curtain. "Hey, don't make a sound back there. I'm going to untie the horses and hitch them in another area of the woods in case we were followed. You've got a good chance of not being seen if everything's silent."

"Katja, who is this man? Get your father right now!"

Hank turned back to Katja's shrug. "There isn't time for this, Kat. Let's go."

"If they haven't followed us by now they're not coming. I'm staying here with Mother."

"Good idea." Hank climbed down from the cart. His shadow was tucked beneath him under the beaming light of a quick rising full moon. He sank knee-deep in snow. It was bitterly cold, with the wind slapping the air, sending snow swirling from its bed. Hank wasn't five minutes from the wagon when he saw deer, a small line of doe looking straight ahead toward the distant sounds, silent sentinels for the dead and dying.

Hank heard something. He turned his head around sharply. It sounded more like human than animal footsteps. He froze, his heart pounding in his ears. He crouched behind a white clump.

Other refuges? No, they came for us on foot. Shit, I haven't even got a gun or a knife.

His eyes darted around the illuminated forest. A lean shadow moved within his peripheral vision.

Hank swallowed dryly. "Scared the hell out of me."

"I just couldn't wait there," Katja said.

"Lower your voice. It'll carry across the field," he whispered.

"How are your feet?"

"Don't feel a thing," Katja whispered back.

"Go back, get off those boots and rub your feet."

"Shut up and keep moving," she said through a smile.

Before they reached the woods' edge they heard more gunshots, then another series followed by a woman's scream. When they got to the forest edge, the moon lit the distant setting like a stage.

"What are they doing?" Katja asked in a strained voice.

"Poor bastards. They're cleaning out the wagons of anything they can find." Rows of refugee men were forced to their knees with wickedly nudging rifles. In unison they all clasped their hands on the back of their heads.

"Don't watch, Kat," Hank whispered, but his warning was too late. The simultaneous sound of rifle fire, the dropping bullet-riddled bodies and the manic screams of women and children echoed across the open field as if haunting apparitions.

Katja's chin dropped. No tears. Only short controlled breathing. The two crouched as motionless as vegetation for over an hour watching the last of the carnage.

"Where do you think they're taking the women and children?" Hank asked, cold breath raw in his throat.

"Let's get back to the wagon," Katja said. "The monsters are leaving."

"We've still got to cross that damn ice, just as we planned. At first light," Hank said, standing up and rubbing his arms to create some warmth. "It's freezing. You're right. We'd better get back to your mother."

~

Hank lingered in the beauty, soaking in the jeweled stars and bold golden moon. "Kat, wait a minute." She turned and rested a gloved fist on her hip.

"Incredible, isn't it? I've never seen a more beautiful night. It's as light as day out here."

She quickly glanced around, unappreciative of what he was seeing. Hank forged through untouched snow to her side.

"What are you going to do when this is over?"

"I don't want to talk about that."

"There's no going back. You'll have to build a new life."

"How the hell do you know there's no going back?" she hissed. "First mother and I will find Father." She shook her head at the soundness of a plan formulating as she spoke. "Then we'll go back to breeding Warmbloods."

"In Trakehnen?"

"I don't know. What in the hell do you care?" She shoved her long mane away from her eye and over her right ear. "You can go back to Sweden and your safe little life."

Hank grabbed her by both arms. "Kat, I'm not a Swede. I told you, I'm an American. Haven't we been through enough together for you to believe me?"

Katja's eyes started brimming over with tears. "Stop telling me that."

"I'm not the enemy, damnit. I care about what happens to you and all these innocent people trapped in Hitler's madness." He threw his arms down to his side. "Oh, to hell with it. Let's get back to the wagon."

Katja stopped him as he turned to go and moved close enough to stare into his cobalt blue eyes.

"I believe you, Hank. Don't say it again or it could get us all killed."

"Or save our lives. Come on, let's get back."

~

"Mrs. Haffmann, where are you?" The delicate weepy voice repeating the same question over and over wafted through the stillness to Hank and Katja before the wagon was in sight.

"Oh no, Hank, something's happened to Mother!" Katja broke into a run with Hank running behind her. "Mother, Mother, I'm coming."

Alena had her arms tightly folded together, her upper body turning back and forth in rapid motions. Katja blazed to her and crouched down at eye level.

"Mother's gone?" The child shook her head.

Katja started shaking the child unaware of how hard her frightening hold was, making Alena mute. "Talk! Talk!"

"Okay, let's settle down," Hank said while struggling to rip Katja away from the child. "Damnit Kat, let the child go. You're scaring the hell out of her."

Katja stopped and loosened her grip. Alena pulled away and ran to Hank, clutching him around the waist of his fur coat. He ran his gloved hand down her hair a couple of times until her bawling slowed down to snivels.

"Now tell us when Mrs. Haffmann left, Alena," he coached gently.

"She…she was calling a man's name. She…"

"Take your time. It's not your fault. Then what did she do?"

"Claas, Claas. Is that the name?" Katja asked through a constricted throat.

"Yes."

Katja hobbled on her knees to Alena.

"Where did she go? Looking for my father?"

The child tightened her grip around Hank.

"It's okay, Alena. Kat needs to find her mom. Can you help her do that?"

"How long ago? What direction did she go?" Katja asked.

"One question at a time, Kat." Hank pulled the girl's grip loose so that he could bend down to her eye level. "How long ago?" he asked.

"Long time. After you left."

"Right after?" asked Hank.

The child nodded.

"That could be hours she's been out here, Katja said. "What direction, Alena? What direction?"

The child slowly raised her arm and pointed straight back from the rear of the wagon. "I didn't leave the wagon, but she started that way."

"I'll go to the right, you to the left and center," Katja said. "Don't call out. There could still be Reds close by."

Only minutes later Katja found what she was frantically searching for. "Footprints. Footprints!" Katja yelled out to Hank.

"Mother, it's Katja. I've found Father. He's back at the wagon waiting."

Katja followed the staggering trail of footprints for another few yards through the thick of trees and night shadows. Her eyes narrowed at what appeared to be a human form only a few paces away.

"Mother? Is that you?" The form didn't stir or make a sound.

"Is that you?" Katja now whispered. A premonition was beginning to fill her with horror. She broke into a run for the unmoving body perched against the trunk under a thick broad-branched pine with only trace-islands of snow at its base.

You hear me? Oh no. Oh Lord, no."

Mrs. Haffmann ice-locked feet were the first thing Katja focused on when she found the frozen form.

Katja dropped to her knees and cradled her mother in her arms.

"Mother, Mother, wake up." The eyes appeared to be frosted glass staring straight ahead as though they were seeing a friendly face approaching. Katja pulled her mother to her breast and rocked her back and forth, too shocked to cry.

"Yes Mother, Father's here for you," she said in a voice cold as death's breath.

Hank circled back to the wagon shortly after he left, realizing the woman would have had to leave traceable tracks. Alena was wrapped in layers of blankets in the wagon, but still shaking from the biting night air.

"I'm freezing," she got out through chattering teeth.

"Any sign of Kat?"

"It's freezing."

"Come on," Hank said softly to the child. "You need to get your body moving to get some heat in it. We'll go find Kat and her mother together." Hank could hardly finish the thought before Alena bolted out from under the blankets and was holding his hand to begin their search.

"If we could just get Kat to take instruction like you do," he chuckled. The two followed the easy path Katja had left, calling out her name repeatedly until they both stopped at the shrill sound coming from the towering pine just ahead of them.

"Here, I'm here." Katja's voice sounded wounded, too much like the voice of the woman he found tied to the bedposts a few weeks before.

"Kat, you all right?" He pulled up a branch releasing an avalanche of snow on him and Alena on their way under the protective umbrella of the branches. What he and Alena saw required no explanation. Death was becoming a daily companion to each of them.

He went to Katja and began prying her away from her mother.

"Come on, kid. She's gone now. Let's go back to the wagon. I'll come back and give her a proper final resting place."

"Wait!" Katja kneeled back down to her mother and lifted her frozen hand from the snow. With some struggle she tugged her mother's wedding ring from her hand, pulled her glove off and slipped it on her own bare left wedding finger.

"I'll save this for you, Mother, to give to your husband as soon as I see him." Katja raised her open hand and lowered her mother's eyelids.

13

Not a trace of Russians. The new line of refugees preparing to cross the Haff was swarming at the three-mile wide frozen ocean's inlet embankment by the time the Haffmann wagon was back on the cart path.

Morning fog hovered over the frozen waterway. Hank, Katja, and Alena silently watched one wagon, cart, and poor souls on frozen feet vanish into the wall of mist just yards from shore.

"God almighty, I wish there was another way to go," Hank said. "Look at the edge. The water's a foot or two deep. We're too damn late. It's melting."

"People are going across," were Katja's first words since Hank returned hours later. Due to the unforgiving frozen ground, Hank had searched out and piled rocks over Mrs. Haffmann's gravesite.

"How do we know? We've never talked to anybody who's made it."

Alena, now sitting between Hank and Katja snuggled up to Katja desperately wanting to believe her.

Hank glared back at the mounting line waiting to cross the ice.

"What choice do we have?" Katja said. "Let's get on with it before we can't squeeze in line."

Hank whipped the reins up and down getting little response. "Noble's not going to make it through the night," Hank said, oblivious to Katja's jerking response to his prediction. "If the colic and starvation doesn't get them, a night standing in a foot of ice water certainly will."

"Shut up. Just shut your mouth," Katja yelled, pulling Alena even closer to her waist.

"Don't listen to him, Alena. He's always full of stories." Katja tucked the mane that constantly covered her eyes behind her ear so she could stare Hank down.

Still haunted by Katja's mother's frozen lifeless body, Hank easily shook off her newest barb, stepped down from the wagon and stomped over to their harnessed team.

His inspecting eye scanned while his gloveless hand felt along every black contour for Noble's swollen glands and other colic manifestations.

"Hey, Kat," he said aloud. "His swelling has gone down. He seems to be getting a little better." Katja slowly nodded, breaking into a slight smile at the way Hank was apologizing without really doing it.

"And Senta, check Senta. She looks thin and tired," said Katja.

The golden chestnut mare's ribcage was protruding in a similar fashion of a wet shirt on a withered old man. Hank felt around the animal's mouth, pulling back a handful of foaming saliva. The eyes were dull as agates. Katja looked up at Hank, craning to watch his body language or a word of encouragement. She got neither. Hank silently climbed back into the wagon, whipped the reins and lurched out onto the ice. The stallions' hooves were kicking up shoreline water and ice as the wagon disappeared into the thick fog.

"My feet are freezing," Alena moaned.

Katja felt around the child's wet shoes. "Alena, these shoes were never meant for the kind of walking we've been doing." She whispered to her loud enough that Hank heard and turned his eyes on the drenched laced leather pointed-toe shoes covering dirty thin pink socks.

"I was looking for Mrs. Haffmann before you came back."

"You should have told me. We could have dried them by the fire last night."

Katja looked up to see Hank's worried look and furrowed brow.

"Better get them off and rub her bare feet, then wrap her in as many blankets in the back as we've got," Hank said, then scratched his bearded chin with one hand while trying to consider further measures to stop encroaching frostbite or worse.

"I've got a dry pair of socks in the wagon. I stuffed them in one of the pots. Hurry, Kat, get in back and help her find them and bundle her up." He tenderly ran his gloved hand over the girl's gold-spun hair. The woman and child climbed into the back, but not before Katja heard Hank mutter, "You've got to tell us when you're wet, damnit."

Hank turned his attentions back to the unending wall of fog surrounding them.

"Watch out!" Hank tried, but had no ability to veer away from the heavily bundled man, woman and child materializing out of the mist not ten feet in front of the wagon.

"Hold up! Hold up!" Hooves skated on ice forcing the three to leap out of the way.

The black-bearded man ran to the side of Hank's wagon seat. "Please take us in your wagon. The axle on our wagon broke soon as I went from shore to the ice."

"I saw it broken down. Get back to it before it gets robbed," Hank said.

"We have nothing. Our horse is dying. She's heavy in foal. We couldn't have made it across the ice anyway. Please. The Russians are right behind all of us. There's no time." The man started climbing up to Hank's seat.

Hank shoved him back down just as Katja climbed back into the carriage seat next to him.

"What's all this?" Katja asked.

"Says he can't go any farther. He wants us to take his family." Hank motioned to the faceless, ghostly outlined woman and child awaiting the verdict of their fate.

"Not this time, Kat. We'd all die if we took them in," Hank said. "There could be hundreds more on the ice just like them."

"I'm sorry, he's right," Katja said to the woman and child. "We can't help you. Go back to your wagon and try to use what you have left in it to bargain for help."

The father of the desperate family hissed. "Nobody will give us a ride. Three before you said the same thing."

Alena poked her head out from behind the near-frozen sheet of canvas. "You can't leave them. They'll die," she yelled.

"Get back under the blankets, dear," Katja said. With some resistance she guided Alena's head back inside the wagon.

"It's hell for all of us," Katja said. "Come on, Hank, we'll have another wagon on top of us any minute if we don't move."

The stranded family disappeared in the fog as fast as they sprang out of it.

"I can't see a damn thing in this," Hank finally said after they had sojourned without a word for more than an hour. Hank shifted so his eyes as well as the tone of his voice indicated his thought.

"Thanks for not making me the bad guy."

Katja shrugged. "We didn't have a choice." She sighed, shivering. "I'm really worried about Alena's feet."

"You know what I like about you, Kat?"

Katja absently rubbed her hands together as if a fire was warming them. "I can't imagine."

"Never thinking of yourself." He paused and stared into the billowing fog. "You're a hell of a woman, Kat."

Katja's usual biting retort took a rest. She surprised Hank by placing a mittened hand on his knee and patting it. "Thank you."

Hank took his time nodding.

"You've lived your life for your father, haven't you?

"What does that mean?"

"Nothing wrong with that. You said he's a high ranking German officer and a Nazi party member?"

Katja mouth grew tight. "You say the words as if you really are the enemy."

"I honest-to-God don't know who the enemy is." He braced himself for battle.

"Hitler is one man. Maybe I don't really know what's been happening since he became Prime Minister, but my father believes in what he stands for."

Hank cleared his throat. "Kat, there's something I have to tell you about your father so you can plan out your life. He…"

"Watch out!" Katja's arm jetted out, pointing to an enormous hole in the ice, a hole that could have only been made from a bomb. Hank tugged lightly on the reins. Noble and Senta were all too ready to stop.

"Jesus. If there's many more of those we're dead when it gets dark."

"There has got to be." Katja started climbing down from the wagon.

"Where are you going?"

"Let's take shifts walking the horses until this fog lifts."

Hank let out a little breath. "At least let me go first."

Katja grinned at him and tightened the fur hood around her neck. "You'd better watch out, Swede. You're starting to put everybody else's needs ahead of yours."

Hank's grimace for an instant turned into a smile. "I'll watch that."

~

They had been on the ice over eight hours before they heard the first of many screams to come.

Katja had nodded off; the reins loose in her hands when the screeching sound cut the late afternoon air and jolted her to erect attention. The fog was still draping itself around them in every direction. Only the muffled noise of wagons and people on foot ahead of them gave a sense of direction.

"I heard a splash, Hank yelled over his shoulder. "Must have been a bomb hole. One of the wagons went in."

Katja peered over the edge of her seat. The wagon wheels were in a foot of water. "Hank, the ice is melting!"

"I've been walking in water for more than two hours. I think it's okay."

"Get back in this wagon."

"No, just a few miles more. This damn fog has got to lift soon. When it does, I'll be by your side faster than one of those village boys who used to ogle over you."

"Henning Henson, get up here right now. It's my wagon and you'll do as I say. Right now!" Katja started puffing like a locomotive building steam. "You won't do Alena and me any good if you freeze to death."

"All right, general, I got the message." He stopped and took high splashing steps to the wagon. Once seated he yanked off his sopping German crafted riding boots and socks more the shape of rags than a foot.

"Can you feel your toes?" Kat asked.

"Lost all feeling in them and the feet just a few minutes after the water started."

"Why didn't you say something?"

"No place for a lady," Hank said in an awe-shucks German-western drawl. He chuckled to himself at how strange he sounded.

Katja had been called an exceptional markswoman, superior horse-back rider, just about everything but a lady. The pink from cold cheeks turned crimson.

"I never thought I would have to tell you this," Katja said slowly as if she was speaking to the hard of hearing. "You've got to start thinking about yourself." She fidgeted in her seat and looked into the nothingness.

Pain was beginning to surge through his feet as if they were resting on fiery branding irons. "Oh shit, damn, son of a bi—" Hank looked up from the bare bluish foot cradled in his hands to Alena's gawking, slack-jawed stare. "Sorry kid, my feet are killing me."

Alena tugged Hank's only pair of dry socks off her feet and handed them to him. "My feet are warm now."

Hank swallowed hard and took the socks. "Get back under those blankets." He reached out and softly clasped the child's quivering arm. "Thanks. That's without question the nicest thing anybody's ever done for me. Now get back under there."

Katja watched tears pool in Hank's eyes. She took a slow quiet breath. "The fog is beginning to lift," Katja said.

Once visibility had returned the ice landscape revealed bomb holes, abandoned carts, and frozen horses lying on their ice deathbed, still in harness.

"Stop!" Katja screamed, then snatched the reins away from Hank. "Look at Senta. She can't move another foot."

Hank nodded. "I know. She was never going to survive the journey across the Haff. I knew it before we left shore."

Katja swirled around in her wagon seat, placing a closed fist on her hip. "Just what else aren't you telling me? You were saying you had something to tell me about my father when we saw the bomb hole. What? What is it?"

Hank looked at the snarl of agony over Katja's face.

"This isn't the time. I promise I wouldn't…"

"Go on, tell me."

Hank looked through her furious glare to the frightened child inside. The child he had held in his arms the night after she had been raped.

"It's your father, Kat. He died in Normandy."

She threw her mane of hair back and forth with each savage word he spoke. "No! No! You know nothing about my father. You're only guessing. Shut up!"

Hank captured her checks in his gloved hands "It's true. Dr. Brunner told me. He didn't want you to know."

Katja stopped all resistance. "Dr. Brunner?" Her question was rhetorical.

"He died in the Allied invasion, Normandy, Kat."

Katja leaped from the wagon to the ice. "Get away from me. All you tell me are lies and horrible things about my country." Her anger turned to visions of her father's dead, abandoned body in some ditch. She put her mittens over her eyes, feebly attempting to block out the horrors.

Alena gave a startled gasp at the sight of her protector and surrogate mother in such pain. "Come back up here, Kat," Alena pleaded.

"Come on, Kat," Hank said. "We're going to stop here for the night. It'll be dark soon anyway. With the fog lifted, we'll be off the ice and on our way to a warm meal and bed in no time."

Katja turned away to walk ahead of the wagon when Senta collapsed to the ice, dragging Noble nearly to his knees.

"Kat, unharness Senta quickly so Noble isn't hurt," Hank yelled.

Katja responded at lightning speed. Once Senta was free of Noble's shared rigging she knelt on the ice to Senta's stilled body and rearing head. Ears back, eyes bulging, and steaming nostrils, the mare was fighting for its last breath. Katja's hand was slapped back by the delirious animal's recoiling head.

"Get away, Kat," Hank boomed while rifling an ungloved hand over Noble to detect any injuries. "Shit," Hank bellowed.

"What?" Katja threw back her hair and cinched a finger between her teeth. "Something's wrong with Noble?"

Senta suddenly stopped her writhing. Her head dropped to the ice with a dull thud.

"Stay in the wagon," Hank barked at Alena. "We're going to walk Noble about a hundred yards from here so we can let Senta rest in peace away from Noble's sight." Without even a glance at Katja for an approving gesture, Hank detached the now vacant harness and re-rigged strapping to accommodate one horse. He climbed in the wagon and pulled back on the reins. Noble slowly backed up, then went forward, leaving the lifeless mare and Katja alone on the ice. Hank stopped the wagon a few paces ahead of Katja, deciding to wait as long as she felt the need to mourn in private.

A moment later she ran to Noble, scanning for signs of trouble, then back at Hank. "Well?"

Hank stood and pointed to Noble's drooping head. "Check the nose."

Katja tugged off a mitten and rushed a hand to Noble's nostrils. She pulled back, fingers dripping in red. "Oh God, he's bleeding! What is it, Hank?"

Hank stepped down and approached Noble from the other side, gently patting his hindquarters and flank.

"Most vets think it has to do with irritated nasal passages." He slowly rubbed the side of Noble's head. "Bullshit. It's coming from his lungs." Hank felt gently under the neck, causing the horse to step back.

"It's okay, Noble." He looked up at Katja's corpse-like expression. "It's called epistaxis and it can be deadly." Katja's face tightened, pinched.

"It's coming from his lungs. Three pounds of oats a day and what the poor beast has been through has made him lose his appetite completely."

"He could die?" she asked in a wooden tone.

"He could. The colic and probably worms could do it."

"When?"

Hank took off his glove, ran a hand through his wheat-blond matted hair and held, then blew out a puff of ice air.

"How the hell am I to know that? It's a progressive thing. He's got to do the work of two. Maybe a week if we can get him to eat." He quickly turned from Katja, but not in time for her to miss mounting tears.

She reached out and rested a hand on his arm. "You've done everything you can, Hank."

"I can't do a damn thing." Hank wiped teary eyes away with furious movements before facing her. "My medical bag was in the other wagon." He couldn't control the muscle twitching in his clenched jaw.

"I honest to God don't know how any of these animals…" He wildly looked around at the grim line of mostly East Prussian Warmblood mares in harness in front and behind them.

"Half the mares I've seen are in foal and starving to death. Their hoofwalls are chewed to bits and they're bloody from the ruddy paths." His breathing was short and jagged.

"Noble, he's the only one we have to save," Katja said.

"No more running him. If we don't make good time, tough. I'm not losing another one." Hank stormed away, scaled the wagon and leaped into the cargo area. Alena cowered at the crazed look on his face and huddled to the opposite side of the wagon. He was whipping through to find the dwindling bag of oats. Once in hand, he raced back to Noble.

He pressed the oats against the stallion's teeth. "Come on boy, open up and eat. Eat, damnit." Katja grabbed his forcing hand.

"You know Trakehners well enough to know they're as sensitive as children. Gentle, Hank." She pried open his white-knuckled fist and eased the handful of oats into hers.

She leaned down and whispered into Noble's ear while petting his head. His ears drooping to each side, indicating sickness, perked up at the cooing sound of her voice. Noble started eating everything she feed him. "Hank," she said in the same velvet tone she used on Noble. "Would you get some more oats? You're going to eat everything, aren't you boy?" Being bested when it came to the care of horses, and by a woman, boiled Hank in rage.

"Get them your damn self!" He charged back to the wagon and sat stoically until Katja finished feeding Noble over six pounds of oats and a bucket of water scooped up from a partially thawed area in the ice nearby.

She raised her voice loud enough for her pouting companion to hear. "Hank and I won't let you die, boy. You're going to make it." Hank's furrowed brows eased at Katja's rare kind words.

~

Dense clouds smothered the full moon. The three occupants of the Haffmann wagon huddled around the kerosene lantern while eating their dinner ration of partially molding rock-hard bread and sharp cheddar cheese.

Katja turned a curious head at the sparkle in Hank's crystal blue eyes.

"I bet you're wondering what I'm so happy about." His guessing game didn't get a rise out of either of the females.

"Let me put it this way. Alena Dreyfuss, besides your parents, of course, name anything you want. Anything."

"This isn't a funny game, Hank," Katja said.

"You'll see. Just trust me a minute and play along."

Katja couldn't resist the untethered joy beaming out of Hank.

"All right. I guess it doesn't hurt to get our minds off the cold." Katja turned to Alena, frantically rubbing her arms to get warmth. "Go on Alena, tell this crazy cowboy your wish list."

"I want to never be hungry or cold again in my life." Alena tapped an index finger to her chin. The game was beginning to get fun.

"I want lots of beautiful dresses and shoes for every day of the week. I want my own riding horse and buggy so I can go on rides anytime I want."

Katja burst into laughter. "Didn't know what you were getting into, did you, Hank?"

"You can do better than that," Hank urged. "What about getting to go to a fine public school and university?"

Katja poked Hank in the side, hard. "This isn't fun anymore."

Hank's eyes fondly fell on Katja. "And you? What do you want?"

"No more games," Katja snapped.

"What if I told you I'm not playing games. What if I told you I have the power to grant you any wish you make, within some reason, of course? I couldn't give you Germany the way it was before the war. You know that kind of thing. But you name it, Kat, and you've got it."

Katja closed her eyes for a moment then opened them. "I'd have my own stud farm in a place as beautiful as Trakehnen. A big home with all the cupboards and closets filled with only the best."

Hank clapped his hands together over the lantern's yellow glow. "So be it. Each of your wishes is granted. How can I perform this miracle, you ask. Come on, somebody ask."

"How?" Alena panted.

"Easy for a multi-millionaire." He narrowed his eyes and leaned into the faces of them both "It's true I own one of the biggest and most profitable thoroughbred breeding farms in America."

Still trying to believe, Katja turned to Alena.

"I have to admit it. You're the best storyteller of anybody I have ever heard."

Hank dropped the smile. "It's true, Kat. I've been trying to tell you since that day I was attempting to buy prized East Prussian Warmbloods from the Haffmann stud farm."

Hank stretched out his open right palm. "Pleased to meet you, Miss Katja Haffmann. My real name is Hank Henson, veterinarian for the internationally famous Kentucky Derby, and sole owner of Sunny Acres Thoroughbred Breeding Farm, Lexington, Kentucky. I'm worth about…Ah, with all my property and stock holdings, about ten million dollars."

"A millionaire?" Alena said.

"Right here in this wagon. I guarantee you both when we get out of this mess, Alena, you'll get even more than you wished for. And Kat," Hank paused, and as he took a breath sank into her molasses-colored eyes made even more rich by the lantern's flame. "Katja Haffmann, you will have one of the finest East Prussian Warmblood breeding and training farms in the new Germany after the war."

"After we lose, you mean."

"Nobody wins in war," Hank said. "I envy how much you love your…Shh."

"I didn't—" Alena began.

"Quiet Alena," Hank snapped. They all sat motionless. "I heard a cracking sound as if the ice is breaking up. I'm going to go out and check."

Katja pulled him back to his cross-legged position.

"It's too dark to see out there." Katja stopped at the unquestionable cracking noise that sliced the air. Alena screamed and threw her arms around Katja.

"That's it. I'm going to check it out."

As Hank rose, Katja pulled away from Alena's grasp to touch Hank's hand.

"Hank, come back to us as soon as you see anything, if you can. It's dark as the Black Forest out there."

Hank climbed out onto the ice with the light-footed delicacy of a tightrope walker taking his first step onto a skyscraper-high rope. He stopped to wait for night vision.

A thunderous noise, like calving icebergs, mixed with a family screaming instinctively made him crouch to the ground to search for cracks.

"Hank!"

"I'm all right, Kat. It was up ahead. A wagon must have fallen through." After endless moments of silently clinging together, Katja and Alena took a deep breath together when Hank poked his head into the wagon.

"Don't see any cracks around us. I think—"

"Help us. Help!" The man's blood-curdling plea sounded less than fifty yards in front of them.

Hank was ready to spring into action, but hesitated and turned to Katja.

"Go ahead, go," she said. He was almost out the wagon when she cleared her throat loud enough for him to turn and see in her eyes what she was feeling.

"I'll be okay, Kat," he said gently, with a smile warmer than the sun.

She slowly nodded and turned her attention back to Alena, crying with raw terror.

Hank leaped from the wagon to the ice and started running in the direction of the continuing loud moaning of a woman's voice. "Somebody please help us!" she hysterically wailed.

The first thing Hank's eyes locked onto was the vast pie-shaped blackness in the ice. He slowed to a walk to see how far out the deadly lines of the crack stretched. Confident he was still standing on firm ice, he slowly approached the woman and two children huddled precariously close to the jagged edge. The woman turned her blanket-wrapped upper body and head in Hank's direction. When the mirage of a man materialized into the real thing as Hank drew near, she threw her arms straight up in the air.

"Please hurry. My husband's in the wagon." She pointed to the protruding half of a wagon wheel on a cart pointed straight toward the icy depths.

"I don't see anybody!" Hank yelled.

"He's there. He was trying to move off the crack when it opened up. He's there! Help him!"

Hank inched his way to the family and peered into the blackness. "I'm sorry, he isn't there any more."

The woman's cry degenerated into a childish whimper. Hank got close enough to see she wasn't much older than Katja with two nearly frozen toddlers. She collapsed in tears against his chest. Hank uncomfortably put both arms around her and held her tight until her manic shaking stopped. Sensing security, the twin four-year-old boys each clamped onto Hank's legs.

"Okay. Everybody comes back with me to the wagon right behind you. We'll get warm and find something to eat."

The young woman tried to turn back to the now wagonless black hole, the silvery pall of death lingering as if a sticky mist above the ice, tormenting, luring the living to join in.

"No, he's gone. You've got to protect your young ones now," Hank whispered in her ear once she was back under his bracing support.

He led them back to Katja and Alena.

Katja and Alena appeared out of the darkness, at first not realizing the entwined man, woman and close-by children included Hank.

"Have you seen a man who…" Katja stopped her frantic plea when Hank pushed back the hood on his fur coat.

"Hank!" Alena yelled and ran to find a spot around his waist. Katja took three stumbling steps back to fully comprehend what was happening, her heart pounding as if an angry fist plunged into her sternum.

"Just until we get off the ice, Kat," Hank said, reading her fearful expression. "They lost everything tonight, including this poor woman's husband."

The mother, with a face as plain as her drab clothes lifted her eyes to Katja.

"We were traveling with three other families from our village. They'll be waiting for us on the other side."

Katja slowly nodded. "Come on, Alena. Let's take some things out of the wagon for the night so we all have room to sit down."

After everybody was shoulder to shoulder in the cramped cargo and passenger space and had shared a modest bite to eat, Hank rose up slightly. He fastened his fur coat and pulled on his leather, fur-lined gloves. The straw-blonde widow lurched out to bring him back down next to her.

"I'm not going back out there," Hank said. "I was just going up to the wagon seat." His low soft words did nothing to break the woman's haunted look.

"What's your name?" Katja said.

"Monika." The ghost of a smile around the woman's mouth urged her to continue.

"Where's your family from?"

"Johannesberg."

Katja glanced at Hank's impatient body language. She glared at him until their eyes connected, signaling the need for patience.

"That's at the bottom of East Prussia," Katja said, light as a sunny day conversation.

"They're going to kill us all for what we've done," Monika said, the edge of her voice as fine as a tungsten blade.

"Done?" Katja asked.

Monika dropped her voice. "The Bolsheviks." She drew three deep breaths. "My husband's brother was with the army fighting in Russia." The woman suddenly jerked back, gasped and put her hand over her mouth.

Katja exchanged places with Hank and draped her coated arm over the woman's shoulder. "Let's not talk about such unpleasant things. When you join your friends on the other side of the Haff and then make it to safety you can begin a new life." Katja leaned down and peered into vacant eyes. She lowered her voice another decibel. "You're young with a long new life ahead of you."

"The Fuehrer was going to use Russia to feed the new Germany. Starve them. We've already starved millions of them."

Hank cleared his throat. "I don't think I'll be able to sleep a wink with the ice breaking that close to us. I'm going to sit up in the driver's seat to watch and listen for any trouble."

Katja pointed down to Alena in a deep sleep against her shoulder. "I'm going to join you," she whispered.

Once a comfortable amount of time had passed for everybody to fall asleep, Hank scooted closer to Katja and leaned down to her ear. "I knew you wouldn't complain about me helping that family."

"How'd you know?"

Hank smiled. "Oh, I know quite a bit about you. Like how much you care about me."

Katja shook her head and fought to keep her voice to a whisper. "Where do you get such ridiculous ideas?"

Hank absently rubbed his chin. "Oh, I saw how you looked at me when I left the wagon. Then you had to run after me, just to make sure I was safe." His blue eyes, bright as neon in the darkness locked on hers again.

"I'm sure you couldn't imagine that we all need each other to get through this alive." Her heart was pumping spasmodically.

"Here I am, an American. Instead of dying for my country I'll probably get killed defending the enemy." He ran a hand through his hair. "Oh hell, I probably deserve it for all the good I ever did in this war, except trying to pluck gold out of the ruins."

"Was that true? This was all about money?"

A mental imagine of Victoria loomed over his thoughts. "I envy you, Kat."

"I'm serious. You'd give your life up for your country—hell, even a total stranger—if you thought you had even the slightest chance of saving him."

Katja looked away. It was obvious she wasn't used to compliments.

"There are some people I wouldn't try to save." She turned to Hank, dropping her smile. "I'd kill Wolf for taking mother's best silver. That bastard's the one who took away the last of her hopes."

"You're everything I'm not." Hank bobbed his eyebrows. "Guess that's why sometimes I want to strangle you."

"You too, huh?" They sat silent, and then laughter started bubbling up to the point they both had to rush their hands to their mouths to not wake the others.

14

"He's not dead!" Victoria Logan's violet eyes had stopped tearing.

The colonel leaned back in his chair and tucked one of his stubby hands into the lip of his suit vest pocket. He took a deep puff of his Cuban cigar with his free hand.

"I thought Hank was—is—your best friend," Victoria said.

"So what are we going to do about it, Vic?" The colonel righted himself in his chair. "You think I don't call at least every other day to see if he's turned up on government or military rolls somewhere?" He thrust both his paws on the edge of his mirror-finished desk, the cigar trapped between the thick digits like a mouse in a spring trap.

"Hell, Vic, I even tried to get word to General Eisenhower in England. Can't get higher than the theater commander of all the Allied Forces."

"You get those pictures of him? Doesn't do one bit of good if people don't recognize him."

The colonel awkwardly rolled himself out of his high-back brown leather and brass-buttoned swivel chair. He shuffled over to the window.

"Come here a minute, Vic." She stomped over in her smartly coordinated forest green wool suit.

"Look out at that track."

"Colonel, you're driving me mad." She tried, but couldn't turn his thick shoulder to her brazen glare. "I've decided. I'm going over there to find him."

The colonel whirled around on one heel. "Oh, no you don't, young lady. That would be more stupid than what Hank did. You know the danger." He stepped behind her and forced her to look out the window.

"I said look straight out there."

"Okay, what's the game?"

"Don't you see the spectacle I've put on to raise millions for the war fund? I've already started mobilizing the racing community into putting on military spectacles the likes of which you couldn't even imagine." Victoria knew him well enough to know this somehow all tied back to Hank.

"Keep looking out there. Can you see the Army bivouac in the center of the field, housing hundreds of motorized vehicles from tanks to jeeps? And platoons of men you can't believe."

As Victoria turned to the gravel voice whispering in her ear, her eyes began to twinkle like opal stones. "And winners and losers will feel obligated to make generous donations to the war chest."

The colonel arched his back and pat his stomach. "You're not only the most beautiful woman in Louisville, you're the smartest."

"What else?" Victoria blazed over to one of two chairs opposite the colonel's desk, and gave an inviting tap on the chair next to her. The colonel turned the chair to fully appreciate her luscious leg lines, and of course, demonstrate his sincere concern.

"I've already had a stack of photos made of Hank. I figure that once contributions reach about a million I'll personally deliver the photos to the Secretary of War in Washington. He'll get them out to General Omar Bradley and his Third and Ninth Armies. Our General Patton is far too self-absorbed with making history to care about one reckless horse trader."

"And President Roosevelt? You're going to get him into the search, too? I wrote him and the Governor, but I haven't heard…"

The colonel gave a hearty belly laugh. "Hadn't thought of him. Of course, even the President will be called in to pay us back for such thoughtful and generous contributions."

He tapped a forefinger against his pursed lips. "Now what's this business about going to Germany?"

Victoria pensively steepled her long, delicate fingers.

"I insisted Hank give me his itinerary before he left. I tracked down his uncle in Stockholm and talked to him a few days ago."

The colonel anxiously rolled his fingers on the fabric-covered arms of the chair. "Itinerary? Vic, why the hell didn't you get that to me? I could have—"

"It didn't help much, but I brought a copy for you. I wouldn't call his Uncle Gustav if I were you. Sounded like he and Hank had quite a knockdown discussion about Hank's plan. He knew less than we do."

"Vic, it'd be crazy to go now. Germany will be surrendering any day. If Hank's still missing a few weeks from now after our drive to find him, I'll hold out a portion of the cash to retain somebody that does this kind of thing for a living to go in and get him out."

Victoria didn't smile. She hadn't since the man she was determined to marry vanished. Her eyes wandered around the colonel's office.

"Hank means a lot to you, doesn't he?" she observed more than asked.

The colonel dropped his signature jovial quip. "Damn, I told him it was a stupid, stupid idea."

"I'm going over." She stood and took a deep breath. "He would have been over there looking for either of us weeks ago instead of planning fund drives and writing letters."

The colonel slowly nodded. "Be careful, Vic. I don't even know if you can find a way to get in. There's no entering East Prussia. My sources tell me the Russians have surrounded it completely." He stood and steamed back over to the racetrack window. "No, you'd never get in. I'll push everything up."

15

Noble was going to live. Hank was sure of it. Katja again stirred an appetite in her suffering stallion. While the wind had been blowing capriciously since daybreak, the cloudless sky was electric blue, a moment to be enjoyed.

Hank stood up in his driver's seat, stretched and scratched his mop of hair and ruddy beard. It was an unfamiliar addition that Katja said made him look older. Anything to keep the enemy from thinking he was a deserter was vital to his survival.

Hank quietly pulled back the cargo drape. His eyes fell to the twin boys still slumbering against their mother's chest. "Beautiful morning. Even Noble's going to have a good day the way he's eating."

Katja's rich gold eyes flickered.

Hank craned his neck ahead and behind. "Kat, can you believe it? This is the first we've had a clear sky to see what we're in the middle of." The still line of refugee wagons and men, women and children on foot were snaked around bombed and thawing holes.

Hank shook his head. "We were lucky as hell not to go down last night. Let's get to shore. What was that?" Hank and Katja's eyes turned skyward.

Horrified, Hank and Katja said at the same time, "Planes."

"Everybody hold on," Hank said, then sharply steered Noble to the right out of the line, trying to pull the load that two horses should withstand.

"Stop! Noble can't pull a thing," Katja boomed. She shot a hand out to capture the reins, but Hank was too quick.

"Sit down, damnit."

Twin-engine Russian Stormavics spitting bullets in even rows roared overhead and circled back. A thunder of gunfire and bombs sprayed up mountain-high ice directly in front of them.

"Come on, Noble." The stallion's oversized lungs and chest heaved under the weight. The valiant creature's life-threatening surge forward dodged a row of bullets that ended less than a foot behind them.

Wagons and carts were dispersing in every direction like ants fleeing stomping feet. The planes broke formation and began riddling individual wagons.

"Hank!" Katja shot a pointing finger out to a growing dark, crooked line springing out from the load crossing it.

"Go Noble, go baby!" Hank's howling command ignited the stallion like it was possessed. Noble broke out from a lugging trot into a full out, eyes bulging, nostril-steaming run.

Katja turned to the blasting sound behind her. A wagon only yards behind them was suddenly plunging into the icy waters.

"God help us," the piercing guttural scream came from a sandpaper-faced, old man standing up in his buckboard seat like a captain going down with the ship.

Noble kept pacing ahead of the fracturing ice until the vast thawing stretch was behind them.

"There's the shore," Hank yelled. The sight of a throng of German soldiers made him pull back momentarily on the reins. Noble reared as far back as the heavy leather and wooden harness allowed, then began sliding and slipping on the ice.

"He'll break his leg," Hank cried and rolled the reins. "Go baby. That's it, off the ice."

The three feet of pooling water at the narrow shoreline where wagons had to exit forced Noble to slow down. German soldiers captured the moment crowding the wagon as it pulled out off the Haff.

"Stop," the senior of the five thickly bundled men yelled and raised his arm to halt. With flashing friendly eye contact, Katja snatched the reins and yanked until Noble stopped.

The soldiers quick-stepped through the mud to her side of the wagon.

"Thank you. Pull your wagon over immediately so the others can get through," the soldier said with a hint of a smile.

"Kat, what the hell do you…" Hank grabbed for the reins, but Katja knuckled down hard as a mad dog with meat between its teeth. She pulled over to a nearby open spot where the ground was hard enough to sustain their weight. Only one soldier retreated behind them leaving the other six to stop the oncoming hoard.

Once stopped, Hank realized the madness had at least momentarily subsided: the planes were gone. Chaos was taking a time out. His eyes just returned from the azure blue sky when the choppy sound of a German officer's voice re-ignited his racing heart.

"Anybody hurt?"

The question seemed surrealistic. The banana-nosed man with deep-set foggy hazel eyes sounded like a caring father to Hank.

Katja lifted the canvas flap behind her. "Everybody all right in there?" After counting nodding heads her eyes turned to the source of the streams of light beaming from the wooden roof of the shadowed interior. An even line of bullet holes had run directly down the center of their wagon, miraculously hitting no one. She righted her position and calmly rested her eyes on the soldier.

"Why did you stop us?"

Large knuckled, bony hands clutched the wood railing. The soldier perched on the step aside Katja to get closer to eye level.

"About ten miles from here there's a hospital with nurses and a couple of doctors who have stayed behind to help out. You'll get a good night's sleep, maybe a little food and proper care for your horse." A wide corntoothed grin spread over the man's face. "You can only stay the night, though. Leave what you can with them."

Hank cleared his throat and leaned an elbow on Katja's lap to get close to the soldier. "What's in it for you?"

The soldier never broke his smile. "Born and raised in East Prussia." He turned a thumb up and over his shoulder to the other deserters. "They are, too." His lips and jaw drooped into sagging jowls. "Women and children have had to stand in two feet of ice water all night. I shudder to think how many wagons…"

Monika popped her head out from the recesses of the wagon. "My husband," she said, tears crowding her throat like jagged rocks. "My husband is gone." Hank turned his eyes from Monika back to the soldier.

"What do you want?" Hank said.

Katja raised a shoulder in an agitated shrug in his direction and tugged a hand back through her tangled hair to anchor it behind one ear. "Not everybody has to get something out of helping other people." She turned back to the soldier and rested a mittened hand on his bare knuckles. "You ought to get some gloves on. Your hands will freeze."

The soldier turned his turkey neck up to the sky and back to her again. "Getting warmer." He furrowed his brow and mumbled, "Getting nearly impossible to cross."

"Have the Russians really surrounded the Province?" Hank asked, finally letting down his guard.

"So I can serve you a purpose, get moving to Elbing, where the hospital's at."

Monika climbed out of the wagon, squeezing herself between Hank and Katja. "My name's Monika Krause. My husband is—was—Berg Krause."

The soldier shot up his index finger. "I bet you're hunting for your neighbors."

Monika collapsed her shoulders and took a deep breath of relief. "Yes, I am. The Hellers or Eisenstadts."

"They said if you make it across they'll be waiting until tomorrow about midday at Elbing."

"How do you and the others survive out here?" Katja asked.

"Oh, if you can help out with a little food it would be appreciated." The soldier glanced over at Hank.

"If you haven't got enough to eat, leave us nothing."

"Can't you see what he's doing, Kat?" Both women turned scorching eyes to him.

"Think about it. A fantasy hospital, almost within reach, able to take care of thousands of us. Your caring neighbors waiting in this fantasy place." Hank dropped his voice and stared directly into the soldier's eyes as he spoke. "It's all a lie to get food. He and the other deserters are starving to death and have found a way to survive off the miseries of every terrified person leaving the Haff."

The soldier shook off the indictment. "You'd better leave now. We'll need this space for the next wagon."

Katja shook her head. "Monika, get in back please, and get out enough food for this kind man and the others to have at least one good meal. He doesn't understand that it's possible to help somebody in trouble without…" She leveled molten copper eyes on Hank and continued, "getting anything out of it."

Eyes wide, Monika hurried to aid the man with such soothing words.

"We'll see." Hank took the reins out of Katja's left hand. "Hurry up back there. The Reds could be back any minute."

The soldier scanned the beautiful contours of Katja's face.

Katja reached a hand down and shook the soldier's hand. "If you're going to stay here you should get out of those uniforms and into regular clothes before the Russians begin clearing the ice on foot."

"Not a lot of clothes available, Miss. We'll be fine."

Katja hesitated, then bit down on her lower lip and forced out the question. "We going to lose?"

The unevenly spaced corn teeth flashed again. "Miss, already have. Just been a slow death, that's all."

"One last question," Hank said civilly. "Ever see two stallions, both chestnut, driven by a hairy beast of a man with thick furry eyebrows and the devil in his eyes?"

Katja sat upright.

"Was he wearing a gray wool coat and all alone?" the soldier asked.

Katja nodded. "When did he cross?"

"He's about a day, maybe, ahead of you. He could be at Elbing, but I suspect you'll miss him."

Once away from the congested exit of the Haff, Monika interrupted the tense silence between Hank and Katja.

"If that soldier was lying, I hate to think how," Hank said to Katja, breaking her train of thought. She looked up at him, her dark brows tugging together in consternation, then turned.

"Did you hear me, Kat? I wonder how Monika's going to handle it if this place really doesn't exist." Hank glanced over, unable to see past the thick drape of hair covering her profile.

"Okay, you don't need to talk." Hank sighed. "You know, you're one of the worst tempered, most bullheaded women I've ever known."

Katja turned hard enough that her long hair flew out and behind her shoulder.

Hank burst into laughter. "I knew that would get your attention. Do you think we can believe that soldier of misfortune?" He slid an arm around her and attempted a comforting squeeze.

"You're not funny." He detected a crack in her anger.

~

Elbing's appearance was getting all too familiar: lonely and bare. Black as death. Decaying, sagging roofs and walls. Toppled chimneys and charcoal-crisp timbers protruding like broken human limbs. Hank and both women moaned as they slowly trudged through a city street graveyard once called Elbing.

"I wish like hell I would have been wrong," Hank said aloud and clearly enough for both mouth-gaping women to hear.

As they wound through skinny cobblestone streets, crowd, wagon, and hoof noise started to emerge.

"Hank, stop the wagon. Everybody be quiet." Katja leaned out of her seat to her right where the noise was coming from. "Hear that? Quick, two or three streets over."

After only one street they halted for the solid backup line of wagons. Katja leaped down from her seat and melted into the masses, shoulder-to-shoulder on the narrow walkway. She returned with a breathy smile and a hand on her heaving chest.

"The hospital." She swallowed hard. "It's only about two blocks away. Let's get in line right now."

"It's really there? "Monika shrieked. She hugged Hank and kissed his reddening cheek.

Katja climbed back into the seat next to Hank.

"Okay, get it over with," he moaned.

A full toothy smile spread over Katja's face. "Oh you mean about the soldier? The German soldier who cared enough to sacrifice his safety for thousands?" Her face was flush with happiness.

Hank tried to hold his growling expression, but finally had to concede. "There's only one thing I hate worse than bossy women." He broke into a laugh. "Oh, forget it. You win."

Katja nodded. "It's about time you started trusting somebody's instincts besides your own."

"Are you done boxing my ears for being careful with our lives?"

She put an open palm on her heart. "I promise I won't say another word about it."

Hank pulled his head back, squinted and wove his fingers through his hair. "Really know how to play it for all its worth, don't you?"

Monika cleared her throat to draw attention. "Can I leave the boys here with you, Katja, while we wait in line? I'd like to try and find my neighbors."

Hank welcomed the interruption and answered for Katja. "Absolutely, Monika. I'll go with you to see about how long we'll have to wait and what procedure they've set up to get a bed and a place for Noble." He was off and gone before Katja could find the appropriate quip.

Hank surprised Monika by taking her hand in his as they walked past a woman rubbing the bare purple feet of a whimpering ten-year-old boy. He sensed that each wagon they passed of mostly women and children had experienced a lifetime's worth of horrors in less than the forty-eight hours it took to cross over the frozen ocean inlet.

A woman in a soiled nurse's uniform stood, arms folded, at the hospital's main door. Hank and Monika nudged their way to the middle of the crowd, all pleading for entrance and asking questions at the same time.

The nurse shot her arms up in the air like a referee signaling a touchdown.

"Listen people. We only have so much room. Form a line and I'll answer questions one at a time."

"Got beds and food for us?" one of the few young men yelled.

"My baby needs a doctor." The nurse stopped waving her arms at the sound of the high-voiced plea. Her eyes turned downward, lower than Hank and Monika could see over the crowd.

"You go right in, dear. See the nurse at the first desk. She'll find a bed and medical attention for your child." The nurse turned her angelic eyes to the still-mounting mob.

"I'm going to say this once," the nurse yelled at the top of her raspy voice. "Get back to your wagons. One bed per family while they last for one night. A hot bowl of potato soup and one piece of bread for everybody. Everybody."

"And our animals?" Hank yelled into the back of a man a near-foot taller than him.

"Horses and oxen only. No cows like some of you have or other animals. We've converted the building next door into a stable. There's enough food to feed your animals one night. It's warm in there, too." The nurse lowered her arms. "No more questions. Pass the word down the line. Now get back to your wagons. No more questions."

Hank and Monika hustled back to the wagon. "

Monika appreciatively squeezed Hank's hand as he helped her up into the wagon.

"Did you find your neighbors?" Katja anxiously asked.

Monika put her hand to her mouth. "I forgot to look after we got the good news."

"I'll watch the boys. Go see if you can track them down. No time to lose." Katja looked up at the cloud-smothered sun. "The storm's moving back in. We'd better hurry."

Hank climbed over Katja and started to step down.

"Where are you going?" Katja grimaced.

"No reason to sit here. I'm going to help Monika. There's a real mob up there. We can both ask around."

Katja softly led Hank back to his seat. "I'll go this time." She angled her chin up as though inviting a fist.

Hank broke into a wide smile and nodded his head. "Good idea, Kat. I'll wait here with Alena and the boys." He lowered his voice. "Alena's been too quiet." The women were walking away when Hank cleared his throat loud enough to get them to turn. "Monika, you and the boys are more than welcome to travel with us if you don't find your neighbors."

"We'll find them," Katja said through gritted teeth.

Raw icy wind had kicked up when Katja returned alone. The tedious wait had already taken two hours and Hank was just reaching the front of the line.

Katja climbed aboard and pressed her lips together. "It's horrible." She pressed her lips tighter and turned away from Hank's fading smile.

"Did you find Monika's neighbors?"

"They're amputating children and women's feet." She could taste the bile rising in her throat.

"They're set up for surgery in there?"

Katja turned from his face and slowly nodded.

"And Monika? You found who she was looking for?"

Katja nodded again.

"We're close enough. I'm going to see about getting you and Alena a bed. I had better get one for Monika and the boys too, just to be sure." Hank cocked his head to get a better look at their stallion. "I'm spending the night with Noble. He might have a fighting chance of making it. I wonder if they have a vet."

Katja found a slippery hold on her composure and began to breathe regularly again. "I asked. They don't, but they said they have everything else. Maybe even vet supplies."

"Mind if I take Alena with me until you go to sleep? She could use some individual attention."

Katja propped up a smile. "This from the man who thought we should have left her behind?" Hank's eyes pained at the reminder. "Don't talk like that. She'll hear you."

Hank studied Katja's openly vulnerable face. He'd always chosen women he knew he could control with even the slightest effort. Women, he for the first time admitted to himself, expected nothing from him except charm and a tender moment here and there. All except Victoria

Logan: the one real feeling beauty who was always desperately searching for something more in Hank than he could find himself.

"You know," Hank felt a trap door open in his stomach, "I've never
even asked you if you've got somebody you're close to."

"That's a good idea to take Alena, soon as we check the wagon in and
unbridle Noble." Her voice was starting to quiver. "Quit staring at me."

"If you'd stop kicking me between the legs for five minutes I'd like to
tell you something."

Katja darted her hand to the canvas behind her and pulled it back.
"Alena, would you like to go with Hank to take care of Noble before I
get us a warm bed for the night? He'd really like your company."

Hank could feel Katja's hand shaking under her thick wool mittens
when he pulled off his gloves and placed his hand on hers.

Katja was about to speak when Alena popped her head out between
them. "I'm hungry."

Hank locked onto Katja's golden eyes. Words weren't necessary.

"Of course you are." Hank lugged Alena up by one arm onto the
wagon seat. "First some hot soup, then you and I are going to baby
Noble like he was back at Trakehnen living the life of royalty."

~

The wail of women and children a floor above the endless rows of
gray metal factory lunchroom tables did little to spur the Haffmann
party's appetite. A half bowl of lukewarm potato-less soup and a chunk
of rock-hard bread raised no complaints from shoulder-to-shoulder,
heads down women and children.

"Where are you going?" A compact woman with a squeezed-in-a-vise,
frowning face queried Katja between bites.

"Hamburg. My uncle's place."

The woman shot a narrow-eyed glance to her right and left. "Did you
hear this? She thinks she can waltz right into Hamburg and find her

uncle." Her jaw dropped like a full sack. "Better find a new destination, dear. Hamburg isn't Hamburg any more."

Hank placed his hand on Katja's leg, abutted to his. She made a jerking, inhaling sound but was embarrassed to react with everybody's eyes turned on her. She tried to slide away, but bodies were wedged in so tight she couldn't budge.

"Yes, we've been told that. How do you feel about being caught by the Allied troops?" Hank said.

Katja began to choke on a gulped swallow of soup. Her hand bulleted off the tabletop and clawed into the hand now rubbing her upper leg.

Hank leaned over, pulled back her hair and lightly pressed his lips to her cheek. "My wife's a little jumpy. Understandable." Katja's short nails clenched as deep as they could, but Hank's hand remained.

"I hope every day I get caught by the Americans or British," the woman said.

Katja released her grip. "You want the enemy to capture you?"

"I suspect just about everybody feels that way," Hank said. "If we can make it across the dunes to Danzig, I think we'll be far enough to escape to the west or be saved by the Allied Forces." Heads around the prematurely aged woman nodded with Hank's reasoning.

Katja huffed and went back to eating. Hank sensually moved his hand under the table along her twitching leg, then returned it to his meal. After Alena had finished eating hers and the balance of Hank's soup, Katja caught him by the arm on their way out of the dingy, cavernous makeshift dining room.

"If you ever touch me like that again, I will place something between your legs," she leaned close to his ear. "My foot."

"Never been much for feet. Long, shapely legs, now that's a different story." He gave her a long, unabashed hungry smile until she finally broke away.

~

"I'll be damned," Hank muttered when he was guided to the horse's quarters two streets up from the village's primary business and residential area. The pitifully ventilated warehouse with fenced areas constructed overnight of random wood from house siding, yard fences and other scrap reminded him more of a shantytown for horses than a care and feeding area.

Hands covering their mouths did little to ward off the strangling stench of manure and filth that slapped Hank and Alena when they led Noble to his narrow, rickety fenced area.

"At least he's out of the wind and snow for the night." Hank turned his stinging eyes down to the child. "You had better go back with Kat. This is no place for a little lady."

While both hands never dropped from her face, she shook her head and turned determined emerald eyes up to Hank.

"Maybe a few minutes then."

Once Hank shoveled out piles of manure from the previous occupant into a manure-caked cart that cost him two marks to use, he and Alena had acclimated enough to tolerate their surroundings.

Hank's wallet, still stuffed with German marks, had finally served a purpose. He went from one stable to the next, paying five and ten times the value for basic grooming supplies, including a hoof pick, grooming brush, and his prized possession that cost him more than one of the stallions he had bought from Katja, a fully equipped horse vet's bag. The stable manager reluctantly sold it for one night's use. The exchange also included Hank's commitment to stay an extra day examining as many horses as time allowed before moving on. Hank hadn't finished shaking the stout, steely-eyed, bald man's hand when Alena bound into the windowless room barren of all furnishings except a desk and two chairs. Her hand clutched her racing heart.

"Noble!" She gasped for air. "He's rolling on the ground like he's crazy."

Hank broke out in a full run, shoving past shuffling feet then whirling himself through the corral's sagging gate directly into flailing hoofs that nearly took his head off.

The second the stallion twisted to roll to the other side, he sprung to the horse's neck and wrapped both arms around, hoisting the horse to its feet. The stallion was too engulfed in madness to respond and whipped Hank over as if he was a professional wrestler.

"Be careful!" Alena screamed from the doorway.

Contorted turns and potentially body crushing, radically swift swerves didn't stop Hank from driving every ounce of muscle and bone to upright the animal.

"Quick, Alena, hand me that bag while he's still stunned." Alena grabbed the handle of the saddle brown leather folding bag with both hands and ran to Hank's side.

"Get away, child."

The stallion jerked its head with bulging, fiery eyes in Alena's direction. Its lips were peeled back, exposing chomping teeth that wouldn't hesitate to bite her hand off. She reeled back and bolted back to the door entrance.

Hank's knowing hands moved swiftly. The bag flew open and out came a hand pump and tube he started snaking up the stallion's nostril. The horse was so shocked it stopped moving and lifted its head, trying to yank it out. The tube was in his stomach before he could overpower his adversary.

With one hand crunching the strap at the stallion's mouth bit, Hank jerked Noble's head down so he could reach the bottle of castor oil. He let the horse's head rise just far enough for him to begin pumping the entire bottle down the tube.

The tube-filled animal stopped flailing, trying to comprehend the foreign object invading its body. While Noble remained still Hank rifled through the bag and found a bottle with less than an inch of chemical dewormer. "Damnit, that won't be enough," he muttered.

Once all the liquid was pumped into the animal, Hank put an ear to Noble's stomach.

"What are you doing?"

"Shh. I can't hear if anything's happening." He finally rose and shook his head.

"Not a damn sound. Normal horses stomachs sound like a tin pan orchestra down there when the digestive track's working." He patted Noble's hindquarters. "He's got intestinal blocking bigger than Cooley Dam." Alena was getting even more confused.

"Oh, that's a dam taller and wider than a western sky back home."

"It's safe to come over and pet him now, honey."

Alena balled her fists and tiptoed to Hank's side. She kept far enough back that only her fingertips made contact with Noble's sweat-dripping coat.

"We have to keep him on his feet or he'll be right back down rolling on the ground again until he twists his guts so much it kills him."

Hank cautiously walked a few paces from Noble to retrieve the bucket of water, sponge and grooming brush.

"One thing at a time. Right boy?" He carefully sponged down the horse's eyes, nostrils and lips. After wiping down its entire body he felt for tendon damage and sighed when the horse showed no signs of lameness.

"You were great, Alena. If we save him it'll be because you got to me in time. You had better get back to Kat, honey. Now I just have to keep him on his feet until we get a chance for the oil to do its work." The child bound her arms around his waist.

Hank smelled of hard work, leather and horses. He ran his hand lightly through her tangled hair and across her forehead. "You need a brush through that pretty hair. Get going now. Kat's going to be worried with you gone this long. I've got to get Noble outside so he can keep walking. We'll get you to the front door, but you'll have to find Kat from there."

~

Shortly after daybreak, Katja found Hank, still walking Noble in circles in front of the warehouse. She swayed her hip to one side, pushed back her long chestnut and auburn-kissed hair and stretched. "Hey American cowboy, not tired, are you?"

Hank stopped; turned and walked the horse through a light dusting of snow the two had endured in the blackness of night. He stared over at her, his face a little more than a silhouette in the breaking light.

"Got to keep him on his feet a few hours more. I cut down his frogs, but his feet look pretty bad."

"He was that bad?"

Hank's eyebrows shot up, as much to prop up drooping eyelids as react to her naive comment.

"Almost lost him." He patted the stallion's flank, then handed the bit reins to Katja. "I'll never know where he got the strength to get us off that ice." He ran his hand along the horse's mane, "But I'll never forget it."

Hank turned from Noble to Katja, then back to the horse. "We owe him our lives and we could again before it's all over." Katja, hand's length away from Hank, joined in petting and murmuring soothing words in the horse's perked-up ears.

"Get him to eat something. He's a walking bag of bones. Keep him on his feet for another few hours and we've got one hell of a horse back." Katja was lost in studying her most prized stallion.

"If I can wrangle up some farrier tools I'll get his hoofs trimmed and shod before we leave." He turned and started for the wagon.

"Hank, wait." When she reached him her lips moved, but the words were trapped inside her pounding heart.

"Yes, Kat?"

"I, you..." She caught the full lower lip between her teeth and stared down through misted eyes.

He tugged off his glove and took her chin in his hand and gave her a long, long look. "Is there something you want to say?"

She grabbed the back of his hair and dragged his mouth to hers. His skillful lips responded without surprise and devoured hers. His hot impatient tongue overpowered her at Katja's first tentative probing tongue.

The fingers she had twined through his hair curled into a hard fist. Her primal taste coursed through his body. She dropped all of her defenses just when he pulled away.

He kept his eyes on hers. "Your heart's pounding. And there's a little pulse right there in your throat." He used his ungloved hand to trace it and feel it skitter. "Jumping so hard, it's a wonder it doesn't come right through your skin and bounce into my hand."

She began pulling him back to her moist lips.

"Are you seducing me?" He purred it out like oozing honey. His smile came slow and potent when her body trembled.

She gradually shook her head. He felt her body jerk and stiffen as he lowered a hand and slid it inside her open coat then pulled every curve of her pulsing body to his. He expected heat or cold. She had both in her. He expected power, for she was anything but weak. He found it all, a rage of passion that slammed into him as if bare-knuckled fists.

He clutched her yard-long hair and brought his mouth down on hers again to feed.

She moaned, a sound trapped in her throat, a sound that reverberated through both their bodies. He couldn't get enough of her mouth. He wanted to devour her very essence.

He was lost in her taste, smell, being. She was holding onto him now, holding hard, moving against him, hips grinding.

He closed a hand over her breast, so firm through her flannel shirt. When it wasn't enough, not nearly enough, he yanked her shirt free of her tight-fitting riding breeches and streaked under to flesh, not caring if his hands were freezing.

The feel of his hand, soft and probing, had the muscles in her narrow thighs going loose, the tension in her stomach and loins pushing towards pain. His thumb flicked over her nipple, ricocheting bullets of heat from point to point over her heaving body.

She went limp, forcing him to tighten his grip. The surprise of her sudden and utter surrender aroused his burning flesh even more.

"We need to finish this." He cupped her small breasts, fingers skimming, stroking as he waited for her eyes to open and meet his.

She fought to suck in air. "I can't." Her lips were a breath away. "I don't think I can."

He lowered his head and nipped at her jaw.

She struggled free and stumbled backward looking around wildly for staring eyes. They were alone.

"Don't touch me." There was a lick of real panic in her voice.

Hank flashed on the naked woman, arms and legs ruthlessly tied to bedposts. Her eyes had the same distant look of horror.

"It's okay, Kat. It's okay. I'll never do what you don't want. Everything's going to be all right."

Steadier, she straightened, faced him. "Don't think that because I kissed you I'm like all the other women you've talked onto their backs. I'm no easy pickings for you to go home and brag about how you, well, did it with the enemy." She gasped and put a hand to her mouth.

Hank picked up and put on his glove then shoved his hands into his coat. He gave her one last long look. "For just a minute there you weren't the enemy."

16

Thick, relentless snow came hard and fast. It buried the last trace of Elbing's cobblestone streets and had tree branches groaning.

After only four hours of sleep on the Haffmann's reserved twin bed Hank was up, and in less than an hour elbow deep in a broodmare too weak to help push out her foal.

Without a word Katja appeared and crouched beside him. "I would have gotten here earlier, but I had to convince the floor nurse you had a commitment to keep the bed an extra day."

Still burning from her 'enemy' remark, Hank shrugged and started pulling again. "That's it, girl, just a little more." He grunted and pulled out the head, the lifeless head.

"Oh, shit. Shit." He steadied his crouch and began hauling the carcass out of the birth canal. Once free enough to grab, Katja took hold and together yanked until they toppled backward still clinging to the dead animal.

Hank squirmed out from under the weight and jumped to his feet. He shook, then started wiping the slime from his arms.

"Damnit," he boomed out in English.

Katja was up and in his face. "Hank," she said in an audible whisper, "Don't speak English. It's dangerous."

"I don't give a damn." The words were like a pair of shotgun blasts in the still of the room.

"Shh," she barely whispered. He clutched her arm and pulled her close. She went stiff at his touch until she saw the pain etched in his face.

"It's too late," he said in German. "It would be a miracle if any of the mares don't have a miscarriage. These animals need more than a day's care." His tearing eyes dropped to the foal at their feet. "Look at him. Completely developed. He probably starved to death days ago."

"I'm accomplishing nothing. We ought to leave right now before the Russians shell this place to bits."

"You don't really believe that, do you?" Katja took hold of his wrist.

"I got the last of the oil to flush them out. About every horse in here has shattered and infected hooves. Cuts and lameness." He took a measured deep breath.

"Does your bag have any Betadine and gauze in it?" He didn't respond. "You still got the pick?" He nodded.

She moved close enough that the iced air of their breath mixed.

"What are we waiting for? There's a lot of work and time's running out. I'll get Alena to join us so she's not alone. She can run us out our meals so we don't have to lose a minute."

Buoyed by Katja's unbridled enthusiasm, Hank moved at lightening speed.

It was late into the second night when Katja finally rose and straightened her aching shoulders.

It would have been hard to explain to someone that spending a frigid January night with Katja in horse stalls kneeling in blood and birth fluid could compete with the best moments in one's life, but that was exactly how Hank felt. He had seen two foals born that lived. And it thrilled him like nothing ever had.

"Sure as hell gets your mind off your problems, doesn't it?" Hank said, standing back with Katja as the newborn struggled to gain its feet for the first time.

"You've got a nice touch with horses, Kat. In fact, you'd make one hell of a vet."

"I don't know about that." Katja rubbed her hands together to warm them.

"Just look at that." Hank slid an arm around Katja's waist, drew her to his side as the foal began to nurse. "Sorry little guy, she hasn't got anything to give."

He put a hand to his aching back. Katja pushed her hand over his.

"What I would give for a hot bath," Hank said as he arched back again.

"You might be able to talk your way into a bath in the hospital. You're good at that. Talking." Hank could see she was working up a follow-up sarcastic comment to lighten the moment when he leaned over and brushed her cheek with his lips.

"Thanks, Kat."

She clinched her fists and moved out of the reach of intimacies. "I think you could get a bath."

He turned his eyes to the rows of unattended animals. "No, just wishing."

Hank's spirit rose with each cut and hoof he tended. While vegetable oil was a poor substitute in fighting colic, Alena had run quarts of it through. Hank had taught women how to pump it through their mares and stallions. He knew they would be gone before the outcome of the procedure proved helpful, but early signs were promising.

"Yes, you'd make one hell of a vet." The soft voice wafting from the shadows behind Katja made her stand and turn.

"Have we got any more bandage wrap?" She returned to the prone mare heavy in foal. "Hank, come here and just look at this tendon. This cut is dangerously deep."

"No more gauze or wrap, Kat." He walked into the glow of the kerosene lantern. "She'll never walk on that."

"What? Go get some. Hurry!"

He made a laughless chuckle. "Not that easy. I've about spent everything in my wallet. Nothing comes free around here." He bent down and squinted at the gaping cut, then reached under both of Katja's arms and pulled her to her feet. She struggled out of his grip and faced him.

Hank looked into her dark, quiet eyes.

They were close enough to the massive open warehouse doors for only a few dancing snowflakes to float between them. Hank looked over at the wall of white framed in darkness like a living painting.

"We can't go anywhere until it lets up. The map looks like it will take at least two days and nights without shelter to get to Danzig and Pomerania."

Katja twisted and bit her lip. "The bandages, Hank."

"We've got to survive the Baltic strand of sand dunes first. Miles and miles of white, then desert."

"I need those bandages."

"The stable manager said this province is run by an old couple he knows who have turned their farm over to helping refugees. We can stay there." His words drifted off.

"Please do this for me."

"The bandages. All right. I'll buy some from one of the nurses with the last of our money." He shot up an eyebrow and twitched one side of his cheek. "That make you happy?"

"Thank you," she said and looked out at the snow.

"Thanks for what? The bandages or the fact that I think you'd make a great vet?"

Katja hunched inside her heavy fur coat. "It's like breathing broken glass in here."

"If you don't take a rest after this mare, I'll stop right now, after getting the bandages, of course."

~

An icy blizzard had only let up briefly when the Haffmann party climbed aboard their wagon and began winding their way through wagons and narrow streets to the outskirts of town. Hank and Katja felt equally or more exhausted than before they arrived. Over forty horses were the better for their stay, they assured each other, before Hank handed the stable manager back his vet bag.

"How long do you think they can keep it going?" Katja asked, looking back at the nearly lone intact building used as a life-saving respite by nonstop swarms of refugees.

"Days, hours. It can't be…" Hank bolted up from his seat. He pointed to the dark belt of trees that clung to the rising foothills all draped in snow.

Katja used her hand atop her brow to cut down the white glare that almost hurt the eyes. The silver of outjutting rock and ridges forming shadows and contrasts made spotting anything extremely difficult. Then she saw them. Like a centipede, the Russian tanks, thirty she could count, were perched with barrels pointed at the masses and hospital below.

"We've got to warn them!" she shrieked.

"No, it's too late." Hank sent Noble into a run and careened around the last city street corner, speeding straight toward an eyebrow-shaped sliver of a stone bridge only wide enough for one wagon to cross at a time.

"Move, get that wagon out of the way," he hollered at the man who was out of his cart and repeatedly lashing his horse with a buggy whip.

A pocked pie-face with flaming eyes turned and snarled at Hank. He then hurled the whip high over his head and sent it slapping the chestnut East Prussian Warmblood stallion's back.

Katja beat Hank down from the wagon. She charged the barrel-chested man and tackled him to the ground. He rolled on top of her before Hank could get to him and drove a sledgehammer fist into her face. Blood spurted out of Katja's nose as if it were a broken faucet. He sprang off her and whipped around to face Hank.

"You bastard," Katja howled. Eyes burning, she staggered up to her feet, causing the man to turn just enough to catch the full impact of her foot between his legs. He curled and was about to drop to his knees when Katja took a step closer and rammed her knee into his forehead. He reeled, toppling backwards. She heard his skull when the back of his head made contact with the metal hub of his cart's wheel.

Katja wildly shook her head, dropped to her knees and collapsed. The snow around her flailing head was as crimson as the bottom half of her face. Alena screamed and was caught in Hank's arms before she could get to Katja.

"It's all right. I think he only broke her nose."

The light flashed in Katja's head like fireworks. She finally steadied her breathing and arched her neck back. She used the back of her wool mitten to ebb the flow of blood.

"Alena, get a towel or something we can clean Kat up with. Hurry." He shot a glance at the unmoving man still propped against the wheel.

"The bastard deserved it," she said, muffled by her mitten.

Hank bent down to cradle Katja's shoulders, slipped an arm under her knees and lifted her. At that moment the sky above them thundered with cannon fire. Katja shot out of his arms and was on her feet.

"Let's get this wagon out of the way," she ordered.

Hank put a finger to the man's neck and didn't get a pulse. He dragged the corpse clear of the wagon.

"Help me unharness his horse." Katja gawked in disbelief at the lifeless face, too dazed to notice the stream of blood dripping from her nose to her boots.

"I killed him?"

"The tanks, Katja. Come on and help me. Now."

All Russian barrels were pointed directly at the hospital. They were barely out of harm's way, but the tanks were on the move.

"Hurry, damnit," Hank said in English, then repeated in German. They harnessed the chestnut stallion next to Noble, again giving them two horses to pull the wagon. They were across the bridge to the ice-smooth road leading toward the dunes and the Baltic Coast.

The trail was cluttered with overturned wagons that had slipped in the steep ditch on each side of the road. Some had been abandoned, while others were brimming with women, old men and children with outstretched arms wailing for someone to have mercy.

"What's that?" Katja asked from a prone position in the back of the wagon.

"Wagons off the road. We can't stop, Kat."

The sound of cannon fire grew to a distant echo when they crested the hillside, then began their descent on a treacherously slippery winding road with less snow each mile they traveled. Once they reached the bottom, Hank pulled on the reins and lifted the canvas flap.

Katja was asleep; the profile of her beautiful face lay softly against the rough blanket. Alena's ashen face was becoming too familiar with horror, Hank thought, when empty eyes met his.

"Climb up front," he whispered. She mechanically rose and with his help was by his side.

"She was crying," Alena said in a wooden tone.

"Kat crying? That doesn't happen very often."

"She said she was ugly with a broken nose."

Hank reached back and lifted the flap. "Impossible. She's one of the most beautiful women I've ever seen. Still is." He winked at the child. "And I've seen a few."

Katja opened her eyes after the glaring face was gone. He just missed her wincing when her upturned lips made her nostrils move.

17

Hank looked over the last of the rolling landscape, accented by patches of snow, ground brush and isolated trees stretching their branches as far from the winds of the Baltic coast as they could reach. On the far horizon was a powder blue and misty white view of a vast ocean with a cresting line of waves lapping the edge of crust sandy dunes.

"Everybody up front. You can see the coast, and the last of the snow, for a while anyway. The Russians are probably patrolling the coast from the sky."

Katja was the first to climb out from the cargo area. Hank's raised brows at the first sight of her face made him groan without realizing it.

"What? What's wrong?" Katja lightly touched her chiseled cheekbones, now puffy purple and dirty custard yellow.

"Kat, if you want to keep that model's face, I'm going to have to tape your nose." While his voice had a smile in it, the meaning had a sharp bite.

"You know how to get to the point without a lot of sweet talk, don't you?"

Gone was the fiery-tempered ruler of the Haffmann party trek. Gone was the razor-sharp quip always less than an inch from his jugular. He wanted that woman back and he was determined he'd do everything in his power to stir her back to life.

"I take it you were never one for girl things like fancy dresses and all that."

"What are you talking about?"

Hank's eyes crinkled in delight. He raised his index finger and chuckled. "There it is. That old fight. Now keep a hold of that. We're not out of the..." He laughed and peered over at Alena, drinking up every word. "Well, I guess we're out of the woods, but not the frying pan."

"What?" his two companions said at once.

"Just an expression."

"The kind of thing you would say around the track at Luxembourg," Katja said.

"Lexington is where my stud farm is. Louisville is where the Kentucky Derby is held, at Churchill Downs."

"Boy, you two dingy women could drive me to drink if I could ever get my hands on any." Katja was still touching her face.

Hank's peripheral vision caught Katja whispering something to Alena.

"Oh, you don't look like a monkey or anything," the child blurted out.

Hank bit his lip to stop from laughing.

"Not another word out of either of you or you'll be walking behind the wagon to Danzig."

"What's that smirk on your face?" Katja asked.

Hank shook his head.

"That's right. Not another word."

Hank winked at Alena and turned an invisible key at his tightly closed lips.

~

With two million people fleeing in the same direction simultaneously, Hank couldn't expect to find any space of time without mounting lines of refugees: the dunes were no exception.

While there was no sign of Russians, wagons, axle deep in sand popped up about every five miles. Hank, Katja and mostly the younger women stopped regularly to lend a hand.

At nearly dusk there was only a string of clouds highlighting a brilliant orange and yellow sunset that shimmered across the Baltic Sea to the Haffmann party's appreciative eyes. Their resting spot for the night, away from the still-moving line of wagons, promised a peaceful time out from the cruelties behind and ahead of them. Once Hank unhitched the two horses, fed them and tied their harnesses to the wagon wheel, he rejoined Katja and Alena on the wagon seat.

Hank broke the serenity first. "Tonight we're going to have a fire. Alena, go gather some wood, will you?" He reached out and touched the tip of Katja's swollen nose as the child disappeared from sight.

"Are you ready?"

"You're a horse doctor. What do you know about correcting human bones that are broken?"

Hank rubbed his chin, carelessly slipped his hand through his hair, and puffed, then blew out the cold night air.

"This can be easy or hard, but we'll manage."

Katja's bottom lip protruded like a child. "Easy for you to say. I'll look like a clown."

Hank gently lifted her chin, taking her face in both hands. "A woman as beautiful as you? Impossible."

Katja's face turned as red as her nose. "You're making fun of me. Go ahead, do what you have to."

The concession was all he needed. His hands moved from her cheeks to a quick pull, grasping her nose between his thumb and index finger, out and across the center point of the bridge of her nose. She gasped at the sudden popping and crackling gristle sound.

"Ouch, you bastard. You broke it again!"

"Had to get it in place." His hands turned to vise grips. "Hold perfectly still." He pulled the tape from his pocket and with one hand and his teeth measured out and bit off what he needed. Lightly placing a scrap piece of gauze he miraculously found in one of his pockets from his work at the Elbing stable, he centered and taped it down.

"Done. Pretty fast, right?"

"How long will it be like this?"

"About fourteen days. The worst will be behind you in a week. It's going to be sensitive and swollen, though, for weeks. And here's the bad news."

"There's worse?"

"Child's play compared to one of our typical days. It will cause you earaches when you lie down for the first four or five days." He moved his head back to analyze the nose alignment. "Looks perfect. Never know it happened."

"What else?"

"Upper teeth are going to hurt like hell when you bite, but there's good news."

She shook her head, then stopped as a pain like a ringing gong bounced from one side of her skull to the other.

"You won't be able to smell so food will lose its taste. And that's the good news. There's nothing to eat anyway. Perfect time to break your nose."

Her chin angled at the mumbling circles he was talking in. She was working at perfecting a sarcastic comment, but his beaming pride with his work made her hold her tongue.

"Can I get rid of this tape soon?"

He shrugged, enjoying his brief moment of control. "We'll see when the swelling goes down."

Katja's probing fingers returned to their constant attempt to grab for her mirror.

"You'll want to lie down. I'm sure you're a little dizzy. I'll get you up when we get the fire blazing. Imagine, we're having a hot meal tonight. After I boil some water, we've got enough to make some kind of vegetable soup."

"I got three fresh bread loaves from the hospital kitchens," Katja said holding her chin up.

"How in the world? Forget it. I should know not to question your powers of persuasion with your tongue or your fist."

~

After dinner, interrupted twice by parties of mothers and children searching out warmth and food, Hank and Katja were alone watching the last fire embers. The night sky was a sheet of deep blue velvet studded with diamonds. A wedge of moon was scaling the far-off sand dunes, spilling its white glow down on the sea.

"I'm glad I planned on company stopping by for a bite to eat." The easy country club manner he spoke made them both laugh, with Katja's cut short by shooting pain brought on with any facial movement.

Hank turned to her molasses crescent eyes, looking like a cat's in the dim fire glow. "I guess this kind of puts a wrinkle in kissing you."

"A wrinkle?"

He moved so close to Katja their hips rubbed. "Sorry, I can't always find the right words in German for saying I would like to kiss you."

"Come here," Hank whispered, turning her around in his arms. He cradled her head against his chest, fingers tangled in the hopeless wilderness of her hair.

"Hank, you asked me if I had somebody at home. Do you?"

His arm stiffened and he brought it back into his lap.

Katja sighed. "It doesn't matter." With her coat slightly open, Hank could see her rapid breathing and feel her shuddering body. "If we live through this, what would we do? I'm not leaving Germany, and of course you'd go home. I don't know what is going to be left of Germany when it's all over, but it would be no place for a rich American." She paused and took a breath, hungering for a rebuttal, but she heard none.

Katja shut her eyes. "Is she rich and beautiful?"

Hank slipped his arm back around her, moving her as close to his chest as her delicate condition allowed.

"So, you do believe me."

"Is she beautiful?"

"Yes, she's beautiful. Pretty nose, too."

Katja lifted the dead weight of his arm off her shoulder. "She sounds spoiled and empty headed."

"Victoria's no idiot. Went to a blue blood college and ranked near the top of her class." He curled his head back and blankly stared into the tranquil night. "She hasn't had it that easy, either. She was treated like a dog by her first husband."

Katja slid away and stared into his darting eyes. "First?"

"Did I say that? She's only been married once."

"You're to be the second husband?"

Hank lowered his head, still shifting his eyes in every direction but hers. "That's kind of where things were leading."

Katja moved away, stood and started for the wagon, half expecting Hank to stop her, but he didn't.

~

It had almost become routine to stop and help push or leverage cart and wagon wheels out of soft dune spots along the seldom-traveled sliver of sand lining the sea. As soon as Hank's eyes opened he promised himself no stops regardless of people's plight until they reached their destination. He was the first to dress and slip out of the wagon.

Katja's eyes were open when he left. They had been open nearly all night.

Stallions harnessed and fed with a piece of rye bread in their stomachs, the Haffmann party's wagon wheels were rolling again, folding back into the nonstop procession all bound for Danzig. Stories of soft beds and hearty meals were at a frenzy as one traveler's story passed to the next.

Hank sighed deeply. He felt whole, a fullness he was beginning to treasure more than power and wealth.

"It's so beautiful," he said loud enough to rouse Katja and Alena. Miles and miles of sand on one side, ocean on the other. "Come on out you two. It's incredible. The sky's so blue it almost hurts your eyes."

Katja appeared before he finished his last tribute to the morning. She watched her breath and shook her head at the cold's unwillingness to even let go of its strangling grip with a sky so brittle blue it looked artificial.

"It's still cold enough to cause frostbite," she threw out, looking at the sky, then Hank, like they were both to blame.

"Good morning to you too, Kat."

She turned away and mumbled something Hank chose to ignore. The less said the better for the moment.

"Another wagon off the roadside," Hank said. He stood, trying to shield his eyes from the morning silhouetting of what was ahead to get a closer look.

"It looks like somebody tried to pull it out with chains and the wagon fell apart." His observation caught Katja's curiosity enough to join in a closer look.

"The hitch is completely detached from the—"

Katja clutched Hank's arm. "I know those. Hurry, hurry up. I need a closer look. I can't believe it!" Katja gasped and reeled back in astonishment.

"Alena, stay down in the back," Hank yelled.

"He's got my father's rifle and shells," she yelled.

Hank craned his neck. They were less than one hundred yards away. "I don't see anybody."

Then she saw him. The black-hairy beast had stolen Katja's mother's last reason to live.

The air seemed thick with death.

"I'll kill him." She uttered each word deliciously slow.

Hank yanked on the reins, bringing the wagon to a stop at a safe distance from being identified.

"Kat, get in the back." Hank clenched his jaw and rubbed his chin. "We're the last people he's expecting. If he's still got that gun we need the advantage of surprise."

"No, he's mine. I've handled him before." She bit down hard on her lip.

"Sure you can handle it?" Before she could answer he was devising the plan of attack. "I'll pull the wagon over and around the other direction so we can slip out—"

"I'll slip out." She squeezed her eyes shut. "I have to do this alone, Hank."

Alena started climbing over the backrest of the seat to join in on a hushed discussion so full of tension it filled her with fear.

"No," said Katja. "Stay here."

Hank's hands weren't gentle as he stopped Katja mid-air. "Come on up, Alena." His voice was rough and his hand on her arm firm. "He has never seen her. We want her out and around the wagon so the only person he spots is a child. A perfect diversion for us, you know, to sneak up."

Katja quickly nodded and obeyed. "Wait," Hank said. He scurried back into the wagon and brought out their only weapon, a six-inch blade pocketknife with the blood-red plastic handles reading 'World Famous Kentucky Derby' on both sides.

Katja shoed it away. "Not our only weapon. Alena, get in back and hand me up that half shovel, will you?"

~

Wolf made a loud sounding yawn and scratched his thick-matted chest. All wasn't lost, he told himself over a piece of cold hard cheese. He turned his gorilla face to the stack of precious possessions that provided more than ample barter to pry his way into another wagon. He surveyed his full box of hunting rifle shells to protect himself, and remaining food. Then he heard something, or someone. His eyes and eyebrows popped open like a jack-in-the-box. A lifetime in shady corners kept his wits wickedly sharp.

He moved silent as a ghost. First the rifle. He wasn't quite sure if there was a bullet in the chamber. Too noisy. He would have to chance that it was loaded.

The sound of one, two footsteps made him inhale and absently rub a hand over his clammy heart.

He decided at the second set of sounds there was one noise he would chance making. His wide, stumpy thumb inched its way up to the cold, rounded metal arm of the rifle.

Katja white-knuckled the rough wood handle shovel at the sound of her father's rifle being cocked.

She crouched lower and silently slipped under the back of his wagon. There was a long moment of absolute silence until Katja's eyes inadvertently locked on two of her beloved stallions. One of the horses let out a shattering noise and, though fully harnessed, tried unsuccessfully to rear up.

"Shh, quiet," Katja automatically sounded. The horse obeyed her slightest command.

Wolf heard it all, including the recognizable high voice able to quiet the animals with one command. He shook his head and smiled. He could be patient. She was now his prey.

"I know it's you out there, Katja," he said in a high mockingly loving tone.

"Just had to come back to me, didn't you? You needed a man who could fill you up." His sour milk breath was getting heavier with each self-hypnotizing word.

"I'm all ready for you, cousin. It's getting hard just thinking about how you are going to enjoy it." He leaned over and put his ear to the floor at the front of the wagon.

"I can see you with that shovel."

The guttural voice directly above her made Katja spring up and slam the back of her head into the wagon so hard she dropped to the ground like a rag doll.

Saucer-wide black eyes watched through the slit between floorboards. She appeared unconscious.

"You're playing with me. I like that. I can't really see you under that heavy coat." A wind whistled its reminder that it was still deathly freezing in the open air. "I think you're just—" Wolf's eyes bulged out like an exotic fish when his head was ripped back to the floor hard enough to break it by the taut, leather strap Hank was crossing around the beast's bull neck.

"Peep show is over, you bastard," Hank hissed in English.

Wolf's digging fingers were too late. The strap was too deeply wrapped around his neck to get a hold. His crouch was too low to lift his attacker's weight and his own off the floor.

Wolf's hands dropped like anchors to his side. Hank started releasing the arched back, forcing his rammed knee into the center of the beast's spine. He didn't know whether the thief was dead or alive, and didn't care.

The strap slithered away from Wolf's neck like a boa constrictor done with its prey. Hank wrapped the three-foot piece of leather he had cut from his own wagon's harness around one of his fists with an end dangling, ready to go back to work. No need. Wolf didn't move.

Hank placed his index finger on the pulse of the heavily bearded neck. At first there was none, then a slow steady pulse.

He lugged both muscular arms back and tied, then retied a knot that would hold the weight of a wagon dangling from a cliff.

He backed away from his victim on his knees and slowly climbed into a slapping gust of wind that shot images of frostbite, hypothermia and death to his mind.

"Kat!" The act of near-murder twisted all sense of time and place. He dashed to her and gently pulled her out from under the wagon. It took what adrenaline he had left to hoist her into his arms and carry her back, while bucking fierce wind the great distance to their wagon. Midway there, he fell to his knees, jarring her out of his arms and into consciousness.

She threw her long hair back and forth, trying to lock into what danger loomed over her next.

"It's all right, Kat," Hank yelled over the shrill whistling wind. "Can you stand?"

She rose as unsteady as a newborn colt. Hank braced her back to the wagon, dry heaving, spitting sand, and squinting through tearing eyes with each step.

Once Katja was safely down in their own wagon with Alena covering her with blankets to keep her warm, she stopped her jagged breathing long enough to turn questioning eyes up to Hank.

"Wolf's tied up in his wagon. Thought I had killed him, but I've got a better plan."

Hank stroked Katja's head. "Alena, our girl's got a concussion," Hank said, while looking at the child.

~

It was midday when the windstorm stopped as fast as it kicked up. Katja was sitting and eating a piece of rye bread when Hank climbed back into the wagon.

"Where have you been?" she asked with a hand to her pounding forehead.

"Changed Wolf's harness for ours and tied your two horses to the back of the wagon with some extra strap." His eyes roamed their already-cramped cargo and passenger area.

"We'll just have to make room."

Katja plopped back to the folded blankets serving as a pillow.

"He's not coming in here," she whispered.

Hank raised his chin and rubbed it. "No, I have to agree with you on that. I was talking about his food, blankets, and of course, your mother's silver set. It's going to be incredibly crowded, but we'll manage."

Katja strained to see, then settled back down after seeing the smirk on Hank's face.

"We'll be off for Danzig as soon as we get things packed."

Even though Katja's eyes were still shrouded by purple-turned-green-and yellow bruises, they made a restless movement that couldn't be missed.

"Oh, you are wondering what has become of your friend, Wolf? I thought we would leave him just as he thought he was leaving us, with nothing but the coat on his back." Hank half-smiled. "We should leave the bastard naked to freeze to death."

"Have you ever killed anybody before, before Germany, I mean?" Katja asked.

"Of course not. My heart murmur kept me out of the War. Not that I tried to get into this mess," Hank mused.

"I shouldn't ask so many questions," Katja said.

Hank put an open palm on her shoulder. "I don't mind." He moved his fingertips to Katja's forehead and lifted her hair back off her sweat-beaded face.

"Kat, we had better face the possibility that if everybody's headed for Danzig like they did Elbing, the Reds could have already taken it out."

With a careful eye Katja studied Hank's face. "You want my approval to break out on our own route."

"It would be a hell of a lot safer," Hank said.

Katja twisted her hands. "After Danzig we'll be well rested and fed. Maybe even get Noble shod."

He knew that look. "I would hate to have you on the other side of a negotiating table."

"Am I that bad?"

He lifted his head and rubbed his beard while taking a contemplative breath.

"Good," she sighed. "Now get this wagon back in motion."

"Not before you tell Wolf we're leaving him here." Katja slowly nodded.

They stopped long enough for Wolf to stumble out of his wagon and start for the back of theirs.

"Where do you think you're going?" Katja demanded.

"I'm getting in back."

Katja leveled a cutting stare at Wolf and shook her head.

"You're not just going to leave me here to die, are you?"

Katja tightened her lips and shook her head.

Wolf ran to the front of the wagon with his hands clasped together as if in prayer. "Don't let her do this," he said to Hank. "I was only trying to survive like everybody else."

"You're a thief and a monster!" Katja snapped.

"You can't do this. You took everything."

With a nod of her head, Katja signaled Hank to roll the reins and start moving.

Wolf leaped to the backboard but Katja quickly shoved a foot to his chest, knocking him backward to the ground.

Wolf clamored to his knees. "Please, please. I'm begging you."

Hank pulled on the reins and turned to Katja. She didn't need to say a word. He started again for Danzig.

~

The temperature had been steadily rising above freezing as they neared their destination. Though it meant mud and slop once they were off the dunes of the ocean coastline, and the wind blew capriciously, it was a moment to be enjoyed.

As the three sat like a family huddled on the wagon seat, Hank thought about the simple, precious joys that people care about, a full stomach and a warm safe place to stay. Danzig meant all of that, if it was still there.

18

They were approaching the outskirts of Danzig when wagons halted at the now-familiar sound of cannon fire.

"Kat, get out the map."

She held her hand up. "Listen. Shh! That's not coming from Danzig. It's coming from the south."

"Hell, Kat. They're on our heels in every direction. By staying with everybody else we're begging for it." He rolled the reins and got the horses, to begin moving at a trot.

"What, what are you doing?" she demanded, quick gusts of cold wind dragging the temperature back down, cutting her breathing short.

"Let's try to get all the supplies we can, shoe Noble, and set out on our own path for Hamburg."

Katja's frown relaxed a bit when one of the first things they saw on entering the untouched-by-battle Danzig main street was a blacksmith's shop.

"Not more than three wagons, only six horses before we could shoe Noble and get moving." Hank drew a deep breath, pleased that his plan seemed to be working out so perfectly.

He pulled up beside one of the blacksmith's customers.

"Let's all go. Alena and I need to stretch our legs too," Katja said. She maneuvered the child to her feet and down from the wagon.

The blacksmith was a little taller than Hank. Just looking at him, Katja could see the man sat as comfortably in a saddle as another man would in an easy chair. After years of forging over hot flames, his wiry arms looked as hard in the glow of his coals as the metal he was dipping and pounding. His hair was golden brown and long, the back of his worn shirt sweat-drenched. His eyes shot up at the sound of the Haffmann party entering his shop. They were sharp as a hawk and set in a face that had the weathered, craggy good looks of a man who would be a Godsend in any out-of-doors journey or crisis.

The man ran his black gloved hand over a scar that lined his chin. His eyes glinted in 'welcome' at the sight of the newest refugee family to enter his world.

"Be with you in a moment, sir, ma'am."

"No hurry," Hank responded with an equally engaging smile. "The bombing. Heard it that close before?" Hank asked.

"For days now."

Hank scratched his beard, wondering why impending death could be shrugged off like nothing more than rain clouds.

"Why isn't everybody—"

"Running off like rabbits?"

Hank and Katja nodded at the same time.

The blacksmith paused and held up a molten yellow horseshoe before their eyes. "That's why."

"You must not have a family to stay here," Hank said.

The blacksmith's grin was enough to make anybody smile. "I'll be with you shortly." He turned his head back down. Every seasoned movement made his work look effortless.

Between customers Hank noticed the blacksmith never took his eyes off them.

"Your turn. How many horses?" the blacksmith instinctively asked Katja.

"Our black stallion has been unshod the entire journey. Check the others, if you have time."

The blacksmith nodded, pulled off his glove and reached an open hand out to Katja. "Kurt Vogel." He turned to Hank and shook his hand.

"If you consider a wife of twenty-eight years and nine children a family, yes, I have one."

Hank's eyebrows shot up.

"Three Vogel generations of blacksmiths worked in this shop. Not stopping when everybody in the country needs us now more than ever before."

Hank grimaced at the man's response.

"On occasion we've let people spend the night with us. House is just behind the shop. Big two-story place."

Katja nodded. "I saw it as we pulled up."

"Why don't you two and the girl here stay with us tonight?" He bent down to Alena's eye level. "Would you like a hot meal of fried potatoes and milk soup? And your own bed to sleep in?" Alena's head never stopped nodding with each invitation.

"No, we've got to move. Those cannons can't be far away. They could be here in hours. Pack your wagon and go with us." Katja flinched at Hank's spontaneous offer.

"Get up to the house now. Tell my wife, Vera, I sent you up." His bright jade eyes rested on Katja.

"That nose still looks sore. You should be the first to heat up some water on the stove and take a bath. You and your," he broke into a wide smile, "husband will get to share a bed tonight."

The blacksmith's playful eyes watched the anticipated objection Katja showed but didn't say.

"That sounds too good to pass up. We thank you."

Hank figured Katja was too punchy to understand the danger in lingering even an hour longer than necessary.

"You hear that?"

They all froze. The sounds of war were gone.

"They're probably on the move to Danzig right now." He reached down and scooped Alena up in his arms.

"Thank you for your generous offer. We have to keep moving."

Katja stepped and locked one of her long legs in front of Hank.

"It's worth taking the chance for a good rest before we start the longest arm of the journey. We are indebted to you, Mr. Vogel.

The blacksmith's eyes bounced from Hank's face to Katja's.

"You two could use the rest."

Adjusting to Katja's edicts was getting easier, especially since he had an opportunity he silently decided not to pass up. The thought of some teasing fun with her when it was time for the two of them to share a bed was worth the overnight delay.

~

Hank tried to convince himself that dining with ten children was going to be followed by more rewards than a full stomach. Eruptive screaming, jabbing fingers and elbows were dismissed by the loving Vogels like they were enjoying company at a private candlelit dinner setting.

Katja rested her chin on her fist when no one but Hank was watching, with a serene smile on her face as she saw the Vogels share the highs and lows of each other's day with attentive tenderness.

After the children fled from their licked-clean bowls to the living room, Kurt Vogel turned his attention to his guests.

"I expected you would both have had a bath by now."

Katja's eyes dropped to her plain white porcelain bowl. Her still-fading purple bruised face turned back up to her hosts.

"I washed up. Thank you," Katja said.

Mrs. Vogel, a still-lean woman despite her brood, rose and gingerly touched her hands to her peppered hair, secured in a bun on the back her head. "I'll be right back."

Mr. Vogel cleared his throat. "You two will be sharing the bed at the top of the stairs to the right. Mother has got it all ready for you."

Hank and Katja looked straight on without a blink.

The blacksmith contained a chuckle.

Mrs. Vogel whisked back into the room with a flowing red, low-necked cotton nightdress in her hands. She came up behind Katja, and over her shoulder delicately laid it in front of her. "I'm sure that will fit. Might be a little short, though, you being so tall."

Katja started shaking her head.

"No, not a gift. Just for tonight. I put water on the stove. Now go up and take the first bath. Your husband will be right behind you."

Hank held back again while watching Katja accept the gracious offers.

Her look of disgust at Hank's sappy grin made the blacksmith have to bite his finger to stop from laughing.

After Katja had slipped away, the blacksmith and Hank were alone at the table. "Let me help you clean up," Hank said, his eyes still avoiding Mr. Vogel's.

The blacksmith drew near enough to whisper, "I could tell she was in love with you from the second you walked into my shop."

"Of course, yes, she is, my wife."

The blacksmith patted Hank on the back. "Your wife. Of course she is. And the little girl is your daughter."

Hank looked away. "That's right."

Hank fed the horses and settled Alena into an attic bedroom she shared with two giggling, poking girls near her age.

The last thing he did before entering the bedroom was bathe. After scrubbing days of exhaustion off his tired body, he cursed under his breath for not asking to borrow something clean, like Katja had, just for the night. He wrapped the towel around his narrow waist, and with folded clothes in hand, slowly opened the bedroom door.

Katja was sitting nervously on the edge of the bed in the flowing crimson nightdress brushing her hair by the light of the fire blazing in the master bedroom fireplace.

Hank suddenly couldn't hear anything over the knocking of his own heart.

"I thought you could sleep right here," she said softly, her hand extended to the two blankets laid out neatly with a pillow in front of the fire.

He closed the door behind him. Her hair was flowing over her shoulders with each stroke of the brush. Firelight streamed through it, and the thin nightdress when she rose and walked over to stand in front of the fire.

His tongue was thick, throat dry. "That should do it. What happened to the tape?"

He re-tightened the towel around his waist.

His throat was closing again, like a bear trap. "You shouldn't have taken it off."

She turned around to him, her taut, lean body leaving nothing to his imagination. "Why?"

He couldn't get his tongue off his toes to respond. He nodded and sat on the edge of the full-size bed. Finally he could speak.

He swallowed as though he couldn't get air. "You look stunning in that nightdress."

"Thank you." She tilted her head down in embarrassment. "I don't usually wear things like this."

Hank started rubbing his sweaty palms together then steepled them into a pointer and rocked them in front of his face. "This is going to be hard."

Katja drew a slow smile. "I don't have any idea what you're talking about."

Though nervous as a schoolboy, he hunkered into a predatory look. "Now what if the Vogels walked in here and found out they had given up their room so one of us could sleep on the floor?" He patted the bed beside him. "Like you said, forget everything for one night."

Katja walked over to him with a provocative gait he didn't know his rough rider companion had mastered.

He lifted his hands to the low-necked dress and began slowly pulling it down.

"Are you going to slug me in the face or kick me between my legs?"

"Maybe. If you go too far."

Hank stepped up to her and tugged the gown back up and into place. His voice had thickened and the sound of it set her trembling. "You look beautiful."

Her arms fell to her sides, and her approving eyes met his. He slowly slid the dress down her shoulders, over her pert, erect nipples, down her waist and let go at the top of her thighs. She shivered at the skim of his fingertips over her skin.

"I don't think I can," she said.

Hank knew what she meant. The nightmares she had spurted out one vulnerable night were always with her. He remembered them vividly. She would wake up drenched in sweat with screams locked in her throat. Always the same: She was naked, wrists bound. She struggled to free herself. Felt the cord bite into her flesh as she whimpered and writhed. Smelled her own blood as it trickled down her bare arms.

He moved back far enough for the light and shadow to play over the lovely lines of her bare flesh. "Don't move," he murmured and moved his mouth to hers.

"Ouch!" She brought her hand to her swollen nose.

Hank again drank in her beauty. There's a lot more than that to devour." His fingertips traveled to the back of her spine and down to her firm, slightly gyrating backside.

"You can kiss. I know that," he whispered between touching lips. "Just use your tongue instead of your lips."

"There's something inside me that died," she whispered.

"I need to taste you." He dusted her green and yellow bruises with feather-light kisses.

"They took it," she sighed.

"No they didn't." He slid his mouth down to her moist, parted lips. "They took nothing because you gave them nothing." He ran his hands down the sides of her narrow hips.

"You can trust me."

"I know." His mouth toyed with hers.

"I'll even stop if you want me to."

"No, just be gentle." Her lips tightened on his mouth the way they had days before. After her darting tongue stopped for a moment, he moved away far enough to see her long and slim, subtle curves and strong angles glow golden in the dancing light.

"You're the most beautiful woman I've ever seen." He cupped a hand to the back of her neck and drew her slowly toward him.

He could see she wanted to lift a hand to cover herself, but didn't. His fingers combed through her hair, letting it fall while his mouth played with hers.

"I want to be the first man to make love to you."

Her eyes opened at that. "You wouldn't be the first."

He ran a hand down to her breast, circled with a fingertip, forced a moan through her lips as his thumb brushed over her nipple.

"That makes it even better. I need to be inside of you."

He slid his hand down over her hip, his fingers trailing lightly toward the center, stroking, awakening.

He watched her eyes grow huge. Her hands moved up to his shoulders for balance, then squeezed him with each stroke of her flesh.

"I don't think I can keep standing up anymore," she sighed.

"Okay." His hands were roaming again, and she was beginning to float. "Hank, we shouldn't."

He trailed a line of kisses down her throat while backing to the bed and wiggling off his towel.

"Just let it go, for tonight. One night." His voice was as deep and soft as rumpled velvet. She fell back on the bed. With a shudder of his own, he took her breast in his mouth. She arched, the breath exploding through her lips. He bit lightly. Her hands fisted in his hair, urging him to ignore her pleas to go easy.

She gasped and released a deep moan. "I want you inside me, too." Her body was fluid one moment, tensed the next as her hips flowed with him. Her scent was clean and pure.

Her raw flavor filled him in ways he had never imagined possible. He took her mouth again. Her tongue tangled like a fighter with his, urging him to get rougher. But somewhere in the back of his mind he knew he had to stay gentle.

He ran his hand up the long length of her leg, stopping just short of the heat, then begin again until she started bucking like a wild animal desperate to mate.

He rolled on top of her and looked into her wide and blind golden eyes when he entered her.

She arched back. He went fast, then slow, teasing along their pleasure until they were both going mad. Everything happened at once. Her arms dropped to her sides. She clenched the sheets and stiffened her body under his pounding weight. The eruption caused her body to buck and shudder while she let free a booming long shriek that neither of them could hear through the thick fog of their passion. Then her body went slack.

Her skin was dewed with sweat, her body soft from total surrender.

Hank rolled over onto his back trying to catch his breath. "I bet they believe we're married now," he said in bubbly laughter.

As soft dawn appeared through the window, Hank's eyes opened slowly. Over Katja's bare shoulder was Alena's beaming face.

"Are you going to be my mother and father?"

Katja bolted up in bed, at first oblivious that she was naked, then she covered her breasts and took a spastic breath.

"Alena, you shouldn't just walk into people's bedrooms."

"Maybe not your parents," the low, gravely voice said, back still turned from Katja. "But we'll be your parents until we find yours. Now come here and give me a little hug."

The child's drooping lower lip jerked back up. She leaped to Hank and pecked his check. "Let's get dressed and we'll see about eating something and getting on our way," he said. Alena's eyes twinkled when she nodded. "And a bath for you, young lady, before we leave." The door was closed before he could finish fatherly orders.

Hank turned around to Katja. She instantly pulled the sheet edge up to cover herself. Her eyes were rimmed in tears.

Hank used his fingers like a comb through his hair. He then tugged on his beard. "I'd cry, too, if I made love to a hairy, ugly beast like me." His smile was too relaxed not to melt down a bit of her shuddering.

He reached out for her arm, but she moved away. "Look Kat, we made love last night. Made love, and it was one of the most incredible experiences I've ever had."

Katja pressed her lips together. "But what do we do now?"

"Survive. And after last night, it's going to be a little easier." He took her hand, lifted it and lightly kissed it. "Now my beautiful lady, let's dress and get the hell out of here."

Katja cocked her head, scooped back a rope of her hair and tucked it behind her ears. She took a deep breath and nodded.

He watched her every move as she dressed.

The breath backed up into her lungs and it took an effort to push it out. "Are you trying to make me nervous?"

"You are incredible," he whispered.

~

Half expecting another meal and slow conversation before they left, Hank and Katja were surprised to find the blacksmith darting around the kitchen with his arms full of plates and bowls. He stopped so fast at the sight of the couple he almost fell forward.

"You've got to get out fast. Those sounds were American and British bombers."

"You said American?" Hank said, unaware he was speaking in English.

The blacksmith's dark eyes narrowed at the stranger's comfort with the foreign language.

Katja quickly cleared her throat. "There you go again." She shifted her eyes to the blacksmith. "He's always showing off his ability to speak English and Swedish."

All three froze in place, each considering their next move.

"You had better go while you can."

From the blacksmith's glare, it was obvious to Hank that nothing got past Kurt Vogel.

19

Hank hitched up the horses and he, Katja and Alena were back on the road in minutes without a word of good-bye or good luck from the blacksmith or his wife.

At a railway crossing, Hank veered away from the main road and began following the tracks. As they vanished from village to woods, the snow grew deeper, the air colder.

The crackle of underbrush and crunching snow and ice under the wagon wheels was all they heard until midday when a whistling sound cracked the serenity.

"Bombers!" Katja reflexively crouched and hid her head at the same time. The ground vibrated as if it were an earthquake, and one deafening explosion followed another. The horses tried to rear up, but were held fast by Hank's white-knuckled grip on the reins.

"Shit!" Hank hissed in English through his teeth.

They braced themselves for the next blast, but heard none. Unable to fathom a plan, Hank nudged the horses forward. "I don't know what else to do. We have to see if it's our—my—troops."

Katja whirled, her face contorted with rage, her eyes alive with it. "Turn around!"

"And go where?"

Katja clutched his arm. "Stop the wagon. Stop right now, damn you."

Hank rolled the reins to step up the stallions' pace. Still following the winding track, they soon found themselves at the edge of a ravine. Massive twisted metal, piled high as a dinosaur's bones across a sliver of a stream at the bottom of a brush, tree and snow-covered divide, was sending up streams of smoke.

"They blew up the bridge," Hank sighed. "That means no ground troops, just hitting escape routes."

"Our escape route," Katja said.

Hank's eyes traveled the embankment and up the other side. "Wagon would never make it. Let's ride along the ledge until the ravine gets shallow enough to cross."

Katja didn't give him the benefit of nodding.

He lifted the canvas flap behind him. "Everything's all right, Alena. No danger to us. Just stay down, honey." He detected enough movement under the blanket the child threw over her body when the first blast went off to satisfy him that she got the message.

Just as Hank had hoped, the ridge descended to where they could cross less than an hour from the railroad tracks.

The wagon jostled down and up the other side with only a few heart-palpitating moments while the horses struggled for solid footing until they got to the stream.

"You're just too damn stubborn to admit I'm doing a good job," Hank said.

Looking straight ahead she gave a slanted-eyes glance in his direction. "I just have nothing to say to the enemy. That is all."

"Damnit woman, we sure didn't need to say much last…" He caught himself, and her still-seething expression. "Sorry Kat, I'm not the enemy and neither are you."

She released her fist-curled mittened hands. Katja blew out a puff of cold air and dropped her pinched shoulders. "We're lost," she said.

The wagon broke through the trees and into the clearing just as the British foot soldiers did the same.

"You there. Halt. Stop that wagon," said a mud-splattered infantry company sergeant. Katja let out a gasping scream and locked her hands around Hank's arm.

Hank ripped free and jumped from his wagon waving one arm.

"Thank God, you're British," he howled in English.

The soldier adjusted his brass wire-rimmed glasses, rubbing even more smears over his vision area. " Damn," the soldier said and whipped the glasses from his face. "Who in the Queen's name are you?"

Hank shot out his open palm. "An American. I'm, ahh, we're Americans trapped behind enemy lines." Hank pressed a hand to his speeding heart, then reached in his inner coat pocket for his papers. "Oh, thank God it's over."

The soldier turned and waved two of his men forward.

"Hold this man while I question him."

Hank didn't resist, welcoming his aggressors with a broad smile. Once held, the sergeant, with wiped-clean glasses, firmly planted them back on his nose and stepped up to the man's grinning face.

"Now what's all this bloody bullshit?"

"Don't hurt him!" Katja yelled in German.

The grip automatically stiffened on both Hank's arms.

"A bloody American, are you?" The sergeant rammed the cocking side of his rifle into Hank's forehead, viciously sending his gashed head backwards. He dangled like a string puppet in the soldier's hands.

Katja leaped from the wagon and came at the men, fists swinging. "You dirty bastards. Bastards." She threw a wild punch but missed the sergeant's darting face. The two soldiers holding Hank dropped him to the ground and locked their eyes and grips on Katja.

Katja pulled away, dropped to her knees and cradled Hank's bleeding head in her arms. "Leave us alone," she screamed in German, but no one understood. "Alena, get down and help," she yelled up at the gawking child in the wagon. The two dragged Hank out of the clearing back to the wood's edge, and with Alena's bracing aid into the back of the wagon.

"Kat, get something to stop the blood," Hank said, dead pale and unable to sit up. "Then wrap it in gauze." He put his hand to his head. "Forget it. We're out of gauze."

Katja pressed a kiss to his brow. "Let me do the thinking for a while." He blinked, understood and cracked a slight smile. "Aren't you always…Oh!" Blinding white light forced him to lie still and close his eyes.

Katja eased out into the open area and turned the wagon to track behind the British soldiers. While never willing to admit it to Hank, she, too, believed they had a better chance surviving if caught by the Allied Forces rather than the Russians.

"Alena, stay up here by me. There will be less trouble if soldiers think we're a family that can do them no harm."

One British regiment after another passed by the smiling and waving woman and child with casual glances or none at all. It was as though they were invisible.

Hank was still asleep when they reached a British-occupied village. Katja gently woke him and lifted his bloody, towel-soaked head.

"That's good, the bleeding's stopped." She leaned into him, making sure he was coherent. "I've got good news and bad news."

Hank blinked a couple of times trying to brush away an aching drowsiness.

"You'll want the bad news, just like you assumed I did when my nose was broken." She playfully nodded for them both. "The bad news is, we're going to attempt to spend the night in a British-occupied village. Bomb holes the size of houses everywhere, Hank. You won't believe it.

And, of course, your friends, the Allied Forces, can't tell you from this dirty, bearded man in near rags." She touched his nose. "If you saw yourself in the mirror, you'd throw a rock through it."

"Thanks for the confidence builder."

"We mean nothing to them, unless we look suspicious. What little scraps of food or valuables we have keeps us safe." She folded the blanket into a pillow and placed it under his head. "You were right, they're safer than the Russians, these stick-in-their-butt soldiers."

Hank struggled out a smile. "Stick up their ass."

"The same thing."

Katja and Alena were soaked to the skin when she found some shelter she and Hank decided would go unnoticed. Just one look and no one would bother to rummage through it. The once charming cottage home had a decayed and sagging thatch roof. The bomb blasted chimney was broken to the north, rough lumps of cemented field stones lying at its base: the sagging and precariously perched chimney to the south. The snow was beginning to smother traces of a yard and garden she surmised was probably the pride of the neighborhood.

The trace of beauty connected in Katja's mind to how all remnants of Trakehnen and the home she was born in were crumbling and soon to vanish. Her mind grew dark, heart cold, as the realization of her isolation and homelessness ripped through her.

Without feeling she glanced down at Alena's dripping shoes. "You'll be dry soon. We'll start a fire, if we can find some dry wood before everything's buried."

Alena lifted one of her feet up and crossed her leg.

"I can't feel them anymore. After they froze the last time, I can't feel them." Katja was jolted out of her spiraling abyss by the child's numb words.

Katja placed her hand on the dangling shoe. "Why didn't you say something earlier?"

Alena shrugged. "Couldn't do anything about it anyway."

"You could get frostbite or gangrene. Let's get you into the house. I want to see those feet.

The snow was turning to sleet. A rumble of thunder made Katja look up at the star-starved sky. "Turning to rain."

While the thunder raged, Katja and Alena braced Hank up and got him to the slightly open front door. Katja kicked it open.

"It'll have to do for tonight," she said, her eyes shifting from a pool of water on the barren wood living room floor. "Alena, get anything out of the wagon we can to warm by the fire."

Hank struggled away and balanced himself on wobbly legs. "Go help her, Kat. I'll be all right in the morning." He felt along the eight-inch gash in his head. "If I could wrap this thing tight enough I'd be up and around in the morning." He eased himself down to the floor and lay in front of the stone fireplace.

Once everything was in, Katja sat down by Hank, took off her dripping coat, grabbed her riding boot and wrenched it off, then heaved it behind her. She reached for the second, gripped the top of it and went into a comic struggle that had her rolling around on the floor. The second boot went flying out of her fingers into the side of Hank's head. She sat there stunned, waiting for his response.

Hank shoved the boot away and turned his head to Alena. "She makes a much better vet than a nurse." His eyes rested for the first time in what seemed like days on the shivering child, frantically pumping her hands on her bare feet.

"You'll get feeling in them soon, when Kat starts the fire," he said, his words as gentle as fingertips.

Alena angrily shook her head.

Hank licked his cracked, dry lips. "If you still can't feel them after they're warmed up, let me know," he said evenly. He turned his head, still touching the cold wood floor. "Kat, would you wrap her in blankets and rub her feet?"

"All right." Katja rubbed her fingers dead center of her brow. There wasn't a headache there yet, but it was building walls around her dark mood.

Even in his nauseous condition, Hank could feel Katja's detachment and depression. What little color he had left drained out of his face when he got to his feet. "I'll get the wood."

Katja rose as well and faced him. "You get right back down. You know we need you better in the morning." She whirled away, wrenched fists at her sides.

The icy rain made her attempts to find anything dry on the way back to the cottage fruitless. She shed her drenched coat as she re-entered the warming room aglow with what looked like broken furniture.

Hank, with Alena on his lap, turned from rubbing her lifeless feet to Katja. "Our girl's feet are freezing."

Katja's eyes darted from what she could now see were broken chair pieces ablaze, back to Hank. "What are you doing sitting up already? I'm capable of finding wood and starting a fire."

Hank dragged a hand through his hair. "This isn't a contest." His eyes shot down to the child's feet and back before Alena was aware of his subtle alert.

Katja quickly took off her wet, clinging clothes and draped them on a chair near the fire. Arms folded, she squatted by the fire to get warm. Moments later she turned her still shivering head, then moved close to her companions.

"Hank, that bluish color looks worse than anything I've had. Can you feel this, honey?" Katja lightly squeezed both of Alena's feet.

"A little."

Katja closed, then struggled to open her eyes again. She got her second wind. "Oh, I can't tell you how happy I am to hear that." She put the back of her hand to Alena's cheek. "You're going to be just fine, baby." She leaned over to the child and kissed her forehead.

"Don't I get one, too?" Hank asked.

Her eyes were heavy, smiling lazily in the fire's glow. "Get some sleep."

"I love it when you order me around." With a chuckle, he settled down next to the cuddled child.

Katja wrapped herself in the blanket intended for her pillow. She plopped her head down next to them, caught between a smile and the fear that her dreams would hurl her back to the monstrous Halloween jack-o-lantern face of the German soldier about to mount and smother her with his foul-breathed tongue. She shuddered and moved close to the child and Hank.

~

When Hank awoke Alena was still braced against him, but Katja was gone. He eased himself up without waking her and rubbed his hands together. All warmth had slipped away with the fire.

The front door flew open and Katja's tall lean body, her arms laden with wood scraps, was silhouetted in the morning light.

"You're up and at it early," he said just above a whisper.

"Things to do," she said cheerfully, and carefully lowered the wood onto the fireplace hearth. Then she stood, stretched and shoved back her hair. "I think we can make this work for your head." She dangled a strip of cloth she had somehow torn off evenly from the bottom of her shirt." She tiptoed over to him and knelt down to his eye level.

He glanced from the fading greenish bruises under her eyes. "What a perfect pair we make now."

Katja pursed her lips and nodded. She ran the cloth around his head twice and used a piece of the same tape roll he had used to keep her nose in place.

"You ought to keep bandages on that nose of yours for at least a couple more days."

She lifted his chin to her dancing eyes. "I'm the doctor today."

"Kat." He stood and guided her into the narrow hallway and first bedroom off the living room. Like every other room in the house, all furniture, even wall hangings, were gone.

"Alena shouldn't hear us in here." Before Katja could speak he moved intimately close and ran one arm around her waist. He knew he could kiss her, but it would have to wait.

"I've got feelings for you, Kat, and they go pretty deep." The plan he had been conceiving since the evening before was hard to get out with her inviting stare. "I don't know what the hell to do with them, but they're there." He released his hold and stepped back.

"I just want you to know that in case anything happens…"

"What are you talking about?"

He scratched the back of his head and ran his hand along his beard. "Should have cut the damn thing off when I had a chance at that blacksmith's."

Katja planted a firm fist on her swung-out hip, waiting.

"I'm getting to it. What I'm about to say isn't up for discussion. We're not the Haffmann party anymore. It's just you, me and Alena." He took a deep breath and blew out a cloud of icy air. "I'm taking Noble to find an American platoon out there. They've got to be close with the British right here."

Katja jerked her head back and forth. "Don't you think I have feelings, too? No." She folded both arms. "That's final. No, we stay together."

Hank lifted the hair back from one eye and secured it around her ear. Her pouting made him break out into a wide smile. "I told you, kid, I'm doing this for all of us. You and Alena stay here. It's probably the safest place we've found yet."

She started building steam like an arena bull.

Hank took a step closer, lifted her chin up with his fingertips and started to brush his lips against hers.

"No," she yanked away. "You try to use me like a toy doll, then throw me into a corner when you're done."

Hank forcibly pulled her into his arms. She was softening. He knew she wasn't aware of it, but she was. Under different circumstances it would have been the time to make love to her right there. He kissed her, letting it deepen, letting himself sink into the struggling, then hungry lips.

Her arms came up, circled his neck. Her body moved convulsively as he gathered her closer. The subtle curves he stroked began to relax under his hands.

He moved his lips a breath away. "Nothing, nothing, Kat is going to stop me from coming back. Forty-eight hours, at the most, then I promise I'll be back and we'll finish this."

Her parched lips went limp at the piercing thought. "And if you do find them?"

His lips brushed across hers again. "I'll make all your dreams come true."

"What if my dreams include you?"

Hank's embrace slowly began to drift away as her last words lingered in the silence.

She shifted her hips back into him and rested her head in the curve of his shoulder. "That wasn't fair. There's nothing either of us could do if we wanted to."

He felt her heart beat, fast, under his hand. "Don't try to make love to me again, Hank. I get all stirred up, and say things."

Hank kissed her forehead. "I liked what you wished for, Kat. But, I'd better go." She tightened her grip around his waist.

"I'll be careful knowing you two are back here waiting."

Katja looked up into his eyes. "Promise me you won't do something stupid and get beat up again." Her head jiggled on his chest from his raspy chuckle.

"You promise not to beat somebody up while I'm gone, and I give my solemn word to keep my end up."

She pushed back in restrained laughter. " Keep your end up?"

"Just an American saying." He patted her on the rear. "I'll be thinking about that end until I get back.

20

Hank wasn't more than an hour away from the village sheltering Katja and Alena when he came upon more evidence of Allied bombing. The ground was creviced as if asteroids had bombarded it. He wondered why British soldiers stood guard over nothing more than rubble and shattered families staggering around like drunks unable to find their way home.

He closed his eyes and mumbled a rehearsal of approaches when he found Americans. There was no interest in refugees. He would have to create one.

"Hello, so good to find another American. Like a fool, I got trapped behind enemy lines. No, I have no papers to prove it." Hank shook his head and closed his eyes. "I am an American. I have information about Berlin that's critical to the War. No, they'll think I'm a spy and shoot me."

"You there, get down from that horse and show me your papers."

Hank didn't need to open his eyes to know what the thick British accent meant. When he opened them soldiers surrounded him. He'd walked right between them in his dreamy stupor.

"Sorry, I was—" At the sound of English he was pulled from his mount to the ground. He was on his feet, fist clenched, before anybody tried to grab him.

The ruddy-faced redhead with an elongated nose even redder at its sharp tip, turned glassy blue eyes on Hank's bloody rag-covered head.

"Oh that, I got it fighting off a German soldier who tried to take advantage of my wife."

A curious eyebrow cropped up. "Your wife? Forget the papers. Get out of our way or we'll shoot you." The soldier raised his head as though calling down the gods. "Arrest this man. He's too young to be anything but a German soldier trying to escape. Have him join the others."

"I'm an American millionaire. Just get me to the Americans and they…"

"He really looks like a millionaire," the soldier spit out between belly laughs. "Just on a little tour of the war, are we, mate? What do you think of it? Bit nasty, isn't it?" The redhead scratched his forehead. "Be careful not to damage this one. There's got to be some bloody story behind all this. Let's get him to Intelligence."

"But I've got my wife and child back there." All heads had turned in disbelief. He was no longer entertainment, just another whining, cowardly deserter.

Hank was gingerly guided back. If he paused, though, he'd get a rifle barrel rammed through his lower back.

A marching line with four rows, twelve deep of skeletal German soldiers and officers were flanked at a safe pace on all four sides by a British infantry battalion.

He hadn't marched shoulder-to-shoulder an hour when the gray bearded man next to him cleared his throat to draw Hank's attention. "What rank?" the Nazi soldier asked.

"No rank," Hank responded in German.

"I'm an American who would cut your nuts off if I got a chance."

Hank glanced at lightening speed over at stiletto-sharp narrowed eyes raking over him. He shuffled over closer to the British private parallel to him.

"I'm not a German," he said out of the side twisted mouth.

"Shut your mouth and march."

"I shouldn't be with these men. They're my enemy too," Hank yelled in English loud enough to be overheard.

Another flanking private turned his head to the English jabbering prisoner. "One more word, kraut, and you're dead."

~

From the route they were marching, Hank surmised the emerging British battalion's regiment size. They were headed straight for Danzig, sweeping German soldiers into a line approaching over one hundred men.

Near dark, they stopped for the night off the road with no village in sight. The captives were herded into a circle on the snow-crusted ground and given shovels.

"Dig in," a bull-necked company leader barked.

Hank turned his eyes to the roar overhead. There was just enough light to see white stars set in a blue circle on the fuselage and wings of the four-engine B-25 bombers.

"Americans, Americans. Somebody help!" Hank dropped to his knees and turned to the motionless German soldiers around him. Not a face gave away who drove a rock-hard boot toe into the back of his leg. As he started to rise an elbow rammed directly into the bandaged gash on his forehead. Blood spread out across the cloth and began a steady stream down into Hank's eyes, mustache, mouth and beard.

The captives cleared away far enough to form a circle to isolate their prey. Hank dropped back to his knees and leaned his head back while wiping blood from his eyes.

"Break it up. Move," said a British platoon leader, armored by two others with pointed semi-automatic rifles.

"Get him on his feet."

"Thank you, God," Hank cried out in English.

They shoved through the wall of German soldiers and helped Hank back to a lone tree with guards positioned on each side.

"Get this man's head taken care of and bring him to the regiment commander," the redheaded sergeant said, then turned and headed for the small frame house being used by the battalion and regiment field commander.

"Who's the highest ranking?" Hank said. "I'll tell him everything."

One of the guards ducked under a snow-laden branch and poked his rifle at Hank. "Shut up."

"Think he'll want to know about Berlin? How Hitler's going to pro—"

The carrot-headed sergeant sharply turned his head at the mention of Berlin. He stepped under the tree and clutched the guard's arm.

"Hold 'im here, mate. I'll see if the commander's schedule is open."

"He'll want to hear—"

"He told you to shut it," the redhead commanded.

Hank nodded and lowered his demanding eyes.

The sergeant was back out in seconds. "He might see him later tonight. Refugees are low priority. Get his head cleaned up and move him to the shack where we've holed up the German officers."

"I can't go in there. They tried to kill me."

"When in the bloody 'ell are you going to learn to shut your mouth until spoken to?"

~

Eight stone faces scanned Hank when he was shoved through the creaking shack door. Hank slammed it, then sat and leaned up against it.

"So, you're an American?" the man with the grayest stubble asked in German.

"I am many things," Hank responded in German.

The self-appointed chief interrogator rubbed his sandpaper chin. "So, you are quick with words. Are you so quick in battle?"

"Would you say the world was won on horseback?"

"You talk in riddles."

"You might influence a tiny little outcome in the war," Hank said, then paused for effect. "I serve the entire German army. Now shut up or face our Fuehrer's wrath."

The German's mouth crimped. "Now I know you are an American, but please continue your charade." He turned to the venomous eyes of fellow officers.

"I am the director of the Trakehnen stud farm, providing every horse in this war for field artillery until the Bolsheviks scorched the land of my home and murdered and raped our women." Hank heaved a dramatic sigh. "Now everything's destroyed."

All was silent. The officers exchanged glances. While he was gazing down, the air was heavy with possibility.

"What do you have to tell about Berlin?"

Hank's head lifted with a devilish smile. "Misinformation, of course. Each of you should do all you can to confuse the enemy any way you can." He could feel the shift in attitude.

"How can you prove you weren't planted in here to confuse us?" a sallow-faced man with dead fish eyes said.

"You see? Confusion gets everybody's thinking cloudy."

The lead interrogator slowly nodded and turned to the other men with a cautious turn of the head.

"We'll be watching you. There won't be any trouble."

The door flew open and Hank tumbled back onto the muddy boots of one of the posted guards. "Get up and follow me." Hank's heart raced faster with each step they took toward the flickering candlelit house.

~

"Sit," the red-haired sergeant ordered, pointing to one of two chairs opposite the only table in the room. "When the commander and regiment intelligence arrive you will only open your mouth when spoken to."

Hank's preparatory thoughts were shattered when the regiment commander stormed past him and sat down at the chair opposite the prisoner.

Hank stood and attempted to salute, shifting from four to three fingers.

The senior officer waved his arms up and down. "Stop. Enough of that. Be seated."

Hank couldn't take his eyes off the pensive hawk-like mask of a face. As the commander lifted long, spindly fingers around a pipe and transferred it to his mouth, Hank smiled.

"You have a striking resemblance to Sherlock Holmes," Hank said in a light conversational tone.

The Englishman squinted through growing balls of smoke at the grime-covered face and beard under the fresh white gauze wrapped around the prisoner's head. Electric blue eyes stopped the inspection.

"The world knows of Sherlock Holmes." He made two quick puffing clouds and set the pipe in its tray. He rolled his chair back, crossed his legs and gradually rested clasped hands in his lap so lightly it was as if he was relaxing them on a case of nitroglycerin. "I have little time. Be clear and articulate. Can you do that?"

Hank nodded.

"Excellent. So you claim to be an American one minute, and have dark secrets to reveal about Berlin the next." He reached over and lifted his pipe out of the tray again. "Which is it?" He raised his index finger. "No more nonsense now."

Hank raked his fingers through his hair. "Actually sir, it's neither." Hank raised his open palm to the commander's hardening expression. "I had to get in to see someone in charge. Yes, I am an American. The name's Henning Oscarson. I am a thoroughbred breeder in Lexington, Kentucky." Hank lowered his hand. " Oh, and I'm also the track vet for the Kentucky Derby and Churchill Downs."

"And you're right, I'm Sherlock Holmes." The commander uncrossed his knees and leaned forward. "Stop the games and tell me what you know of Berlin before Intelligence beats it out of you."

Hank shook his head. " Please give me a chance to explain myself." Hank's polish was tarnished and he knew it. "I'm worth millions. People know me. Colonel Matt Winn, president of Churchill Downs, can verify that I'm missing."

"And you have papers?"

Hank shot his hand into his pocket, then stopped.

The commander rested his elbows on the chair armrests and interlocked his hands until the knuckles were edged in white. "Don't tell me, you lost them."

"I didn't lose them, but they don't prove what I'm saying."

"Give them to me and I'll decide that."

Hank inched his way into his western jean pocket.

The commander critically studied the oversized silver belt buckle that flashed when Hank arched his back to pull out the folded papers. The commander stood and leaned over the table at Hank's American-looking pants and shirt.

Hank's eyes followed his. "Oh, Levis. The pants. Not much good when you're up to your ass in snow, though." He smiled, yanked the soaked folded papers out of his pocket, and slid the square across the table.

"They should still be readable."

The commander opened up and flattened out two pink typed sheets of standard legal-sized forms.

"You are quite the chameleon, Mr. Oscarson. Now we have you as a full-blooded Swede named Henson." He handed the papers back to Hank and returned to his pipe and seat.

"I can explain. I changed my name to protect my relatives in Sweden if I got caught."

The commander calmly held up his wristwatch close enough to read its hands. "You've got five minutes to tell me about Berlin or this conversation is over."

Hank took a jagged breath. He felt dizzy and weak. "What I know I'll only tell an American officer. I will tell you, knowledge of this could speed up the end of the war."

The commander dropped his voice an octave. "Does it have to do with Hitler himself?"

Hank nodded.

The commander sat back in his seat, gritted teeth showing the first crack in his smooth demeanor. "Ridiculous. You play me for a fool, sir." He signaled one of the two posted guards to take the prisoner away.

"I leave you a choice: I return you to your German friends or you have our protection." The commander lifted his pipe, deeply sucking the hot ember. "I'll give you a while to think about it outside tonight."

"I don't have time. I've got to get back," Hank gasped, unable to struggle free from the guards.

The commander held up an open palm signifying the interrogation was over.

"He's daft. Get him out of my sight."

"There's a woman and child. They need me."

"Quickly," the commander snapped at the sergeant. "I have no time for this rubbish. No more desperate refugees. Let Intelligence take care of this. Damnit, don't waste my time."

~

Hank pulled the British military provided blanket up to his chin, eyes open, mind reeling. Granted, the tree he was ordered to sleep under blocked the snow, but did nothing, nor did one blanket, to halt the bone-chilling cold.

He hadn't seen the first rays of daylight when he was kicked and pulled from his spot to eat a tin of canned meat and fall into formation.

Hank was marched separately from the other prisoners, raising focused hatred for the traitor.

Even to stop and eat, Hank was separated, but placed within eyesight of the German leaders. They pointed at him, mimicking how they were going to slit his throat, mouthing, "You will die," all under the ever-attentive eye of the redheaded sergeant. He was always within a shadow's length away from Hank.

Two days from his capture, Hank was brought before the commander again. Seated next to the regiment commander was a gangly, small-headed man who made Hank think of a praying mantis. It had to be Intelligence.

"Are you ready to be honest with me?" the commander asked. "I must warn you. If you are not tonight, you will sleep with your Nazi friends." He said it as calmly as a chat across a neighbor's fence. The praying mantis absently started tapping his drooping lip with an index finger.

Hank pounced from his chair to the edge of the table, untainted hate in his eyes. Two guards stepped forward and forced him back to his chair.

"I told you, I'm an American! Check it out, for God's sake, before it's too late."

The commander sat silent making smoke circles with his cigarette, while looking in every direction but at the prisoner. "You told me a lot of outrageous things." He glanced at the approving praying mantis, then signaled the redhead. "Take him to the German officer's dugout."

"They'll kill me, damnit. I'll...dig in somewhere else. Please, they'll kill me."

The commander's calm had returned. He narrowed his glare at his prisoner's wild eyes. Once Hank was removed he turned to the redhead who had witnessed every word of the exchange. "What do you think?"

~

Hank stopped his struggling by the time the guards arrived at the German officer's self-dug hole in muddy earth. He gulped the cold night air furiously until only his hammering heart could give away his fear.

The only open spot left for him to sleep in the black oval ground was near its center. A paper-thin folded blanket marked his designated spot. He was too exhausted to resist lying down. None of his predators moved. He silently stepped over and around them to get to the center of their lair.

Hank squatted on his sparse sleeping square, peering at the blanketed mounds for any movement.

"I know you're awake." The words were like a shotgun blast in the deadening silence. "They learned nothing from me or I wouldn't have been sent back." Still no movement. "Do what you will, but know I serve the Fuehrer." The last words he spoke played back like bubbled-up bile until he finally drifted into sleep.

~

The claws tightening around Hank's throat were squeezing the last life out of him by the time his bulging eyes popped open. His arms and legs were staked to the ground by the pressing weight of four of his attackers. Death would be silent, quick. Hank arched up and was shoved back down to the cold-as-a-grave earth by the strangler's full-body press.

His mind flashed on Victoria Logan, effortlessly riding a stark white Trakehner stallion in dressage exercises at his Sunny Acres performing arena. Suddenly he felt himself rising and hovering over his writhing body. Katja and Alena were sitting next to him on folded knees oblivious to the horror.

Then a flash of blinding white light.

Then nothing.

~

"It kind of looks like the bloke. Hard to tell with the dirt and beard, though." The voice was distant, British.

The world began coming back into focus. Hank didn't know if he was dead or alive. Alive, he suspected, wincing. Dead shouldn't hurt. Air rushed back into Hank's lungs upon consciousness and he sucked it in greedily. Awareness of his body came back, pain by pain. He opened his eyes and gasped at the face less than an inch from his. It wasn't the face of anyone who'd be found in heaven. No, the face that stared down at him was the face of a long-nosed Englishman. The eyes staring into his may not have come from hell, but had likely seen it.

"Not too popular these days?" the British field medic asked. "Another minute and you would have been gone. Just lucky I poked my head in when I did."

A picture of a clean shaven, cocky-looking man with a bit of a mischievous smile was held up inches from Hank's squinting, blurring, then focusing eyes. The face kept nodding, then looked over at the command sergeant major. "He's going to make it."

Hank jerked up ready for the next German soldier attack, then took a deep jagged breath. He was in the commander's tent with two guards posted at the curtain door.

The commander pulled a chair up from his portable table strewn with maps and two lanterns next to Hank's cot.

The commander clutched and shook Hank's shoulder. "You can thank Sergeant Beck here." His head shot up to the carrot-headed man to his right. "He not only joined in saving your life a few minutes ago, he wouldn't take no for an answer. He took it upon himself to reach the nearest American artillery division to see if they knew anything about you."

"It seems, old chap, you're some kind of celebrity. Word had come from General Omar Bradley himself that it was a high priority to find and return you to American troops immediately. There was even something about President Roosevelt."

Hank shook his head, not sure if it was another illusion before death.

"Sorry about all this. What in bloody 'ell are you doing here anyway?"

Hank sat up, his hand to his raw throat, and tried to mouth Katja and Alena's names, but couldn't be understood.

"Wait until morning and…"

Hank violently shook his head and mimed writing on a piece of paper.

"Sergeant, get this man something to write on."

While his hands shook like he had palsy, he slowed down to ensure each potentially life-saving word was legible.

"I came on a horse. I need it back. Black stallion. I need clearance papers until I get to the Americans. Draw a map of where they are. I must go back and get a woman and child."

The commander read each word aloud to insure no confusion. "I'm sorry. I have instructions to return you to the Americans immediately. They'll probably route you to Paris by truck, then fly you to England and back to the States."

Hank rocketed to his feet, knocking the commander back and off his chair.

"Sergeant!" the commander yelled.

Hank was grabbed by three officers and forced back down off his wobbly legs.

"They need me," Hank mouthed through a half-audible voice. "I have to go back."

The commander stood up and hovered over Hank, his shoulders pinned to the cot. "It's less than four hours to get to an American division. I'm sorry, but it wasn't a request that you be returned, it was an order."

"When he settles down get him a shave so he can be identified by his picture. A good meal, too. Meat and potatoes, that kind of thing."

"I have to go to them," Hank screeched with his hand to his throat.

"I understand, sir. We will prepare you in every way to be presentable for the Americans. I am sure they will agree and make your passage safe."

Hank fell back, limp.

"You can let go of him," the commander ordered. As the flap on the canvas medic tent closed, he turned back to the man stretched out on the cot. "The worst is over. Try to rest."

Hank sat up with his hand clasped to his throat. "Not for them."

"Who is 'them'? Your wife and daughter? I got no word about you traveling with anyone else."

Hank lifted his chin. "Good people, caught in…" Hank pleaded.

"They're Krauts?"

Hank shook his head. "No, they're people who…" The commander's unyielding jaw had made its point.

"Thanks," Hank silently mouthed to the fiery-haired sergeant next to his commander. The officer nodded and pointed to Hank's mud-caked boots.

"Get this man a decent pair of boots before he leaves. Make sure his horse is fed, whatever we've got that it'll eat."

~

Hank and Noble rode alone in the back of a camouflaged troop movement truck. Less than four hours later the truck pulled into an evacuated village with little left standing from air and ground attack. Hank lifted the canvas curtain back far enough to see streams of smoke rising from the rubble and lifeless bodies in German uniforms still fresh from battle.

He dropped the flap and clutched his neck while arresting the bile filling his aching throat. The too-real visualization of his own dead body was more than he could stomach. A sudden stop jolted him out of his waking nightmare. He gathered his composure by focusing on Katja and Alena.

Less than four hours since his true identity was discovered he was standing, clean-shaved in new boots, in front of the American artillery commander.

"Everybody took you for dead, Mr. Oscarson." The commander stuck out his hand. "I imagine you've got quite a story to tell," the rounded, balding general said while directing a string of mud-splattering tanks around a sizable bomb hole.

Hank cleared his throat and dug his nails into his palms. "Sir." His throat was raw with pain. Hank held it while he forced out each word. "I must be allowed to return to a village less than a day's ride, if you'll loan me a jeep. It's a woman and child. I owe them my life."

The commander's arms kept flailing like a New York traffic cop. "Saved your life, you say?"

Hank nodded. "Please sir. The village is already British occupied. I'll get them and get right back."

The division commander dropped his arms and whirled around to Hank. "I haven't even thought about how the hell we're going to get you out of here." He shook his head. "We're an advance troop, goddamnit. You're in the middle of a war, not some country town."

"A jeep, General." Hank choked out.

"Take the damn jeep and get your ass back here fast. We're not stopping for you."

Hank paused, shocked that the general had conceded.

He ran his hand up in another salute. "Thank you, sir."

"General Bradley will probably be furious if he hears we found you and let you get away. What the hell? Get moving."

"Watch my horse," Hank said over his shoulder while a foot soldier was leading him to the vehicle.

"What in the hell are we going to do with a horse?" the commander growled.

After getting official identification papers and giving harried instructions on how to care for Noble, Hank scavenged a sizable pile of K ration cartons, each complete with tins of canned meat, cheese, peanut butter, jam, crackers, cigarette packs and gum. With an American army helmet on his head and perfect fitting never-worn military issue boots on his warm, new wool sock-covered feet, he kicked up rocks, ice and snow at foot-to-the-floor speed until the village was in sight.

He jolted to a stop in front of the near-collapsed house. Just days before he, Katja and Alena had huddled in it, not sure they were going to live another week.

Hank sprang over the closed jeep door and stormed into the house.

"Katja, it's me. I'm back." His face was hot, his heart leaping at the sound of calling her name. "Alena. Hey, it's me, Hank." He craned his neck and turned his ear up, waiting for a gushing response. All he heard was the incessant dripping from the leaky ceiling onto the soggy living room floor.

"Come on. I have food and a truck. We're safe." Still not a sound but his pounding heart.

His eyes raked the room. There wasn't even a trace of when he had been there. The fireplace ash was fine and no indications of when the last ember died.

A sickening wave of fear welled up in Hank's chest.

They could be anywhere. I'll search every house for them. No, wait here for them to return. No, they would have started a fire. They're out searching for me. Jesus, the wagon and horses are gone. Hank held the edge of his open palms to his throbbing temples.

"Don't worry, they're safe," he said to the empty room.

He ran from the house and his feet flew out from under him on the last step. His churning arms did nothing to stop the back of his head from slamming against one of the steps. "Oh, my God!" He rolled into a fetal position on the ground, then on to his back. He pressed his gloved fingers to his eyes, shuddered once, and took a long deep breath. Tears that even the icy air couldn't stop began draining from his eyes.

"Okay, I have a jeep. I can find them." He rolled over and up to his feet. "Why didn't I see you on the road coming here?" he asked the ominous, rumbling sky. "They never left, that's why. They never left the village."

He hopped in the jeep and fish-tailed around the corner, lurching to a stop in front of a gathering of British soldiers huddled in front of the still-standing village tavern.

"We got caught with our knickers down," one of the young soldiers said through a whisky-coated throat.

Hank pulled his American clearance papers out of his pocket and flashed it in front of half blurry eyes.

"There's some right pretty little things around here, there is," one of the soldiers said, then leaned on Hank's shoulder.

"How'd you hurt your head, mate?"

Hank shoved the soldier away. "Listen to me, damnit. This is important. Any of you see a tall brown-haired woman. Young, good looking, about my height. She was with a girl about ten-years-old."

"In a wagon?" one of the soldiers asked.

"Yes, yes, that's it. With one harnessed horse and two tied behind."

The soldier made a jiggly nod. "I told you the women around 're are something to look at."

Hank grabbed the young drunken soldier by his uniform lapels, causing the others to tighten their hands on rifles nearby.

"Hold on there, Yank," the soldier said, blinking madly in surprise.

"The woman and child, they're mine." He dropped the soldier back off his toes. "Sorry, I need to find them. They're freezing and hungry."

"It was yesterday morning about three blocks from here near where the market, food store must have been before the bombing." The soldier turned from Hank to his half-alert companions. "You seen that hole? It was huge."

"What were they doing? Look like they were leaving town, begging for food? What?" Hank demanded.

"Now how in the 'ell am I to know that? We can't help you find one bloody woman and child." He waved his arm up in a circular motion. "There are homeless people on every street corner in the village." He paused. "Wait, we've set up a soup line at the other end of town. They could be there. Set up tents, too." He curled his lower lip and nodded. "That's where you'll find them. I'd bet a holiday in Paris on that."

The soldier hadn't overstated the swarm of tattered homeless who survived the bombing. An international Red Cross tent and vehicles were clustered in a field at the eyebrow of the village ruins.

Hank roared up to one of the trucks and nearly pulled the brake handle off when he stopped. He stood up in the jeep to gaze down on the menagerie of hunched-over bundled bodies of all sizes and shapes.

He put his hand to his mouth to be heard over the biting, whistling wind. "Katja, Katja Haffmann! Kat, it's me Hank!

Katja's head whirled from the portly Brit with a veiny, button nose as red as the potatoes he was scooping out of his steaming pot to her plate.

"Katja!" Hank yelled again while standing on the hood of his jeep.

Katja dropped her plate, turned and tucked a tumble of wild hair behind her ear. Alena's dark eyes went wide with the same flash of surprise.

"Hey, wait a minute, young lady. Have you had your head in the loo? Those are perfectly good potatoes."

They both burrowed their way through and out of the crowd.

"Hank, Hank!" Katja yelled. She brought a hand up to press it over her trembling lips. Desperation and tears began swimming in her eyes.

"Kat!"

Their eyes met, hers brimming with pain and confusion. She froze for a surrealistic moment, then shot up like she was frantically guiding in a small plane to land. "Over here."

"Holy shit!" He pulled off his helmet and waved it over his head, sprang down from the jeep and swept them both into his arms. The tears kept spilling over her lashes.

"Oh, thank God, I thought you'd gone after me," Hank pulled back, and just as Katja opened her mouth he grabbed the back of her head and pressed his lips to hers, hard. She hadn't caught her breath when he was down in a crouch with Alena's arms wrapped tightly around him.

"I love you, Alena. Thank God you're safe," he whispered in her ear.

Katja ran her hand through Hank's hair. When he rose up she kissed him on the cheek. "You got a shave. I could hardly recognize you." She lightly ran her hand along the contours of his jaw. "Oh, I knew you would come back."

She breathed him in deeply, then wrapped herself around him, and pressed her mouth, warm and firm, to his. They lingered in the kiss, and then Hank tipped her face up.

"You and Alena, come back to America with me." Katja winced and fell limp in his arms.

Hank moved away and raised both hands. "I know we said it would never work, but come on, Kat." Hank turned with a slow waving hand. "Look at this. There's nothing left for you two here." Her brow furrowed and lips pursed. Hank put his arm around her and led her and Alena to the jeep.

"I got food. Probably not as good as that hot slop you were just about to eat, but…" He looked up with sparkling blue eyes. "Consider this the beginning of both of you getting every wish I promised." He leaned down and whisked Alena into the back seat. "No more wagons."

"The wagon and horses?" Katja said, still mortified by his proposal.

"Thought about that. The horses will be faster than the wagon. We'll load up everything important…" he glanced at Katja's darkening face, "like your mother's silver, in the jeep and all travel together back to the American troops. They've got to be close to us by now."

"You have it all figured out," Katja mumbled behind hands she had pressed to her face. The tears were crowding her throat like jagged rocks.

"There is just one problem. You didn't include me in your figuring. I am not giving up the horses. And Alena has a mother and father who need her."

"Kat, we can make it all work."

"We are going to Hamburg and," she said, her eyes darting from Alena to Hank, "Some of us remember our promises."

Hank's face went ashen.

"I'll lead the wagon back," Hank said. "You have to agree to let the Americans help us out."

"What can they do for us? Give us a motorized escort to Hamburg? There is nothing they can do."

Hank slammed his open palm into the steering wheel, turned the key and revved the engine. "Only save your life, like they did mine. Germans are dying by the millions, if you hadn't noticed. From here to Hamburg is a fiery hell." He pounded the steering wheel again, threw an arm over the seat and backed up.

Hank recklessly sprang over ice-hardened ruts and mounds of the open field leading to the wagon and horses.

Katja took off her glove and tentatively placed her hand on Hank's bouncing knee. "Thanks for coming back."

"You actually thought I might leave you two out here?"

"Can you see why we can't go back with…" Katja's voice was shaky, vulnerable. She put a trembling hand to her mouth.

Hank put his foot on the brake at the wagon and yanked up the brake handle. "You think I just offered to take you and Alena into my life without giving it thought?"

Katja shrugged and squeezed her shoulders together more in fear of what he was going to say next than the chill of the encroaching evening air. She desperately needed his warmth, his strength, his hope. Instead, she moved even deeper into retreat from his lure.

"Kat, are you listening to me?" He could feel her passion simmering beneath her stubborn resistance. "For once in your life quit giving orders and really think about what I am offering you." She clutched one of her arms and jerked a glance back at Alena, leaning close enough between them to hear, but not be noticed.

Hank shifted his attention back and forth between the two people who had finally untethered a lifetime of harnessed emotions. "I'm serious about you both coming back with me." He turned to Katja and put his hand on hers. "You'll both be out of harm's way until the war ends. Isn't it obvious who's going to win yet, Kat?"

Katja shook her head. Tear-filled eyes gradually lifted to his. "What are you saying?"

"He wants to get married," Alena said.

"I, I wasn't, ah, I…" Hank gulped and slipped his arm around her shoulders.

Scalding tears squeezed out of Katja's near-closed eyes. "No he wasn't, Alena."

Hank took a deep breath. "All I'm thinking about is getting you two out of here. You can't be thinking of going back to that damn wagon to starve and probably freeze to death." Hank grabbed Katja by both shoulders. "Money makes it possible to do anything. Everything you two wished for can, will, happen now. We're safe." Katja's tear-lined cheeks started to fill with a slight smile.

"Yes, Kat, imagine. You never want to leave Germany. All right, I'll live with that. When the war's over we'll sweep all of Western Germany for the best Trakehner stallion and mares left standing." His enthusiasm was infectious. Katja raised a shoulder in a careless shrug and tugged a hand behind her tangled hair, anchoring it in a loose knot. He detected a slight smile at the corners of her mouth.

"Yes, and a stud farm like you won't believe."

Alena tugged on his coat sleeve "My parents?"

"Yes, Alena, if it takes an army to find them, we will. You'll get everything you asked for and more."

Hank stretched his arms over his head. "My God, we made it," he boomed out.

Quaking like a schoolgirl, Katja's head started nodding up and down faster and faster as his soothing, warm promises poured over her. The three of them threw their arms around each other and hooted like war dance Indians.

Hank held Katja by both shoulders at arm's length. "The first thing we're going to do is find a way to transform you." He glanced at Alena. "And you, into something that resembles a female."

Katja lifted her chin and dragged her hands through her hair. "Do I look that bad?"

"There's got to be some kind of currency people will take. They told me I could fly out to England, then back to the States. I'll buy you two the prettiest dresses in London."

The color drained from Katja's face. "Noble, what happened to…"

"He's fine. He's waiting for us with the Americans." Hank scratched the stubble starting to spring up from his shaved chin. "I haven't figured out how we're going to get the horses to safety yet, but there's got to be an answer."

Hank kept his eyes on Katja, his moves slow as he brushed his fingers down her check. " We're all going to be fine.

21

Victoria's teary eyes turned down to the airline ticket set on the desk before her. Destination: New York, then on to London to begin her search for her missing fiancée.

Her head reared up at the sound of the brisk continual knock at the door.

"You in there, darlin'? You're cutting it pretty short if you're going to be ready in time for the party. Victoria, you all right in there?" Victor Logan said.

"I'll be up in a minute, Father."

Wealthy commercial real estate developer Victor Logan had always kept a proper Southern distance between his emotions and matters of the heart. Of late, he had instructed his obedient wife to lift Victoria's spirits. He wanted his daughter's mind off the assumed-dead brassy Swedish-American millionaire he never approved of anyway.

"The governor always puts on a helluva party. Plenty of beaus. Come on, dear, open this door and get ready," Mr. Logan said.

"Can you arrange for me to talk to the Governor, Daddy?"

Mr. Logan tried to turn the locked handle again. "Unlock the door, dear."

A moment later Victoria was at the opened door. Her usual radiance had turned to a ghostly pallor with dark under-eye evidence of little sleep.

"You'll want to put on some makeup, beauty."

"Arrange for me to talk to the Governor, please, Daddy."

"And why would you want that?" Mr. Logan cocked a disapproving eyebrow. "I see…Mr. Henson."

Victoria lowered her eyes. "Never mind."

~

Like everybody else attending the ball, Victoria knew Governor Andrew Hampton rode into a first and second term singularly on the merits of his Confederate decorated great-great-grandfather, whose chivalry at Gettysburg had grown from memory to myth to legend, at least among his descendants. The Governor's mansion was considered the quintessential tribute to the South's glory days with its gated white-pillared majesty and immaculate gated ten-acre grounds. The Governor's Ball the Logans had been invited to was Kentucky's social event of the year.

Mr. Logan scanned the cobblestone circular driveway when he stepped out of his Rolls Royce and shoved the keys into an attendant's hand. He breathed a sigh of relief as Kentucky's U.S. Senator Brolin passed by and nodded with a tight-lipped smile just when Victoria, aided by her father's hand, stepped out into the crisp winter night air. The senator softly gasped at her flawless beauty. She was wearing only a sophisticated form-fitting black full-length gown accented by her mother's teardrop diamond necklace.

Victoria slightly bowed to the senator, causing just the reaction she had hoped for to set her plan into action.

"Oh, Senator, would you be my escort into the party?" Victoria asked.

The senator first glanced over at Victor Logan for the approving nod. "Of course, Miss Logan. I would be honored."

Victoria took his arm in hers, and moved close enough to the senator to brush hips once or twice on the way into the Grand Ballroom. She leaned over to the senator's ear and whispered over the small orchestra's violin music. "I really need to see the governor alone for a few minutes, if you could arrange it."

The senator's Adam's apple popped up and down like a teenage boy. "I don't know if that's such a safe...I mean, being alone with the governor. You know how he is with beautiful women."

Victoria moved away far enough for the senator to see her conviction. "Don't worry about me. I know what I'm doing."

Moments later the governor, bubbly with big-eyed enthusiasm, was kissing Victoria Logan's outstretched hand. "I understand you would like a few moments alone with me." He craned his neck to see his wife was surrounded and well out of sight.

"What I have to say needs to be said alone," Victoria whispered.

The governor's eyes steered hers to one of two doors in the ballroom, leading to a marble staircase going to the bedrooms on the second floor.

"No, not up there," Victoria said coyly. "Haven't you got a main floor office or something?"

The governor's palms were beginning to sweat in anticipation. "Of course." His eyes skimmed from one end of the ballroom to the other for an inconspicuous exit. "This way." He guided her to his library, locking the doors behind him. He glided to the fireplace hearth. "Please, have a seat." He motioned her to the saddle leather couch in front on the flames. "Let me round us up a drink."

Victoria stood in place near the door. "That won't be necessary."

The governor looked puzzled.

"I need your help to find Hank Oscarson. Nothing's worked yet. We need more pressure. I tried to reach you at your office, but I couldn't get through."

"You're getting through now." The governor's insinuation was obvious.

"I need you to plead with the president to send out an all-points search."

The governor slowly sauntered over to Victoria with his hand up. "Hold on there, princess." He placed his sweaty hand on her bare shoulder. "What are you going to do for me if I agree?"

Victoria sensually moved her hand up to the cleavage of her strapless gown. "I'm going to rip this apart and scream," she said in a breathy voice.

"I don't understand," the governor said.

"I think you do."

"Get the hell out of my house! Right now!"

Victoria reached for the front of her dress. "Then it's a no."

The governor dropped his tensed shoulders and sighed. "I like you, Victoria, and I don't think I want to cross you." He turned his eyes upward and paused. "I'll see what I can do."

"I'm going to walk out of here making sure everybody sees me go right out the front door. The next move's yours."

The governor smiled. "You've got what it takes for politics."

"I'll do what I have to, to get Hank home safely."

~

"Better wipe those eyes," said Colonel Matt Winn. "You're going to drip all over your destination." He pulled his fashionably folded pocket handkerchief out and lightly patted down the airline ticket locked between her quaking hands.

"Why didn't he reach me first? I've gone through hell waiting..."

The colonel guided her to his office couch.

"I haven't heard a word from him either. Here, read the telegram I just received less than three hours ago." He placed the half sheet on top of the ticket that he hurried to buy for her moments after he got the news.

She sniffed, cleared her eyes, and read the telegram out loud.

Colonel Matt Winn.

Good News. Word arrived from Ninth Battalion that Henning Oscarson has been found. In good health and being flown to London, then New York and back to Kentucky ASAP. Best, General Omar Bradley.

The telegram was like a talisman, as if merely touching it might bring him back sooner.

"When…When will he be in London?" Tears swam back into her eyes.

The colonel took her by the arm and helped her rise and collapse into a wailing cry against his chest. "Now, now, dear, it's all okay now. You'll have your Hank back in no time. That's why I've got you flying out tonight."

"Go with me, Colonel," she murmured.

His belly bounced as he made a wheezy chuckle. "Victoria, Hank would never forgive me. When you two get your arms around each other…I envy Hank on your first night back together. I hope he's still got enough strength left in him."

22

The veins in Hank's neck stuck out in livid ridges.

"Bullshit! I want to see the commander right now."

Lines of restrained tension soared across the first lieutenant's smooth chiseled jaw. He searched out anybody in or within earshot of the commander's quarters at the back of what was once a village restaurant. They were alone.

"Listen, mister. You're damn lucky we found space for you on the next plane out."

"That woman and child have to go with me. They're my…"

The lieutenant's lips curled in disgust. "Your what? Sure as hell not your wife and child. They're Krauts. The enemy is how we fondly refer to them."

"I have money."

The lieutenant spread and locked his legs. His solid arm shot up with fists like sledgehammer heads. "Hold it right there. You make me sick. Man your age should be fighting for his country, instead of screwing…"

Hank swung wildly, but was too slow. His fist was caught midair and hurled behind and up his back.

"I'm going to forget that happened because you're supposed to be someone important." Hank could smell his hot spearmint breath at his ear. "You're just a pathetic coward hiding behind your money and a woman's skirt."

"What's going on in here?"

Hank's arm was released at the sound of the field commander's voice. The first lieutenant went to a rigid salute. "Nothing, sir. Mr. Oscarson tried to take a swing at me, sir, when I told him he couldn't take the woman and child with him."

"Is that right, Mr. Oscarson?"

"I owe them my life. Please, sir."

"I understand they are refugees from East Prussia."

"Yes, sir."

"He tried to bribe me," the first lieutenant snapped.

"Lieutenant, check on the woman and child's provisions to insure they have adequately warm clothing and food before we move out." The lieutenant lingered to hear more.

The commander's friendly moss-colored eyes set in a proud Nordic face turned to Hank.

"Nothing's fair in war. It's the best that can be done for them. You have to think of yourself."

"Can I make one request, sir?" Hank struggled to force out the right words first.

"I...I'm not going until I see them to safety. We need a truck and supplies to last at least two to three weeks."

The commander flinched at a suggestion that guaranteed repercussions if he acquiesced.

"I've seen your picture more than a Betty Grable poster. Absolutely not. My orders come from as high as the White House to get you home safely, if possible."

"I'm not leaving without them."

The commander locked his hands behind his back and paced back and forth in silence. "Are you aware of international laws regarding harboring or marrying the enemy? Both are illegal."

"I wasn't, sir. Besides, they're not the enemy any more than women and children anywhere in the world when their men go to war. I'm not getting on that plane, sir."

"Lieutenant, no more rough stuff. Do as I ordered for the woman and child and get Mr. Oscarson to his plane right now. We're holding it up. There are men dying on that plane." He walked up to Hank with thunder in his eyes. "Men who are dying for their country."

"Can I have a few moments alone with them to say goodbye, sir?"

The commander nodded, turned and left.

Hank slumped in defeat. "Please bring them to me in here and give us some privacy."

"Be quick about it."

Katja and Alena were laughing and exchanging whispers when they entered the tent, empty of everybody but Hank. He waved them close to him without making a sound.

"Listen," he whispered in German. "They won't help get us all out of here, so we have to slip away." Katja's breath hitched once.

He leveled his breathing. "Now listen to me. Leave right now, preparing everything in the wagon. Leave the road and head for the woods. Act like you're fine about me going."

Stomach pains bent Katja at her waist. "You're going?"

"Please, hush up and listen. Get the wagon ready as fast as possible. I'll go without resistance to the plane. After the guards leave me alone, I'll find a way to slip out of the plane before it leaves the ground and catch up with you. Once it's gone, they've got to keep moving. They won't stop to try and hunt me down." He sternly lifted Katja's chin and glanced down at Alena. "I'm not leaving until we're all safe. Now go."

Katja stood up, charged by Hank's determination. She looked at Alena and they both nodded. She pulled Hank into her arms and let out a long, steady breath. He made sure his eyes did not meet hers.

"Go, fast as you can."

"Look at me," she demanded. He hesitantly focused on her golden eyes. "If you can't get off the plane we'll be all right."

Hank tore away from her embrace. "Not an option. Now go." He walked them to the entrance of the tent and hailed the lieutenant to come.

"Lieutenant. We worked everything out. You're right, they'll be fine if you'll load them up with food.

"Only have K rations."

"That's great, Lieutenant. Enough food and drink to last them three weeks. They need some more blankets, too."

"We can handle those requests. Are you ready to go? The plane's about to leave."

"Absolutely." He turned and gave a quick embrace to his two companions. Alena bit her lip, not to smile when he winked at her before they parted.

"Would you walk me over to the plane, Lieutenant?" Hank asked after the females had left.

"Sorry about the mix-up, Mr. Oscarson. I'm glad you've returned to your senses."

"Let's get to that plane. I can't wait to get home."

A puzzled look crossed the lieutenant's face, then disappeared along with his caution. He motioned to have the civilian escorted to the plane and left without turning to see the orders were carried out.

"Name's Oscarson," Hank said with an outstretched hand to the soldier to his right.

"Poulson," the young private responded and heartily shook his hand. "I understand you're some kind of hot shot back in the States."

"Kentucky is my home. Yours?"

"Michigan."

A man was being carried on a stretcher up the ramp when the two flanking soldiers and Hank arrived at his ride to go home.

"I've got it from here guys." He turned to the private from Michigan and winked. "Unless you want to try and sneak on with me."

The private chuckled. "What a dream that would be. Goodbye, sir. Have a safe trip."

The privates weren't twenty feet from Hank with their backs turned when he charged away from the camp, disappearing into the flat gray light of a late winter's afternoon.

23

Sexy and not too formal, Victoria told herself while unpacking one of four suitcases the old London Hilton Hotel valet had set out for her.

"All right, which negligee do you like best?" she asked herself, almost in reach of her absent lover and fiancée. "Yes." She held up the sheer off-white satin and lace shorty with matching silk panties.

The outfit would be a hip-hugging black skirt and silk blouse with a neckline that accented her generous breasts. The hair back. No, she decided to leave it loose and free for him to run his hands through. A colorful scarf teasingly draped around her neck would finish the look. She slipped into her tallest heels and dialed the front desk for a taxi to take her to Heathrow Airport immediately.

For the fourth time she unfolded and read Hank's arrival time, including how long the shuttle was expected to take from the military airfield to Heathrow's VIP waiting room. She glanced at her watch. He would be back in her life in less than an hour and a half.

~

Dozens of stumbling, gawking soldiers took more than a passing glance at Victoria Logan, even before she crossed a shapely leg in the airport's VIP lounge.

"Any word? He should have been here by now," Victoria asked the receptionist.

The young fluffy-haired blond cleared her throat. "It looks like the flight got in about twenty minutes ago, ma'am. He should be walking through that door any time now."

In her mind Victoria could see herself letting out a long throaty moan, the sound that always aroused him, spurred him to quicken the pace. He loved to watch her when she rode him, the way her lush, raven black hair rained down off her shoulders. She could see those flashes, flickers of pleasure in his cobalt blue eyes, as she would thrash around wildly, completely consumed by his every move. She could see herself wrapped around him like a silky vine.

"Miss Logan. Miss Logan." The voice was deep, authoritative like her father's. She looked up at a brass-buttoned coat full of colorful bars, stripes, and ribbons.

"Miss Logan, I'm Colonel Peterson. Would you join me in another lounge for a moment?"

"What is this? Hank? Something's happened." She ran a hand to her throbbing heart. "He's had an accident? Killed in a plane crash…"

The stiff soldier lowered to the seat as if he wore a back brace. "No, ma'am. Please, come with me." He offered a hand to help her up, but she was on her feet before he was.

"What is it? Tell me." She couldn't get another word out of her constricting throat.

"Okay, we'll just sit here." They both sat back down.

"First, are you his sister? A relative?"

"His fiancée. Please, sir." She took a jagged breath. "Get on with it."

"Well, first, he's okay. At least he was less than twelve hours ago." The colonel began to excessively clear his throat. "He was, now mind you it's entirely possible the word we got was scrambled, but—"

"Damnit, say it!"

"Ma'am, he was delivered to one of our infantry divisions by an advance British regiment. He had a woman and child with him he tried to bring back, but wasn't allowed. He reportedly just up and ran off with them." He shrugged. "Disappeared."

Victoria's fingers fell open. The crumpled itinerary of her fiancée's arrival time floated to the floor.

24

British planes by night and American planes by day. The roar of war overhead and around the tattered parade of over fifty refugee wagons was ceaseless.

"Kat, we should reconsider this idea of going to Hamburg."

Katja jerked back her hair. "I never asked you to stay."

"It's okay." Hank touched her gloved hand. "Remember the stable manager in Elbing?" Hank said.

Katja nodded.

"He said he got word from family in Hamburg that it's been bombed like no city in history since the summer of '43. I didn't know it when you first said Hamburg, but it's where the Reich turns out fighter planes, ball bearings, naval ships, you name it. This place has been blown to bits, Kat."

Katja shook Hank's arm. "Look." She pointed to a clump of wild flowers triumphing out of the mud at the side of the trail. "It's just about the first of March."

"Great, now we'll be axle deep in muck instead of snow," he said.

Katja lifted the canvas partition behind her. "Alena, come and sit with us." She lifted her eyes to coral pink clouds painted on a deepening blue, then down to a pansy springing up miraculously in the thick forest: splashes of yellow and purple teasing the mountain ridge.

Once Alena was settled in between them Hank joined in the game of searching out any other signs of spring until darkness closed over a shared illusion of peace and safety. Hank steered away from the line of wagons settling in for the night in a meadow at the border of thick woods and a pond just released from winter's icy wrath.

Exhausted, but full of renewed hope, they crammed into their wagon bed space.

After Katja trusted Alena was asleep, she cleared her throat. "Hank?" she whispered. "You awake?"

"Yes."

"How are you going to go home once we reach my uncle's house?"

"I haven't really thought about it."

"Stay with us until the war is over."

"That won't be long." Hank sighed and fluffed up one of three U.S. Army issue pillows Katja had managed to slip in with extra containers of K rations.

"I know," Katja said. "Everyone else knew a year ago when the Allied bombing started tearing everything apart."

Hank braced himself on one elbow, struggled to see through the tangled hair covering most of Katja's face. "Then you agree about Hamburg? Last I heard, the Allies haven't taken it yet, so they're probably still bombing the hell out of it."

All Hank heard for a stilled time was Alena's deep breathing.

"I have no place else to go."

"No other relatives in the west?"

"My father's other brother, but they never spoke. I heard about him a few times, but he and my father hated each other. I never knew why." Katja stretched out her arms and clasped her hands behind her head.

"You have beautiful hair, Kat. I've never told you that, have I?" He lifted his hand across Alena and plucked a spiraling handful of thick naturally wavy hair away from her slightly embarrassed face. She brought her hands down to stop him, but his touch was too tempting. She gently moved the child's arm from her waist and sat up.

She tossed her thick mane back and he watched her arched chest heave in and out in the dim light from a sliver of the new moon.

"You were finally out of this mess." Her heart hastened and palms started sweating. "Why did you do this?"

Hank laid back and crossed his outstretched legs like a cowboy by the campfire. He turned his face to her and crinkled one eye with a devilish smile. "Is your memory that poor?"

"What if I don't want you to?"

"You do. You're lucky Alena's between us," he whispered playfully.

Katja giggled loud enough that Alena stirred, then sighed and fell back into a deep sleep.

"Stop talking like that," Katja said. Her resistance couldn't have pushed away a mound of feathers.

"I need to kiss you."

"Hank, you're impossible." She eased back and grinned blankly at the wood-slatted ceiling, then drifted into sleep.

As always, that was when the nightmare started.

~

With American, British, and Swedish papers, only road blocks and bombed-out roads and villages caused any long delays in the four days it took them to reach the outskirts of Hamburg. The goblin-gray sky was made even darker by massive billowing smoke from a firebomb-roasted and corpse-piled city more than a year beyond being on its knees.

Katja watched in horror over her own nail-bitten fingertips. A silvery pall of death lingered like a sticky mist above the ground. "If there is a God, He's punishing us," she said.

Hank jerked his head around in all directions from their hilltop vantage point. "Looks like we've got a break in the bombing." He pulled one of Katja's hands down from her blood-drained face. "Do you know where your uncle lives?" He stared at the plumes dotting every area of the sprawling city. "I don't want Alena to see this if we're actually going into the belly of this mess."

"I don't want to get in back," the child snapped. Her pupils were stormy, dark.

"God knows you've already seen more than a lot of soldiers in battle." He reached down and pulled her close with his hand not holding the reins. "Let's not make it worse." Alena's pleading eyes turned to Katja, who was unfolding her Hamburg map with the inked circle where her uncle lived. She glanced at the child and back to the map.

"You heard him, honey, get in back."

Hank hardly noticed that it wasn't rain falling from that dark sky, but snow. It fell with thunder rumbling, then broke into a rage.

Thick, heavy flakes were a welcome curtain between them, and horrors so close they could almost touch them.

They eased down switchbacks into the madness of what was once one of Europe's most cultured and beautiful cities, boasting more than a million inhabitants. The dead were piled as arbitrarily and inanimately as rubbled brick. Young and old stone faces stared back at them through haunted eyes as Hank stepped up the pace over what were once paved roads. Even in the heavenly innocence of fallen snow, the air was heavy as lead with the smell of death, smoke, and hopelessness.

Hank's eyes rested on the stark beauty of a woman and two daughters huddled together on a city street corner. They seemed oblivious to the cold, to everything. The young woman's furrowed full dark eyebrows and flowing black hair accenting a flawless, motionless face and hypnotic eyes made Hank flash on Victoria Logan. He yanked on the reins.

Katja looked from Hank's glazed eyes to the beautiful woman.

"Alena, hand up a couple of the containers of food for this family," Hank said.

"Hank, I don't think you should."

He turned like a stranger on her interruption, then climbed down from the wagon and placed, like an offering, the food at the toes of the woman's buttoned boots. The little dark-haired girls snatched up the treasures. Hank bent his bowed knees slightly forward, expecting at least a nod of acknowledgment or appreciation, but the beautiful face never moved.

He began backing away, but was stopped by the wall of black and gray overcoats building a line behind him.

A hunched-over, pepper gray-stubbled man, with cheeks that looked like he was sucking in air, spoke with animated shoulder movements, never removing his hands from his overcoat pockets.

"You have more?" he asked in a raspy voice.

Hank needed both arms to part the crowd and scale the wagon to avoid being pulled back down. Katja already had the reins.

Hank was on his feet. "Let go of those, Kat!"

Men and women laden with teeth-shuddering children wrapped around them bulldozed their way to the front of the circle that completely surrounded the wagon.

Hank side-mouthed Katja in a calm voice. "Another minute and they won't be asking. Let's try to give them half of the ration boxes."

Because it made sense she nodded and pasted on a strained smile. "All right, let's move slowly. I'll get in the back and wait with the rifle for whoever tries to overtake us while Alena hands them out to you."

"An excellent suggestion." His eyes raked the stirring, mounting mob.

The flaw in their plan, revealing they had a wagon full of food, instantly drew masses of refugees like sugar lures ants.

Hank tapped the rifle barrel just off the right of his hip. "Hand it up here, Kat. There's no other way out."

The crowd had grown manic, shoving and breaking out in fistfights and hair pulling to get to the front of the circle. Even the horses tied to the back of the wagon and in harness were being sized up as food.

Hank had to cock and fire three overhead shots to silence the growing mob.

"I will kill any man, woman, or child who doesn't allow us to pass right now." His eyes narrowed to bead in through the snow on anybody who would dare test his mettle. The masses slowly backed into lines crowding both sides of the wagon as they passed.

Hank whirled around to Katja. "This! This is what we've almost died to get to. Where the hell are we?"

"What was that about—the woman?"

Hank got the horses trotting until they were a safe distance from the mad crowd.

~

"How far? Where the hell are we?"

From the tilt of Katja's chin, Hank didn't expect any answer until he responded.

"She reminded me of somebody back home."

Katja nodded, her stomach churning from fear to shock.

"That was our food. You could have gotten us killed."

"You're right." Hank took a deep breath and opened his mouth to the icy coolness of the falling snow. "It was a mistake, Kat. I guess that's all I can say."

They moved on in silence, both healing from their mistakes. Katja kept her gaze above the ground level horror.

"Stay in the back, Alena. We'll be there soon," she said.

"Two more streets over." She gasped when Hank tugged the reins right and they rounded the corner. Molten steel oozed like a giant monster over everything in its path. Hank threw his arm around Katja and pulled her to his chest. "Sorry, Kat."

"We've got to find it!"

"That's got to be at least four blocks long. They must have lived by a bombing target." He stared into the five-foot and higher mounds filling what was once a street.

"There's no way in. Let's get out of here before the bombing starts gain."

The snow was turning thick, wet. Katja pushed her nose to her map and pointed in the opposite direction.

"Just tell me where we're going." Hank said. He leaned over and wiped the mounting snow off her coat shoulders. "Let's think of Alena, Kat. She handed out all but two of the ration boxes. If we don't freeze, we're going to starve to death."

"Lubeck," Katja said.

"What? Oh, the village is Lubeck?"

"My father's brother lives just outside of it, right on the flatlands of the Baltic coast."

"Sounds nice."

Katja's head drooped. "I don't know. It's nothing like Trakehnen. No mountains, lakes, forests."

"It will be all right, Kat. You're family, whether they've seen you before or not." He rolled the reins to step up the horses. "About how far?"

"About a day's ride, if they're still alive."

25

The white world, brittle with frost and plumes of breath-made clouds began to melt into spring near the sparsely vegetated coast, allowing uninterrupted travel time to Lubeck.

The once-bustling town of nearly a quarter million people was eerily untouched by the claws of war.

Hank pulled Alena onto his lap. "You know what this could mean? You'll be safe. We can sit out the rest of the war. No reason for anybody to bother with anyone here. Nothing to conquer."

He arched his back but got no respite from piercing pain running from his shoulders to his lower back. "I am dying for a real bed."

"You're sure planning on a lot from people who may have moved or run away, for all I know," said Katja.

"Okay, okay, just let me dream a little, will you?" He snuggled Alena to his chest. "Hot food. All we can eat and a warm fire. How much farther?"

"I think we're looking at it. See, the white stables and big and small houses over there. They've got a view of the ocean." Katja motioned to halt the wagon. "Not right on it, but it can't be more than a mile or two away."

Hank gave Katja a curious look.

"My aunt wrote my mother regularly, since the brothers never talked."

"Then she's going to be our ticket in."

~

Daniel and Else Haffmann looked nothing like Katja had imagined. Her father, over six feet tall with an aristocratic nose and thick wavy hair, was the antithesis of Daniel, with his rounded, pinkish face, watery blue eyes, and thinning blond hair. His wife wore every wrinkle of a tough life fighting the weather and earth with a toothy smile. The two stood at their front door like strangers at a bus stop, watching the wagon approach, then halt in front of their house.

"Looks like he had excellent pasture land," Hank mused.

"You two stay here," Katja said, placing her hand on Alena's knee. "Let me ease into our shocking proposal."

She jumped down, opened her mouth, shut it again, and swallowed. "We've never met…"

Else threw her arms up in the air and shrieked. "I know you. Your mother sent me pictures." She launched an elbow into her puzzled husband's side. "Your niece, Daniel. Katja, your brother's girl."

At the mention of the unspeakable, Daniel Haffmann's lips curled down. He gave a quick nod. "Damn Nazi."

"And the little girl. I didn't know you even got married," Else said while gawking at the man with a child on his lap.

"Else," her husband said. "That can't be hers. Look how old that child is."

"Oh, I'm so foolish. Please come in out of the night air and stay."

Not knowing what to say and doing everything she could to avoid eye contact with her father's enemy, Katja bowed, turned, and waved Hank and Alena down from the wagon.

She turned back to Daniel's cocked eyebrow.

"My husband," Katja said loud enough to signal the charade. "He was a famous veterinarian from the Trakehnen stud farm."

Hank extended his hand with the kind of broad smile that even forced Daniel to send his lips twitching upwards.

"Pleasure. We've come a long way." He directed everybody's eyes to Alena. "We adopted her. Long sad story…" He ran a hand through Alena's hair, then locked on to her eyes. "Sad because we had to wait to get her in our lives instead of having her from when she was a baby." Alena listened, first in confusion, then beamed.

"All of you come in," Else said, jabbing her husband again to confirm her invitation. "Can't say we have much, but what we do we'll gladly share with family."

"Come in," Daniel spit out with an echo of resentment in his tone.

Else leaned into Katja and whispered. "He read every letter your good mother sent," she giggled. "He would sneak them, but I saw him."

After stabling and feeding the horses, the three lingered over the healing refreshment of washing their faces and hands in stove-warmed water.

Else directed Alena to her own private bedroom and Hank and Katja to the larger of the two guestrooms.

After the guests nervously stared at their laps while waiting with Daniel for a hot potato soup dinner, Else seated them, sitting opposite her husband at the end of the table. "See something familiar about Katja, Daniel?"

Daniel shot a quick glance in Katja's direction. "What are you talking about?"

"Your brother, dear. Doesn't she look a lot like him when he was young?"

Daniel stared long enough to connect a distant resemblance. He signaled his wife to change the subject.

"How are your father and mother? We haven't heard a thing," Else said.

Daniel cleared his throat to command attention. "Yes, how is one of Hitler's most loyal followers?"

Katja slowly lowered her spoon. "That's what the fighting was about?"

"And what better reason?" Daniel snapped.

Hank hesitated, then plunged into getting the painful subject behind Katja as fast as he could. He turned to Daniel. "Your brother...he...was killed fighting in the Normandy Allied invasion." His eyes shifted to Else. "Katja's mother died during our journey. We all almost died."

Agony spread over Daniel's ashen face faster than spilled milk on a tablecloth. He slowly stood, one hand cupping his stomach. "Excuse me." His wife's eyes followed his every pained movement as he shuffled out of the dining room and up the stairs.

Else lifted her head with eyes closed and began to rock. "Oh, this war. It's slowly killing us all." She leveled her eyes at Katja. "We've eaten all our winter food. Eaten every animal, even our horses." She glared at the lone potato protruding from the watery broth in her soup bowl.

"All horrible news. We stopped listening to the radio months ago, after the Hamburg bombing started." Else reached out and clasped her hand over Katja's. "Daniel blames it all on Hitler. You will, of course, stay here with us. Your journey is over."

"You've got the ocean a short walk from here," Hank said. "What about fishing?"

"You could get killed. Some villagers already have," Else said.

"But Lubeck..." Hank interrupted.

"Planes fly by and shoot at boats or people fishing the shore. You never know when they're going to come. Nobody's fished for over six months."

"Nobody's going to starve," Hank said, accepting that Katja might never forgive him for what he was about to do.

~

Hank knew what most don't, that a horse can smell a human's fear. The chestnut stallion's nearly 360 degree vision sent his ears straight back when Hank, rifle low to his hip, sauntered up, patting the horse on his flank and speaking in a soft, low voice.

"I'm doing you a favor, boy." He ran a hand along the rack of bones protruding from the starving animal's ribcage. The horse relaxed at his master's soothing tone and touch.

Hank gulped back the sickening feeling surging through him. Killing the German soldiers would haunt him less than destroying the animal that had kept them alive.

He had driven a bullet in the chamber before he entered the barn. One shot through the side of the head and they could earn their keep for weeks. He took a few more steps back and leveled the rifle at the stallion's head. At any given moment Hank could tell what was going on in a horse's head the same way he understood colors and smells. And he knew it was mutual. The air was thick with the inner battle Hank was mounting to pull the trigger. The stallion responded to Hank as if it was aware of its final sacrifice. It stood perfectly still as though wanting to ensure the shot hit its target.

"Stop!"

He held his aim but turned an eye to the silhouetted woman whose shadowed face didn't need to be seen for him to know the horror filling her eyes. Volcanic adrenaline turned his verve to quivering arms and a twitching trigger finger. The barrel waved its way down to his side, then dropped from his hands to the stable's dirt floor.

He took a deep, jagged breath and put a shaking hand to his forehead.

They stood motionless about five yards apart. For a long moment all they could hear was their labored breathing.

"I thought," he swallowed. "I thought you had gone to bed."

Katja nodded. "Yes." Her voice was fainter than air. "It took me awhile to understand what you meant at dinner."

Hank turned his head to the chestnut stallion they had picked up near the end of their journey.

"You have to get outta here," Hank ordered.

She stepped close enough to pick up the rifle off the ground. "It's not fair for you to carry the weight of this alone." Before Hank could respond she raised her father's prized elk hunting rifle to her shoulder and fired. The stallion stood motionless as though she had missed, then dropped to the cold earth.

Hank knew she wanted to go to him, but couldn't move. He stepped toward her and took the rifle out of her locked hand. Watching him draw near, she reached out to grasp him like a drowning soul. He enclosed her in his arms, clinging to her until she was saved.

The wave broke over her, convulsing her with sobs that shook her very bones. He felt her quake and held her more tightly to him, burrowing his face to find hers, feeling, tasting the salty tears that streamed on her cheek and smoothing, soothing them with his lips. When he felt the quaking subside, he slid his face through the pressing wetness and found her mouth.

He kissed her with a depth from which neither of them could turn back. He held her face in his hands that he might kiss her even more deeply, reaching in until their souls made contact.

"Just hold me," she whispered.

She moved her hands from his neck down, up under his coat. Hank was too engulfed to even twitch at the gnawing, icy fingers. Then his hands searched out and held her the same way, making her tremble at his touch.

They leaned apart to get their breath and look at one another.

"I can't believe you did it," he said.

She turned her head to the dead animal and with one finger touched her dry lips. "I can't either."

He took her by the hand and led her to the stable doorway. "I have to be with you tonight."

"I've got to bleed him and dress him out right now." She lowered her head and nodded at the gruesome duty she knew she couldn't perform.

Hank lifted her chin until her eyes caught the slanted light of the slivered moon. "You'll wait for me? It could take a good part of the night."

"Sleep won't come easily tonight. I'll wait."

Near daybreak Katja dressed and slipped away quietly to the barn. She gasped at the sight of Hank, splattered in blood up to his elbows, kneeling at a water bucket with a bar of soap in one hand.

He leaped to his feet at the sound of her entrance.

"I told you to stay away."

"I just wanted to see how you were doing. It's almost morning."

Hank could see amidst her tangled hair teary eyes that hadn't closed since she left him.

"Sorry, Kat. You scared me. Never butchered anything before let alone a huge animal." He blew up and puffed out his cheeks while pressing a hand to his lower back.

"I'll run you a hot bath," Katja said.

"That would be perfect."

After his bath and a clean shave, Katja led Hank, clutching his waist-wrapped towel in one hand and folded blood and dirt soiled clothes in the other, to their room. She sat on the end of their bed, yanked off her boots, and started to unbutton her shirt.

Hank was watching every move: she wanted him to.

The light from the window set aglow her naturally golden skin when her shirt fell open to her breasts.

In the momentary blindness when he turned his head to the side to release his towel, he felt her hands on his chest.

"Shh, you can hear everything in here. My uncle is sleeping next door." She put an index finger to her cracked lips to still him.

She held his gaze and took off her blouse. Her breasts seemed fuller to him than he remembered. They were firm, her nipples hard and set high. He put his hands on them, and then his face, feeling pulsing signals shoot through her with each brush of his lips.

"Please, now," she whispered.

He pulled the aging quilt from the bed and opened the sheets. She lay down and watched him slowly join her. He felt no shame, nor saw any in her.

Her eyes were on fire like a cat's caught in the light of a yellow moon. They had a glazed hunger that even exceeded his own. She lay back and lifted her hips for him to tug off her panties. They were of a creamy, functional cotton. His fingers danced across the soft bulge within them and pulled them gently down.

The triangle of hair was thick and dark amber. He lowered his head and traced a line at the edge of it, then ran his tongue up and circled the belly button on her concave, heaving stomach. The brush of her thick hair on his face and her warm, sweet, just-bathed smell were intoxicating.

They surveyed each other in their nakedness, letting their eyes roam and feed with an incredulous suspended, mutual hunger. The many meals he'd passed up to ensure enough for her and Alena had taken their toll on an already-lean frame.

She pulled him down to her pulsing hips. She searched for his hardness and closed her fingers on it. It excited him even more to see she felt momentarily free of such things being instruments of cruelty and torture.

He opened his eyes wide and glanced down at Katja's legs slowly spreading open for the pounding collision of their flesh.

Katja stuffed the corner of her pillow in her mouth to stop from screaming when he finally entered her. His loins shot a hot surge that swept slowly through the entire length of her body, then wrapped around her brain, springing her into fireworks of brightness the harder he rammed.

He moved on her with the same kind of centered confidence he had brashly flaunted since the first day they met, only now it focused exclusively on her.

Their eyes locked on each other. He could see flickers of fear, then pleasure in her face as she lost herself. She lifted and wrapped her knees around him to quiet any of his fears that he was feasting too deeply on her.

No matter how much she gave, he wanted more. Her moan came again, a booming, rusty sound of delight that echoed off the walls and pumped through his blood like a cutting whiskey.

He let her take over, set the pace, let her shudder back into control. She leaned over him. Her hair curtained his face, her hands braced on both sides of his hips.

"I want to make you crazy." She lowered her head until her lips were a breath away from his. "I want to be the only woman to make you beg."

She stopped moving, then stepped up her gyrations to a slow, torturous pace. Her mouth took his in quick, playful kisses that gradually deepened and heated up. When his hands were wound in her hair and his back arched, she moved away from his mouth. He repeated his quick and slow rhythm all the time, watching her dazed eyes.

He knew what she wanted, needed, now. Her moves grew more and more wild and desperate, mirroring the emotions and words that had been raging inside her for weeks.

He released a thunderous moan when he erupted, sweat-dripping flesh to sweat-dripping flesh.

"Oh my God, Katja." When he could speak more than a couple of words, he turned his lips to her cheeks. "You win," he whispered. He lost his hands in her hair when he turned her face to his.

"I think I can stop worrying about you letting yourself go again."

Beautifully relaxed, she braced herself on her elbows and looked down at him. "I feel safe with you." She kissed him before she rolled lazily to her back.

"When I get back to the States…"

"We've been through all that, Hank. Please, not now."

~

When a man tiptoes out of a darkened house and he knows he's awakened by moans of ecstasy, he feels like a fool. Or extremely fortunate. Hank was debating which course to take when he faced Katja's uncle in the morning on the way back to the stable.

"Damn," he mumbled, inching his way up on his bowed legs. He could have woken up with her lying along his body, nestled in the shelter of his arm. He could have felt her breath on his skin and the soft rise and fall of her breasts against him, her right leg tucked over his and the warmth of her belly against his back. Instead, he was again arm-deep in blood butchering the meat into portioned cuts for prolonged rationing.

Until Hank had fallen in love with Victoria, like most men, he had always slipped away like a thief of flesh. It seemed, for him, prompted not so much by guilt that it meant too little, but fear that the comfort of the companionship women seemed often to need was more than he had to give. Victoria was the first woman to understand his base instincts and love him without judgement. Yearnings for her were again beginning to entangle with Katja Haffmann.

He wiped the sleep out of his eyes and bolted for the house, disappointed when he found Katja up, fully dressed, and down in the kitchen with Else planning how to stretch out the cold storage room full of horse meat.

Never in their brief night of quenching hunger had she shown any sign of regret, knowing they had no future if they lived to see the war end. What he feared most that with the dawn would come, if not regret, some colder new perspective.

"Good morning ladies," he said, seating himself on one of six kitchen chairs.

Katja cleared her throat and spoke at a rapid pace without making eye contact. "We were just talking about the new meat and how to best use it. And how to tell Alena what I've done."

"We've done."

Katja turned to Hank. "She's going to be really upset."

Hank scratched his unruly hair, dipped in gold dust from the light of the morning sun. He glanced at Katja's chafed chin and cheeks, then rubbed the poorly shaved bristle-hard stubble on his face. She caught the association and blushed.

"I could use another shave," Hank said.

Else's eyes rolled under raised eyebrows. "Father's got an extra straight-edge razor I'm sure he'd give you." She rubbed her hands together. "When he hears what you two did to put meat on the table for all of us less than a day after arriving, he'll be so happy he'll shave you himself."

Hank's smile plummeted at the returning thought of Alena. "We could have a little funeral service. I could set up what looks like a grave mound and have Alena believe the stallion died. Then…" He stopped at the two shaking heads and startled faces.

"Shouldn't lie to her, should we?" He scratched his upturned chin. "She can handle it. I'll tell her as soon as she wakes."

"I think Hank has a good idea to have a service. We should. He gave his life so we could live."

Hank anxiously slipped into the small pale yellow bedroom where Alena was still sleeping in the lone twin bed. He sat down, making enough noise to wake her.

Startled, Alena sat straight up. "What? What happened?"

~

Hank clasped one of her hands in his. "Everything's fine, honey. I just need to talk to you a minute."

Alena rubbed her eyes, yawned and stretched.

"I've got some news."

"You're leaving us?"

"No, no, of course not. We had to take the chestnut's life so we could all have enough food to stay here."

Alena shook her head while trying to comprehend what he was saying. "You killed him?"

Hank closed a tightened grip on her quivering hand. "Someday you'll understand."

"No I won't."

Hank paused and put a hand to his brow. "I probably won't, either."

~

Whether it was the blue sky, growing signs of spring, or grandeur of the rolling pastureland abutting vistas of the ocean shores, everyone except Alena was in good spirits as they gathered outside the stables for the funeral service.

Never having turned his eyes upward except to survey impending weather, Hank felt less than comfortable in trying to string together more than mindless chatter. With the elder Haffmann being an atheist and Katja undecided, the job was his.

He crossed his hands at his waist and lowered his head. The circled group followed. "We're gathered…" He cleared his throat and lifted his eyes. "Everybody, please lift your heads and open your eyes." He shifted his weight from one foot to the other. The refreshing sound of birds chirping nearby filled a long silence.

"I don't know the right words to say in a prayer, but it's easy to give a tribute, as I'm sure you, Kat and Alena, can do to such a brave animal." Hank stopped and slowed his breathing. "I've spent my life more dedicated to horses of every kind than to the human race." Hank looked at the crude wood stake that had been pounded in the ground to symbolize the horse's death.

"It wouldn't be right to speak of all horses today. This morning's tribute belongs to the East Prussian Warmbloods like this one, who have, without resistance, given their lives for people like us. As if the snow, ice, and stony roads weren't bad enough for unshod horses, they've dragged us across every kind of twisted and jagged piece of earth in Germany, leaving them with bloody hooves, and bloated and collapsed stomachs full of worms and colic from malnutrition. They've spent weeks without shelter, left harnessed and unfed to face the day and night in temperatures that would kill a person left in such a way in less than twenty-four hours. A broodmare in foal, placing my safety over its own, carried me to safety from the bullets of low-flying planes." Hank's throat tightened.

Katja moved closer and looped her arm in his. "These magnificent horses' courage has been the only thing millions of us have been able to depend on," Katja said. "Let the death of this stallion stand as a monument to that courage, in giving the ultimate sacrifice, its life, to make ours possible." Katja breathed deeply and gazed up at the sky, then down at Alena.

She pointed to the ground as though the stallion lay dead at her feet. "You can't explain the beauty of Trakehnen to someone who hasn't, didn't see it before the war."

Hank could feel her begin to slip to the ground and tightened his bracing support. He rubbed his hands together. "All right, let's look at this as a celebration. A beginning of better things to come."

~

Hank dreaded the inescapable reality that each day the war stretched on brought the next slaughter closer. An agreement that the four adults and one child would ration the horse meat to last four weeks meant carnivorous eyes would soon turn on Noble.

26

Katja's eyes narrowed dangerously, causing Hank to clear his throat and move, subtly he hoped, out of range. He shoved her relatives' kitchen chair back a bit and glanced again at the dome-shaped mahogany cased radio emitting a static signal sound between emergency broadcasts.

"Why can't you believe a word you hear, just because it's in German?" she wailed, then slammed her coffee cup to the table, splashing out the last of it.

"You mean you believed the radio reports you got in Trakehnen about how well the war was going right up until cannon shells nearly blasted your farm to bits?" Hank furiously shook his head. "Unbelievable. If you haven't woken up to the fact that Germany lost a year ago, you'd be the last one."

Katja's head whipped around, and her eyes seared Hank where he stood. "What is unbelievable is that I've given myself to a man who hates everything I've lived for. Everything has vanished. Totally destroyed."

To her surprise, Hank sympathetically nodded.

"My home, my mother, my Nazi father. Trakehnen. All lost forever." Katja leaned on the table with both hands on her temples. She sat staring, motionless.

"You couldn't understand," she said in a distant voice.

"This isn't about a trip to town. It's about us, isn't it? For the past month you've known the war's going to end at any minute, and you're afraid of what happens next."

Katja bolted out of her seat and jabbed Hank hard on the shoulder right when his chair was tilted back. He tipped over making a crashing sound and booming yelp.

She darted her eyes around to see if anybody was entering or near the kitchen. Hank scrambled to his feet, then poked her right back.

"You think the world is yours for the taking." She angled her chin up as if inviting a fist. "You can go to hell."

"I've done what I had to."

That snapped it. A roaring temper was unleashed before Katja could take a breath and suck it in. Her fist shot out in a full-rounded swing before she could stop it. It sent Hank's head back with a nasty jerk, leaving a rising red mark on the side of his jaw. He teetered back on his heels, almost falling butt first on the tiled floor.

"I'm sorry. I shouldn't have done that," Katja stammered.

Hank rubbed his chin, crinkled his eye, and then gave her a smirky smile. "I was warned about that mean right hook before our first tangle," he said with a shake of his head.

Katja puffed out her lower lip and dropped her eyes. "Well, you deserved it."

"I can count on one hand the number of times I've gotten my way since we started this picnic outing," Hank said.

"Go ahead and get yourself killed in town, but don't take Noble."

"He's safer with me than your relatives."

Katja's breathing was beginning to return to normal.

"Kat, I'm going, and that's final. It's just Lubeck, for hell's sake. Not more than a two-hour ride. The Allies have taken it. I might be able to get word out that I'm safe." He rubbed his swelling eye where she had belted him. "Kind of."

She gritted her teeth trying to build up steam.

Hank stayed respectfully silent. He could feel the torrent of her emotions, but kept busy shunning the thoughts that, in the gold of dawn, had forced him from the warmth of her flesh bonded to his backside, to long walks on heavy dew-covered pasture grass, preparing for the inevitable. He had a ritual now of walking to a flattened stone overlooking the vast, torrid Baltic Sea. Once the Haffmann farm was back in sight and the spring sun fully bathed everything in its crisp warming light three hours later, his emotions and thoughts were still as tangled as seaweed.

Judging it was safe, Hank stepped forward. He started to offer Katja comfort before he saw in the glint of her eye that was premature.

"Noble's all I've got when this war's over."

Shrinking a little at the tone, Hank began to open his mouth, but knew there was no more to say. He marched from the kitchen with Katja at his heels. Noble's riding saddle needed cinching three buckle holes higher than the well grooved line for a horse living on more than three pounds of oats a day.

"I won't be long and—"

"The last time you said that you were made a prisoner and almost strangled to death."

Hank mounted Noble and leaned over to her. "Come on, Kat, admit it. You're worried about more than Noble, aren't you?" He beamed a cocky grin.

Too furious to speak, Katja spun on her heel and stalked away.

~

Hank never saw her watching him ride off through the well-hidden shadows of the living room window, but other eyes did.

Katja jumped at the throat clearing behind her. She turned to Else's understanding eyes.

"Are you ready to talk about it yet?" Else asked.

Katja closed her eyes for a moment, then gingerly rubbed her throbbing temples.

"Daniel was thinking he was going to hook up your last horse to a plow for spring planting."

Katja's eyes leaped with fire. "What? I thought I made it clear nobody, nobody does anything with Noble without my permission."

Else propped one elbow in her hand and rested it on her chin. She said nothing, but her knowing glare made Katja swallow hard.

With Else at her heels, Katja walked to the kitchen and dropped down onto a kitchen chair.

"Who is he? I know he's not a German," Else said gently.

She was about to speak, then hesitated. "He's Swedish."

Else nodded. "Can I heat up some water?"

Katja shook her head. She lifted a finger to ebb the tears in her burning eyes.

Else rose, and from behind wrapped her arms around Katja and rocked her. "Is he going to marry you?" she whispered.

Katja shook her head, as Else knew she would. "Returning to his wife and family in Sweden, I suppose."

"Maybe," she said and sighed.

~

Hank rifled his pockets for his British and American papers. He took a deep breath and handed them both to the suspicious British soldier blocking his path. "And you have the bloody guts to fly into Germany the very moment the Russians storm East Prussia?" He held the two clearance and explanation papers up for scrutinous examination.

"Everything seems to be in order. Been through hell, I'll bet."

Hank nodded. "Thanks for not taking this drill any further." Hank rubbed his hands together. "When did you take Lubeck?"

"The Krauts been dropping like flies. You have been out, haven't you?"

"German radio transmissions have Hitler bravely defending Berlin," Hank said.

The soldier eased his stance and placed a hand on Hank's shoulder. "I've got some news for you that you're not going to believe, chap." He tilted his head and studied Hank head to toe.

"You're probably the last American to hear this. Hitler's dead. The bloody bastard died before the Reds finished taking Berlin."

"Took Berlin?"

The soldier nodded. "Took it three days ago. We finished up with Hamburg a week ago." He shrugged. "Not much of a fight."

"We saw it." Hank's eyebrows shot up. "So the war's over?"

"Far as the bloody Nazis, it is. Don't go forgetting the Japs."

"Then I'm safe to…How can I send a message, telegram, something quick to the States?"

"You might have to go on to…No, follow me. We'll get you word back home somehow."

~

Katja was anxious, but Alena was nearly uncontrollable when she learned the man she had long ago adopted as a second father had again placed himself in danger. "Why didn't you stop him?" she screamed inches from Katja's face at the kitchen table. "You don't even care." She knocked a kitchen chair over when she bolted for her bedroom.

"She tried, darling," Else yelled loud enough that the child, lingering at the top of the stairs, could hear.

Katja waited, but didn't hear a slamming door.

"Where did he run off to?" Daniel growled. "We saved enough seed to plant, but stopped short with no horse."

Katja's lips were vibrating. She struggled to hold back a response by crossing her arms hard over her stomach.

Daniel shoved a piece of pan-fried horsemeat to one side of his mouth and waved his fork in Katja's direction.

"There are a lot of unanswered questions about that man of yours."

"And you're not going to make your niece any more miserable by sticking your nose where it doesn't belong," Else said, leveling her eyes at Daniel. "Are you?"

"Just the same. You've lived under my roof for over two months and I deserve to know what's going on. Don't think I don't know you're not married. I knew it the first night I heard you two—"

Else cracked his words with a near-comical falsetto clearing of her throat.

"I expect some answers," Daniel said, then swooped the last bite on his plate into his mouth and stormed off, muttering condemnations.

~

Near noon, Katja, sitting in a comfortable front porch rocker, flicked her eyes up to the brittle blue sky filling up with threatening rain clouds. She had stopped fighting off her heart beating like a snare drum, and flowed with silky, sensual thoughts of Hank.

Everything he had done since sharing her bed every night had made her feel different. Frightened, then secure; lighter, then heavier. Even the screaming nightmares were being replaced by dreams of Trakehnen magically transformed back into paradise.

She wondered if she looked different, to herself, to him. There was no denying she felt different. All the horror of the past few months had been set aside since they had arrived at her uncle's farm, an oasis from reality.

She was still blankly smiling when Hank came into view, kicking up earth and stone as he thundered up the muddy road to the house. Before he even dismounted, his wildly happy eyes told it all. Reality was back.

He leaped down, not bothering to tether the reins to the hitching post at the front steps.

"Kat, you're not going to…" He bent down and gave her a quick kiss. "Let's get everybody together. I've got some news you won't believe." She paused and nodded. She would believe.

~

Katja wasn't around when Hank and Alena returned from another one of his mysterious one to three day absences. The only clue he gave as to their whereabouts was that he needed to get affairs in order.

The two waltzed into the sun-bathed kitchen, whispering between giggles. Katja had barely said a word to Hank since he announced that Field Marshall Montgomery had accepted the Germans' unconditional surrender and life could begin again. She had moved out of his bed to share the twin with Alena and was focusing all of her waking and sleeping blistering energies on getting herself to move out of his life.

27

Hank felt alone as Katja's prey when Alena left the kitchen.

The mumbling, jutting jaw and the violent and methodical way she wielded everything she touched in cleaning the Haffmann house were less than subtle ways of demanding an explanation.

"How long are you planning on staying?" Katja said as she put an iron skillet back on the kitchen shelf.

Hank looked up from the New York Times he had paid handsomely for in Hamburg. "This war isn't even close to getting over." He shook his head and folded the thick paper in two. "I liked it better when I didn't know anything."

"When are you leaving?" She still hadn't looked at him since he had entered the house.

"I don't know if I am." He waited for a response, but got none. "Depends on how you like your new place and how things go with the investigators I hired to speed things up assisting the Red Cross's search for Alena's parents."

Katja turned and gave him a strained look. "What new place?"

"Oh, you haven't seen it yet, have you? I showed Alena on the way back from Lubeck. Only about, say, five miles from here."

For a moment she didn't know what to say. "You didn't answer my question."

Hank rose, went to the kitchen sink, leaned against it, then crossed his legs and folded his arms. "It's called Baltic Acres, if it suits you. Your Trakehner breeding farm. Of course, while the title in your name spells it out that way, I'm open to changing it." Katja's jaw dropped in disbelief. "Did you hear me, Kat?" Hank dropped his arms to his sides, then reached over, and gently pulled her to his chest.

At his touch Katja closed her eyes and blindly let his fingers trace a delicate path from her temples to the corner of her mouth. When his fingers reached her lips, she parted them and hungrily let him explore their rim.

When she slowly opened her eyes, she found calm, certainty, and need as legible as her own. He moved his hand to her back and began rubbing. They hadn't made love in days, and even his slightest touch, smell, made her loins ache for him. He put both hands in her hair, drawing her head back into the curve of his shoulder and neck. His arms gradually closed around her.

In the instant before their mouths touched, Katja had the sudden urge to say she was sorry, that he needed to forgive her for cheating them out of what little time they had left together.

He could see the thought taking shape in her eyes. Before she could utter a word, he shushed her softly.

He ran his rough road-dirty hands up the back of her shirt while whirling in the sweet wet taste of her glistening mouth, feeling the warmth of her breath on his face.

"We still have right now," he said.

She looked down, then moved back and took one of his hands in hers and nodded.

"What's this about a new breeding farm for Katja?" Daniel burst in, not hesitating to shatter whatever was happening around him. "The little one said it was a secret she couldn't tell Katja." He broke into a belly laugh. "But we couldn't shut her up."

Katja still didn't look up. Through the dark arch made by her falling hair, Hank could see the tears lining her cheeks.

"I'm not really surprising you, am I, Katja?" Daniel boomed.

She shook her head, still not looking at either of them. Hank took hold of her hand and led her to the kitchen chair.

"I wired my, well, I had money wired through the Deutsche Reichsbank in Hamburg, all I needed to buy a two-hundred-acre spread right on the coast. Still need to get up more barns, corrals and that kind of thing, but, Kat…" He lifted her chin up to his eyes. She looked at him at last and smiled. Her eyes never left him while his eyes sparkled and danced with each vision he laid out. The land was going to be transformed into the finest Trakehner stud farm in the world, using resurrected Hamburg as her sales hub for all of Europe.

Her fixed stare finally broke away when Hank sprang from the table to retrieve Alena. He brushed his lips against Katja's hair before he left, leaving her breathing hard and hungry for where the night would surely lead.

~

"Here we are," Hank announced, gathering everybody at the kitchen table. He rose and stood behind Daniel, placing his hands on wincing shoulders unaccustomed to such familiarity, especially by a man. "Daniel and Else Haffmann. For generously sharing your home with us when all else was lost, I have set up a bank account in your name, Daniel that only requires your signature to verify. A sum of internationally exchangeable currency totaling fifty thousand dollars in American currency will give you the resources to buy new animals and ample farm supplies to start better off than before the war. If not, there will be more."

Daniel furrowed his eyebrows trying to comprehend the unbelievably generous offer from his adversary.

Hank then stood behind and placed his hands on Else's shoulders. "I insist that in order to receive this money, Else has to join Katja and Alena in buying new clothes for herself."

Else ran a hand to her giggling lips. "Don't be foolish. I don't need anything."

"Else, it's a condition of getting the money. Get at least three or four new outfits." His eyes turned to Katja's, laughingly anxious as a child's. Even Daniel's eyes sparked with humor.

"There haven't been any dresses for sale for over a year in all of Germany, I expect," Else said, still blushing.

"I want to see all of you in the prettiest clothes post-war money can buy before leaving, except you, of course, Daniel!"

Hank stopped at the deadly silence created by his slip of tongue.

"Where are you going?" Alena asked.

"No need to get into that. Let's concentrate on getting all these things done. I'm selfish enough to want to see each of you realize your dreams."

"Oh! Oh!" Alena sputtered with her arm waving to get attention. "Can I go with you again?"

"Not where he's going. Right, Hank?" Katja asked quietly.

"Can you go to round up stallions and mares that have survived the trek from Trakehnen? Of course you can, Alena. Can you join Kat and me when we meet with builders to complete her new stud farm? Absolutely. It's the three of us, like always." She ran to his arms and sat on his lap.

Daniel Haffmann had quietly taken every aspect of the spectacle in with a face flushed with curiosity and growing indignation. "You're an American, aren't you?"

Hank bridled at the remark, spit out like a foul taste.

"We don't want your filthy money. It's covered with the blood of our women and children."

Katja bolted to her feet, fists clenched. "Don't you dare talk to him like that. It was our horses that kept meat on your table. We would have never survived, a woman and child, if he hadn't half-starved and been frozen for weeks trying to get us to safety." Katja's face was turning red, then purple.

Hank moved to her and held down her waving arms.

"Hamburg, Dresden, Berlin," Daniel said with a frigid stare. He turned his snarling face to Katja. "His people slaughtered your father."

Katja broke away from Hank's gentle grip and wielded her pointed index finger like a knife blade, in front of her uncle's crazed eyes. "We, we started the war. We murdered Jews, gypsies, anybody who didn't fit an insane new Aryan world conceived by heartless maniacs. You were right about my father." Katja stopped, wide-eyed in cutting realizations. "Even Wolf understood what was really happening."

"Who's Wolf?" Else asked.

Katja lowered her head. "We will be the ones spending the rest of our lives trying to apologize for what we've done to this world."

"Get out! Get out of this house with the American right now. Not another minute..."

A porcelain plate exploding into a thousand pieces against the kitchen cabinets silenced the madness. Else raised another plate to hurl if she didn't command total silence.

"Daniel, I have never told you this before, but shut your mouth, or they won't be the only ones walking out that door. You have suffered with this man, eaten all your meals with him, and now benefit from his generosity. Nothing he has ever done since entering this house has been anything but unselfish and sensitive to everybody in this room." Her face lit up in bitter triumph. "Now not another word about anybody going anywhere." Else reached one of her small arms up and around Katja's shoulders, pulling her to her side.

"This is our niece and the man and child she wisely loves." She put a hand to her heart and took a deep breath. "I want you to think about that." She eased her tensed shoulders, let her arms fall to her sides, and plopped into the chair.

Stress lines were carved deep into Daniel's brow. His eyes took on a wounded look. He slowly rose and climbed the stairs to the solitude of his bedroom.

"I planned on Kat and Alena moving into their new place soon, anyway," Hank said to Else, burdened with what she had said to her husband.

Katja's growing exuberance plummeted at the words "their place". The moment Hank's attention turned to Else she quietly rose and left the room.

~

Hank tugged at the wagon reins when he reached the rise above Baltic Acres. Katja stared down in fascination and wonder at the valley below. Lush spring green grass covered the floor of the valley and swept upward to a seaside vista of rolling pastureland that sparkled with leftover morning dew. She marveled at the crisp, freshly painted white pastureland fences, corrals, and paddocks, two expansive horse barns, and some sixty yards from the horse quarters, a regal two-story white clapboard house. A veranda supported by white posts that circled all four sides accented Katja's future home. The buildings were all nestled together like pearls in an emerald shell.

Splattered against the glorious carpet were random clumps of pink, red, yellow, white, and purple wildflowers, ablaze with rich hues. Their sweet perfume mingled with the fresh morning sea breeze.

The land was breathtakingly beautiful and so much like Katja's lost world of Trakehnen, she began to cry. How could one stretch of pastureland remind her so much of another? She wouldn't have believed it was possible, yet there it was, spread out before her like a dream.

The melancholy vanished as quickly as it had come, and she suddenly felt tremendous peace and contentment. Tranquility wrapped around her like a warm quilted blanket. Her hunger for home abated with each breath she drew.

She could stay here forever.

The realization jarred her. She immediately forced herself to block out life without Hank Oscarson.

"Aren't you even curious about how many horses you have? Your income's going to depend on it," Hank said.

"Hank, it's too much." Katja swallowed hard.

"Kind of hoping you'd say that." He took a deep breath and nodded in full satisfaction. His investment was already paying dividends. He rolled the reins and began down the winding road leading to the estate.

"You've got eight stallions and twelve mares," Hank said. "Believe me, Alena and I had to scour a big stretch of land to find those."

"I'll pay you back after you leave."

Hank pulled the reins sharp bringing them to an abrupt stop. "I owe my life to you. I'd say we're more than even. Besides, who said I'm leaving?"

"What?"

Hank broke into his sure-fire country boy smile. "I'm going back to get things in order if I'm living here a good part of every year."

Katja's eyes welled with tears. She couldn't speak.

28

Hank was leaning on the corral fence watching the team of workers gliding through their finish work to realize the bonus he had promised them if they met his outrageous completion deadline. He heard Katja and turned to see her walking his way with two cups of steaming coffee. She could see apprehension in his normally broad smile.

Not an hour had gone by since she first laid eyes on the property she had renamed Noble Acres, that Katja hadn't heightened every sense to retain for a lifetime his smell and touch as they lay beside each other each night in her new four-bedroom house.

With Alena's widowed mother found by Hank's bloodhounds en route to live with them, she knew it was a matter of days before he would be gone. She feared a change of heart when he got back home. It was terrifying.

"I made some coffee," Katja said.

"Thanks."

"Kat?"

"What?"

He swallowed. "I just wanted to say that whatever you're fearing, whatever you think or want to say, it's all right."

"And what do you feel?"

Hank was about to respond when he spotted a dust cloud line snaking its way across Noble Acres' hilly countryside to the main house.

The black Renault sedan roared to a standstill not ten feet from Hank and Katja. When the dust settled out stepped Victoria Logan.

"Holy Jesus!" Hank yelled. "Victoria, what are you doing here?"

Hank turned his eyes back to Katja, gawking at who she instinctively knew to be her long haunting nemesis.

Victoria absently dusted off her smart-fitting periwinkle suit and adjusted the silk scarf loosely adorning her neckline.

"The colonel tracked you down through a banker friend when you started drawing off your fortune." Victoria scanned her surroundings, stepping past Katja like she wasn't there. She nodded in disgust. "This is where you've been piling your money?"

"Vic, we've got a lot to talk about," Hank said softly while cautiously approaching her.

"Oh, I'd say that's an understatement." She glared over his shoulder at Katja. "I just had to see your face while you told me everything." She turned for the car. "I'll be staying at the only hotel—if that's what they call it—in Lubeck. You've got one day before I fly back." She again burned her eyes into Katja's. "That should be enough time to come up with a hell of a story."

Before Hank could conjure up a response the dust cloud was on the move again.

Hank couldn't hide his excitement and shame from Katja. She stormed up to him and planted a fist on each hip. "I can't live like this and neither can she. I'm glad she found you here."

"You know I have to see her, after all she's been through."

Katja threw her hands up in the air. "Absolutely, but do all of us a favor. Be honest with yourself first."

~

Hank paced back and forth in front of the post-war converted two-story hotel Victoria Logan had rented for one night.

Was he wearing the right clothes? To buy a suit to dress up would crush Katja's feelings. To show up in any of his threadbare clothes would insult Victoria.

While the midnight blue suit was second-hand and the jacket a size too large, it was too late to consider changing once again.

He looked up and saw Victoria had been watching him from her opened top floor window, probably since he had started lingering in front of her lodging.

"It isn't going to get any easier," she yelled down to him. "I'll be right down."

Hank's throat felt as if he was trying to swallow a baseball. When he opened the door, Victoria was standing halfway up the staircase to the second floor.

"We can talk more privately in my room." Her tone was cold, instructional.

He sat in the room's one fabric covered reading chair. She sat on the edge of the bed, erect, looking proper and damn mad.

Her voice was even and controlled. "After personally getting every-thing in motion to find you and literally save your life, is it not fair that I at least deserve some kind of acknowledgement?"

"I can't imagine what you've been through," Hank said.

"And know you're going to say that I can't imagine what you went through. How, in trying to protect and save the woman and child, you just couldn't help falling in love with her." Victoria lowered her head.

Hank could feel her stoic resolve cracking wide open.

"I cried for you. I fought for you." Her head shot up spilling tears from her glistening blue eyes. "I even blackmailed the governor to find you."

Hank slowly approached her and sat by her on the bed. "I'm so sorry this happened to us, Vic," he murmured.

She lifted her delicate shaking hand and placed it on his. "It doesn't have to."

~

"Look at me, damnit. Let's get it over with," Katja snapped.

Hank lifted his head and then slowly exhaled. He ran a hand through his hair while looking at, but not seeing, Noble Acres at the bottom of the valley from where they stood. "I love you and always will." Then he squinted at the sun and gave a little shrug that almost made her heart burst. "I just thought you ought to know that."

She wrapped her arms around him to deeply swallow every word she knew would soon be his last. She covered his lowered face with kisses.

"I want you to take Noble with you," she whispered.

"No, no way."

"I'm worried about Alena. She loves you like a father."

"I'll never stop seeing her," Hank said in a non-negotiating tone.

"You'll return with our finest mare and Noble. You wouldn't understand, but it's better if you go together." She gave a hollow laugh. "Didn't exactly work out the way you planned, but you got what you came for."

"More. A lot more."

He kept his eyes firmly on Noble in the distance as the magnificent animal pranced around its spacious paddock.

"It's best you go. It could have never worked for either of us leaving home forever."

~

That night while she slept in his arms, he lay listening to the drumming of the summer rain on their bedroom window and tried to do what she had told him they must, not to think beyond the moment, just to breathe it all in. But he couldn't.

The heat of the morning sun roused Katja from a warm slumber. She stretched without opening her eyes, her fingertips searching out the last morning embrace of her companion.

Her open palm rifled across the sheet to the edge of the bed. She was alone. Her eyes shot wide open and she vaulted upright. "Hank!" The nightstand. A folded piece of paper leaned against the alarm clock on the nightstand with the word 'Kat' meticulously scrolled in fancy cursive. Her stomach fluttered, then knotted. She barely made it to the toilet before she threw up.

29

Victoria had personally planned the wedding down to the napkins. It was going to be the first wedding to take place at Churchill Downs, and surely would outshine any to follow.

Colonel Matt Winn bubbled over at Hank's suggestion that he be the best man. As soon as he heard the wedding was still on, less than a month after Hank's return, he suspected he and his track might play another major role in his two favorite people's lives. He had taken action to remove a wall and put bay windows in the main dining area where he envisioned the couple would exchange vows. No less than two hundred close friends, including the "who's who" list in the world of racing, would attend.

If Victoria had declined his offer to use his facilities for Hank's homecoming reception and later the wedding ceremony, he would have been in a bind. He would have had to call back the editors of *National Equine*, newsmagazines and his regular menagerie of newspaper reporters he had already primed for the juicy postwar wedding of a returning war hero.

Of course, the colonel hadn't bothered to bounce off Hank his slightly exaggerated and totally prefabricated stories of how his best friend brought home a prized black Trakehner stallion and bay Trakehner mare, but like always, he made it the story of the month.

The colonel orchestrated a returning hero celebration feast that only a man who worshipped food could conceive. It was the hottest social event in Louisville with Kentucky's wealthiest and most influential clamoring to get an invitation. Dom Perignon champagne would flow. Russian caviar, Alaskan king crab, salmon and halibut would be flown in fresh for the extravaganza. A full orchestra would back up the melodic sounds of track regulars, Frank Sinatra and Vic Damone.

Hank could tell something was going on as soon as his fiancée, dressed in an all-revealing backless black silk evening gown, stepped into his Mercedes convertible. Victoria's smile sparkled as much as the diamonds around her neck.

Hank jumped out and released the canvas top. "Sorry, I wasn't think-ing." He leaned back into the car. "Let me be the first of many this evening to tell you that your dress is a killer. It's going to make every woman hate you and every guy drool."

She nodded curtly. "Thank you, sir. I only want one man drooling." She patted the driver's seat. Her perfectly manicured cherry red fingernails shimmered under the interior car light when he swung open the door.

~

Hank popped the lid securing the car's canvas top and connected it. "That should be better. I don't want the wind to blow on a Matisse while it's still drying."

Victoria flicked her lush raven-black hair. "You still pile it deeper than four horses stuck overnight in a horse trailer."

~

The line of chauffeured limousines, Rolls Royces, and classic cars lining the circular drive leading to Churchill Downs' main dining building astonished Hank.

He glanced down at his black double-breasted suit. "I'm underdressed. Why didn't you tell me this was a black tie affair?"

Victoria's fingertips touched the cuff of his sleeve. "You look perfect."

"Right."

"Hank, don't talk about that woman and child tonight. Okay? It would be embarrassing."

"There they are," the colonel yelled over the swarming crowd at them. "Over here."

Hank's steam was building to confrontation by the time the colonel had freed himself to see his guests of honor.

"Vic." The colonel lost his chin in his walrus neck when he reached out and kissed Victoria's hand. "What can I say? You're gorgeous as always."

Hank's irate glare was less inviting. "Who's the press here for?"

"A returning hero. You, of course."

"I've been back for over a month." Hank pulled the colonel aside and leaned to his ear. "I'm anything but a hero. Shit, Colonel, you know I hate this kind of thing."

Victoria cleared her throat. "Yes, Colonel, you know Hank likes to be the only one to shock people to death with his actions." Hank caught her cool stare from the corner of his eye.

"I've got you seated at the head table." The colonel looked past Hank at Kentucky's governor and wife, just stepping out of their limousine. "Don't worry, Hank, no speeches or anything like that."

"Colonel," the governor yelled.

"Okay, maybe I'll say a word or two. You'll only need to say something if you want to. I think it would be appropriate considering everything." The colonel peered over Hank's head again. "Governor Hampton, so good of you to come. You know Hank, of course."

The permanently tanned and well-toned man approaching sixty stuck out his diamond-ringed hand. "Howdy, Hank. Good to have you back in the saddle, boy." He shook Hank's hand as though he were a muscled ranch hand. He shot a glance over at Victoria.

"Beautiful. Beautiful," the governor said hungrily while feasting on Victoria Logan. Hank sensed the way he said it made Victoria feel dirty. She tightened her entwined arm around Hank's.

"She's a spitfire, that one," the governor said leaning into Hank. "One more month, and she would have carried you out herself."

The colonel had shared all the details of Victoria's passionate attempts to find him, as well as her altercation with the governor.

Hank turned to Victoria. "Thank you, dear."

The governor cleared his throat to break the moment. "A lot of hero talk going around. Killed how many Germans?"

Victoria elbowed her fiancée. "You didn't kill anybody, did you, honey?"

Hank pursed his lips while flashing on his hands and chest splattered with the blood of Katja's rapists. "Yes, I did."

Victoria pulled away from Hank's escorting arm. "What other surprises have you got for me tonight?"

Hank shrugged and took her hand. "I'm here, aren't I?"

"I would have loved to have taken a few Nazi or Jap scalps," the governor said, interrupting their quiet exchange. He shoved ahead through the crowd without awaiting a response.

"Stupid bastard," Hank said loud enough for the nearby colonel to hear and enthusiastically nod.

"Unfortunately, they'll be at our table." The colonel shrugged. "Widest spread in Kentucky and narrowest mind."

The resplendent maroon-carpeted ballroom, accented in massive gold leaf mirrors and circular ten-foot crystal chandeliers, was filled to capacity with tuxedoed and gowned Southern blue bloods and wealthy Thoroughbred owners.

Through Hank's eyes, the evening degenerated with each pompous exchange of small talk he suffered through at the head table, made worse when the colonel stood and waddled up to the microphone. The last notes of Sinatra's "I've Got You Under My Skin," still lingered in the air of the low-lit room. The colonel tapped the mike, then cupped his hand above his eyes to see beyond the hot spotlight.

"We've got quite a crowd here tonight." The audience burst into applause. "Besides the sheer enjoyment of such a spectacular evening at America's best track, the evening is also steeped in another kind of tradition." He paused and dropped his voice an octave for effect. "The American hero. It's hard to find a street and hometown where there isn't a World War II son or father with stories of personal heroism."

He took a deep breath and long swallow of water.

"But we're only talking about one of those stories tonight. Hank Oscarson, will you stand up?" The spot rotated over to Hank, leaving him no choice but to rise and wave, tentative as it was.

"Hank's passion for horses even overpowered his fear of death. Surviving everything from imprisonment and near starvation, to saving women and children, our guest of honor is truly one of America's finest."

The room again burst into applause. Hank waved away the chant of "speech, speech" until all quieted down. Moments later all six couples at his white linen covered table had settled back into casual conversation.

The governor's booming southern drawl carried through every ear. With each double-neat scotch, his voice and opinions grew louder.

"We've got a damn haberdashing idiot at the helm. Hell, the man was bankrupt more times than a prostitute's been laid. FDR, there was a great American. We wouldn't have crushed those Nazis without him and Churchill." A fidgeting, frail, and bespeckled lieutenant governor nodded.

"If it had been up to me, I wouldn't have left one Kraut standing."

"That includes women and children?" Hank said from directly across the table.

"Hank," Victoria warned.

"What? You bet. Every damn one of them."

Hank threw down his napkin and bounded to his feet.

"Listen, you ignorant son-of-a-bitch, I resent you making remarks about our president, and it burns my ass even further when you talk about killing innocent women and children whose only crime was that they were caught between bloodthirsty assholes like you."

The governor's nostrils flared like a caged bull.

"I heard you stayed over there for some German woman months longer than you had to." The governor dragged all eyes over to Victoria.

Hank shook his head and lowered his eyes to his beautiful, humiliated companion. "I'm sorry you have to hear such trash, Vic."

He reached out and clasped her trembling hand.

"How could you let this happen? Of all nights," she whispered.

~

Two days from the wedding, Hank headed from the main house toward his corrals and show arena. Victoria had just gotten back from a long morning ride and was taking Noble through some preliminary lateral work dressage exercises. Since the stallion's arrival with Hank, she had had her eye on the next Olympic trials. The fact that the magnificent animal had no show training was compensated for in her mind by her feelings toward the courageous animal that had nearly lost its life bringing home a man she was beginning to realize was twice the man he had been before he left.

"Hey, get off that horse! Right now!"

Victoria turned her head. At first she couldn't believe it. The thunderous command was coming from her fiancée.

Hank stalked to the center of the arena, close enough to snatch Noble's reins. "Never, never get on this animal."

Sensing more than she wanted to know, Victoria clenched her teeth. "Why? Because when you see me on it you think of her? The only woman you love so badly it's driving us both crazy?"

"What in the hell are you talking about?" Hank yelled while she dismounted and walked Noble over to him.

Hank patted and rubbed Noble's neck, avoiding Victoria's accusing glare.

"Come on, Hank. Get it out. This is about more than a horse, isn't it?"

"Her name's Katja Haffmann," Hank volunteered for the first time since their all-night talks and tender lovemaking.

"And she wasn't just one of the refugees you escaped with, was she?" Victoria's voice got thin and high. "Was she, Hank?"

Victoria's white-cotton-gloved hand rushed to her lips as he silently led Nobel back to his stall.

30

For the first few weeks after Hank had left, Katja had kept the note he left by her nightstand and read it before closing her eyes.

> Dearest Kat,
>
> I've taken a coward's way out of not saying goodbye in person. You already know how I feel about you. You know I won't be able to say your name without it ripping my heart out. You know a part of me is dead and always will be when you're not within touching distance. You know I can never speak of, or see you again without making every wrong decision for both of our futures. That's why you know I have to leave this way. Kiss Alena for me, and reinforce that I really will make arrangements to see her at least twice a year. Make Noble Acres your new heaven on earth.
>
> Always, Hank

Alena had found a similarly beautiful note of love and lifetime commitment next to her pillow. The woman and child had spent many nights holding each other to ease their loss. Katja kept the notes under pressed glass for their protection and life-lasting endurance.

Alena's mother soon learned to never mention the American's name at Noble Acres. Katja had taken Hank's parting words to heart and formed a self-kept secret bond with her lost love to never have the name Hank Oscarson cross her lips again.

Katja not only accepted the return of the screaming nightmares of ghoulish raping German soldiers, but almost welcomed them each morning she had made it through another night without Hank's torturing presence.

Tears would well up in her eyes all times of the day, and she was powerless to stop them. Katja kept her arms around Alena more than even her grateful mother felt natural.

Else and Daniel Haffmann were near-nightly visitors since Hank's departure, with not even an "I told you so," glance from her uncle.

Near dusk Katja was at her kitchen sink peeling potatoes and onions while singing to Alena, who was scratching out a drawing of the Trakehnen she and Katja daily kept alive in their imagination, if not memory.

The child proudly lifted up her colored pencil drawing full of blue sky, beaming sun, trees, a lake, and horses.

"That's absolutely beautiful, kid."

Katja paused and turned her head sideways at the surprised and pained look Alena was giving her. Hank had often called her "kid."

"Alena, that's very good."

~

Katja had taken off her work clothes and slipped into a lavender halter-style cotton sundress she had bought to please Hank before he left. Now she wore it to stay cool on hot summer evenings. She slipped her bare feet into flat leather sandals, lazily walked out to her front porch, and began her nightly sunset journey up the winding dirt road to look back on Noble Acres from the spot she had first beheld its breathtaking majesty.

Seated on her favorite flat rock for overlooking her property, she surveyed what she had accomplished the past six months since her benefactor's departure. With the generous sum of money Hank had left on her kitchen table, she had bought twenty more mares and ten more stallions. She nodded in satisfaction that she was within three mares of having the same number of Warmbloods they had bred on the Haffmann stud farm what now seemed a lifetime ago.

"I'm paying you back. Every American dollar of it," she declared to the low whistling sea breeze.

Katja turned at the distant sound of galloping hooves. The ground swell behind her made it impossible to see who was rapidly approaching.

Her heart betrayed her by leaping with anticipation.

"Stupid!" She scolded herself for still being haunted by even the slightest sound.

Just then a carriage breaking through a cloud of dust appeared on the horizon of the distant hill. Katja put an open palm to her brow and squinted to see the carriage was led by two horses. Trakehners, she bet by their size. A black and bay. It was traveling at lightening speed. Katja's heart pounded like a locomotive in anticipation. It had to mean news, big news. Maybe bad news.

"Noble, God in heaven, it's you!" She clutched her chest. While easy to spot the horse, bouncing up and down on the buckboard was a man, shaded by the slanted yellow light of the setting sun.

Too soon her fantasy crumbled, as the familiar face of Hans Jager, Lubeck blacksmith, came into view.

She ran to greet her beloved horses. Hans tugged on the reins about a hundred yards from her front door.

"What's the hurry?" the refined-featured man asked. "Hop in, and we'll get these beauties to where they belong." She gave a lingering hug around her horse's neck.

Hans couldn't help but see the disappointment on her face when he first came into view. His smile only grew larger.

"Get in the carriage." Once she was seated next to him he continued. His eyes lit up as if a match had just been put to a candle inside them. "I have a note." He nodded after he said it. Her brow furrowed at the news.

"You had better read it fast," Hans said. "It's from an American." He shoved the folded note into her open palm and closed her drooping fingers over it.

She sat stunned. "An American?"

"Hurry, dear. There's reason to my insistence."

Katja wanted to save it and take it in slowly, like sipping an aged wine, but she couldn't. She gradually laxed her thumbs. The note was on plain white paper folded without an envelope. She held her breath and opened it and took it all in with one glance.

> Dear Kat,
> Get out of the carriage right now.

Her tear-brimming eyes met Hans'. He knowingly nodded; this time fighting back tears himself.

Katja leaped down, and not fifty paces behind her was Hank on another stallion in full stride, waving, with his wide country smile that could only mean one thing: more than her beloved Trakehners had found their way home.

About the Author

Lon LaFlamme is a former AP wire service and daily newspaper reporter. He was CEO of one of the largest marketing communications companies in the western U.S., receiving numerous national advertising and public relations awards. LaFlamme has served as marketing professor at the nation's largest private university. He divides his time between Seattle, Washington and Salt Lake City, Utah.